GLIMMER TRAIN STORIES

EDITORS
Susan Burmeister-Brown   Linda B. Swanson-Davies

CONSULTING EDITOR
Roz Wais

COPY EDITOR
Scott Stuart Allie

TYPESETTING & LAYOUT
Paul Morris

COVER ART
Here We Are *by Jane Zwinger*

ESTABLISHED IN 1990

PUBLISHED TRI-ANNUALLY
in April, August, and November by Glimmer Train Press, Inc.
P.O. Box 80430, Portland, Oregon 97280-1430
Telephone: 503/221-0836   Facsimile: 503/221-0837
www.glimmertrain.org

PRINTED IN U.S.A.
Indexed in *Humanities International Complete*
Member of the Council of Literary Magazines and Presses

Glimmer Train (ISSN #1055-7520), registered in U.S. Patent and Trademark Office, is published quarterly, $38 per year in the U.S., by Glimmer Train Press, Inc., P.O. Box 80430, Portland, OR 97280. Periodicals postage paid at Portland, OR, and additional mailing offices. POSTMASTER: Send address changes to Glimmer Train Press, P.O. Box 3000, Denville, NJ 07834-9929.

ISSN # 1055-7520, CPDA BIPAD # 79021
DISTRIBUTION: Bookstores can purchase *Glimmer Train Stories* through these distributors:
       DEMCO, Inc., 4810 Forest Run Road, Madison, WI 53707   ph: 800/356-1200
       Peribo PTY Ltd., 58 Beaumont Rd., Mt. Kuring-Gai, NSW 2080, AUSTRALIA
       Small Changes, P.O. Box 70740, Seattle, WA 98127   ph: 206/382-1980
       Source Interlink, 27500 Riverview Center Blvd., Suite 400, Bonita Sprints, FL 36134
       Ubiquity, 607 Degraw St., Brooklyn, NY 11217
SUBSCRIPTION SVCS: EBSCO, Divine, Subscription Services of America, Harrassowitz, Swets, WT Cox, Blackwell's UK.

Subscription rates: Order online at www.glimmertrain.org
or by mail—one year, $38 within the U.S. (Visa/MC/check).
Airmail to Canada, $48; outside North America, $62.
Payable by Visa/MC or check for U.S. dollars drawn on a U.S. bank.

On July 6, 2013, sixteen-year-old
Wang Linjia died after the San Francisco
crash landing of Asiana Airlines Flight 214.

The day before, Wang posted on her blog,
"Perhaps time can dilute the coffee in the cup,
and can polish the outlines of memory."

We dedicate this issue to writers and
thinkers; we are better, larger, for them.
We dedicate this issue to Wang Linjia.

Linda & Susan

Submitting Work to Glimmer Train

Your short-story manuscripts are welcome all year. To make submissions at our site, go to www.glimmertrain.org and click on the yellow *Submissions* tab. Complete writing guidelines are at the site.

SUBMISSION CALENDAR

January............**Standard** submission (up to 12,000 words). No reading fee. Payment for accepted stories: $700.

Very Short Fiction Award. Any length under 3,000 words welcome. Prizes: 1st place – $1,500 and publication, 2nd/3rd places – $500/$300 and possible publication.

February.........**Short Story Award for New Writers**. Most entries run from 1,500 to 6,000 words, but any length up to 12,000 words welcome. Open only to writers whose fiction has not been published in any print publication with a circulation over 5,000. Prizes: 1st place – $1,500 and publication, 2nd/3rd places – $500/$300 and possible publication.

March............**Fiction Open**. Any length from 2,000 to 20,000 words welcome. Prizes: 1st place – $2,500 and publication, 2nd/3rd places – $1,000/$600 and possible publication.

April..............**Family Matters**. Any length under 12,000 words welcome. Prizes: 1st place – $1,500 and publication, 2nd/3rd places – $500/$300 and possible publication.

May...............**Short Story Award for New Writers** and **Standard**

June...............**Fiction Open**

July................**Very Short Fiction Award**

August...........**Short Story Award for New Writers**

September ......**Fiction Open** and **Standard**

October..........**Family Matters**

November ......**Short Story Award for New Writers**

December.......**Fiction Open**

One of the most respected short story journals in print, *Glimmer Train* is represented in recent editions of the *Pushcart Prize: Best of the Small Presses, New Stories from the Midwest, The PEN/O. Henry Prize Stories, New Stories from the South, Best of the West*, and *Best American Short Stories*.

We love being the first to publish a great story by an emerging voice. Let us read yours. If you're a subscriber, you know that we go to some lengths to honor and support our contributors and their writing.

Stories accepted for publication are presented in a highly regarded print publication where literary short fiction persists in the real world and beyond the next post.

CONTENTS

With my pet chickens, in the backyard of my childhood home in Florida.

Laura van den Berg's debut collection of stories, *What the World Will Look Like When All the Water Leaves Us*, was a Barnes & Noble "Discover Great New Writers" selection and short-listed for the Frank O'Connor International Award. Her second collection of stories, *The Isle of Youth*, is forthcoming from Farrar, Straus & Giroux in November 2013. She lives in Baltimore, where she is finishing a second collection of stories and a novel.

ANTARCTICA

Laura van den Berg

I.

In Antarctica, there was nothing to identify because there was nothing
left. The Brazilian station at the tip of the Antarctic Peninsula had
burned to the ground. All that remained of my brother was a stainless
steel watch. It was returned to me in a sealed plastic bag, the inside
smudged with soot. The rescue crew had also uncovered an unidenti-
fied tibia, which might or might not have belonged to him. This was
explained in a cold, windowless room at Belgrano II, the Argentinian
station that had taken in the survivors of the explosion. Luiz Cardoso,
the head researcher at the Brazilian base, had touched my shoulder
as he spoke about the bone, as though this was information intended
to bring comfort.

Other explanations followed, less about the explosion and more about
the land itself. Antarctica was a desert. There was little snowfall or rain.
Much of it was still unexplored. There were no cities. The continent
was ruled by no one; rather it was an international research zone. My
brother had been visiting from McMurdo, an American base on Ross
Island, but since it was a Brazilian station that had exploded, the situation would be investigated according to their laws.

"Where is the bone now? The tibia?" I'd lost track of how long it had been since I'd slept, or what time zone I was in. It felt very strange to not know where I was in time.

"In Brazil." His English was accented, but clear. It had been less than a week since the explosion. "It's not as though you could have recognized it."

We stood next to an aluminum table and two chairs. The space reminded me of an interrogation room. I hadn't wanted to sit down. I had never been to South America before and as Luiz spoke, I pictured steamy Amazonian rivers and graveyards with huge stone crosses. It was hard to imagine their laws having sway over all this ice. It was equally hard to believe a place this big—an entire fucking continent, after all—had no ruler. I felt certain that it would only be a matter of time before there was a war over Antarctica.

"It's lucky the explosion happened in March." Luiz was tall with deep-set eyes and the rough beginnings of a beard, a few clicks shy of handsome.

"How's that?" My brother was dead. Nothing about this situation seemed lucky.

"Soon it will be winter," he said. "It's dark all the time. It would have been impossible for you to come."

"I don't know how you stand it." The spaces underneath my eyes ached.

My husband hadn't wanted me to come to Antarctica at all, and when our son saw where I was going on a map, he had cried. My husband had tried to convince me everything could be handled from afar. *You're a wife*, he'd reminded me as I packed. *A mother, too.*

"Did you know about your brother's work?" Luiz said. "With the seismograph?"

"Of course." I listened to wind batter the building. "We were very close."

I couldn't stop thinking about him as a boy, many years before everything went wrong: tending to his ant farms and catching snowflakes in his mouth during winter. Peering into a telescope and quizzing me on the stars. Saying tongue twisters—*I wish to wish the wish you wish to wish*—to help his stutter. We had not spoken in over a year.

Luiz clapped his hands lightly. Even though we were indoors, he'd kept his gloves on. I had drifted away and was momentarily surprised to find myself still in the room.

"You have collected your brother's things, such as they are. There will be an official inquiry, but you shouldn't trouble yourself with that."

"I'm booked on a flight that leaves in a week. I plan to stay until then."

"The explosion was an accident," he said. "A leak in the machine room."

"I get it." Exhaustion was sinking into me. My voice sounded like it was coming from underwater. "Nobody's fault."

I had flown from JFK to New Zealand, where I picked up a charter plane to an air strip in Coats Land. There had been gut-popping turbulence, and from the window, I could see nothing but ice. Luiz had been the one to meet me on the tarmac and drive me to Belgrano II in a red snow tractor. I'd packed in a hurry and brought what would get me through winter in New Hampshire: a puffy coat that reached my knees, a knit hat with a tassel, leather gloves, suede hiking boots. I'd had to lobby hard to come to Antarctica; the stations weren't keen on civilians hanging around. When I spoke with the director of McMurdo, I'd threatened to release a letter that said details of the explosion, the very information needed to properly grieve, were being kept from the victims' families. I knew Luiz was looking me over and thinking that the best thing I could do for everyone, including my brother, including myself, was to just go on home.

"Are there polar bears here?" I felt oddly comforted by the idea of spotting a white bear lumbering across the ice.

"A common mistake." He drummed his fingers against the table. He had a little gray in his eyebrows and around his temples. "Polar bears are in the North Pole."

"My brother and I were very close," I said again.

There was a time when that statement would have been true. We had been close once. During our junior year of college, we rented a house in Davis Square, a blue two-story with a white front porch. Our parents had died in a car accident when we were in middle school—a late spring snowstorm, a collision on a bridge—leaving behind the grandparents who raised us, and an inheritance. My brother was in the earth sciences department at MIT, and I was studying astronomy at UMass Boston (I was a year older, but he had been placed on an accelerated track.) Back then I thought I would never grow tired of looking at the sky.

When it was just the two of us, we did not rely on language. He would see me cleaning chicken breasts in the sink, and take out bread-crumbs and butter for chicken kiev, our grandmother's recipe. After dinner, we watched whatever movie was on TV. *E.T.* played two nights in a row, and *Maybe it was just an iguana* became something we said when we didn't know what else to do, because even though we had been close, we never really learned how to talk to each other. Sometimes we didn't bother with clearing the table or washing dishes until morning. We went weeks without doing laundry. My brother wore the same striped polos and rumpled khakis; I showed up for class with unwashed hair and dirty socks. His interest in seismology was taking hold. He started talking about P-waves and S-waves. Faultlines and ruptures. He read biographies on Giuseppe Mercalli, who invented a scale for measuring volcanoes, and Frank Press, who had land named after him in Antarctica, a peak in the Ellsworth Mountains.

It was at MIT that he met Eve. She was a theater arts major. They dated for a semester and wed the same week they graduated, in the Somerville courthouse. I was their only guest. Eve wore a tea-length white dress and a daffodil behind her ear. She was lithe and elegant, with straight, blond hair and freckles on the bridge of her nose. When the justice of the peace said "man and wife," she had called out "wife and man!" and laughed, and then everyone started laughing, even the justice. I wasn't sure why we were laughing, but I was glad that we were.

There were three bedrooms in the house. It might have seemed strange, brother and sister and his new wife all living together, but it felt like the most natural thing. Our first summer, we painted the walls colors called Muslin and Stonebriar and bought rocking chairs for the porch. We pulled the weeds that had sprung up around the front steps. All the bedrooms were upstairs. When I was alone in my room, I played music to give them privacy. At dinner, I would watch my brother and Eve—their fingers intertwined under the table, oblivious—and wonder how long it would take them to have children. I liked the idea of the house slowly filling with people.

That fall, my brother started his earth sciences PhD at MIT. He kept long hours in the labs and when he was home, he was engrossed in textbooks. Eve and I spent more time together. She lived her life like an aria—jazz so loud, I could hear it from the sidewalk; phone conversations that sprawled on for hours, during which she often spoke different languages; heels and silk dresses to the weekend farmer's market. She always wore a gold bracelet with a locket. I would stare at the oval dangling from her wrist and wonder if there were photos inside. I helped her rehearse for auditions in the living room, standing on a threadbare oriental rug. I got to be Williams's Stanley Kowalski and Pinter's Max, violent and dangerous men. I started carrying slim plays around in my purse, like Eve did, even though I had no plans to write or perform; the act alone felt purposeful. I learned that her father was an economics professor and she had majored in theater to enrage him, only to discover that she loved the stage. I'd never met anyone from her family before.

One afternoon I went to see her perform in *The Tempest* at a community theater in Medford. My brother had been too busy to come. She was cast as Miranda. Onstage she wore a blue silk dress with long sleeves and gold slippers. In one scene, Miranda argued with her father during a storm; somewhere a sound machine simulated thunder. Everything about her carriage and voice worked to convey power and rage—"Had I been any great god of power, I would have sunk the sea within the earth…"—but for the first time, I noticed something was wrong with her eyes. Under the lights, they looked more gray than blue, and her gaze was cold and flat.

Afterward, we drank at The Burren. The bar was bright and crowded. A band was unpacking instruments from black cases. We jammed ourselves into a small table in the back with glasses of red wine. Eve was depressed about the production: the turnout, the quality of the lighting and the costumes.

"And the guy who played Prospero," she moaned. She had left a perfect lip print on the rim of her wine glass. "I would've rather had my own father up there."

When the waitress came around, she ordered another drink, a martini this time. She took an eyebrow pencil out of her purse and drew hearts on a cocktail napkin.

"What do squirrels give for Valentine's Day?" she asked.

I shook my head. My hands were wrapped around the stem of my glass.

"Forget-me-nuts." She twirled the pencil in her fingers and laughed the way she had during her wedding, only this time I caught the sadness in her voice that I'd missed before.

She put down the pencil and leaned closer. At the table next to ours, a couple was arguing. The band tuned their guitars. When she spoke, her voice was syrupy and low.

"Lee," she said. "I have a secret."

In Antarctica, I shared a bedroom with a meteorologist from Buenos Aires. Her name was Annabelle and she talked in her sleep. Every morning, I had a three-minute shower in the communal bathroom (it was important to conserve water). I took my meals in the mess hall, with its long tables and plastic trays and harsh overhead lights. I sat with the ten Argentinean scientists who worked at the base; we ate scrambled eggs and canned fruit and smoked fish. They spoke in Spanish, but I still nodded like I could follow. The five scientists from the Brazilian station always sat at their own table, isolated by their tragedy, which I understood. After my parents died, it took me months before I could carry on a conversation with someone who had not known them, who expected me to be young and sparkling and untouched by grief.

Four of the Argentinean scientists were women. They had glossy dark hair and thick, rolling accents. In Antarctica, I'd found that personalities tended to match the landscape, chilly and coarse, but these women were kind. There was a warmth between them, an intimacy, that made me miss being with Eve. They lent me the right clothes. They let me watch the launch of their meteorology balloon from the observation room, a glass dome affixed to the top of the station. The balloon was white and round and looked like a giant egg ascending into the sky. In broken English, they told me what it was like during the darkness of winter: *The sun*, they said. *One day it's just not there. There are no shadows. You have very strange dreams.* They included me in their movie nights in the recreation room, which had a TV, a small library of DVDs, a computer, and a phone. Once it was *Top Gun*, another time *E.T.* Everything was dubbed in Spanish and when I didn't get to hear the iguana line, I started to cry. I didn't make a sound, didn't even realize it was happening until I felt moisture on my cheeks. The women pretended not to notice.

I started wearing my brother's watch. No matter how much I cleaned the metal, it kept leaving black rings around my wrist. With my calling card, I phoned McMurdo, only to be told that the scientists who worked with my brother had departed in anticipation of winter; all they could offer was the date he left and that their reports indicated he'd been in good health. I started pestering Luiz for a meeting with everyone from the Brazilian station, with the hope that they had more to tell.

"An interview?" he'd asked, frowning.

"No." By then I'd been in Antarctica for three days, though I felt it had been much longer. "A conversation."

The day of the meeting, I dressed in thermals, snow pants, wool socks, fleece-lined boots, a hooded parka, and thick red gloves that turned my hands into paddles. I added a white ski mask that covered everything but my eyes. From Annabelle, I'd learned it was called a balaclava. She had given me a laminated sheet with a drawing of a human body. Arrows pointed to what kind of layer should cover each part, to avoid frostbite.

When I first stepped onto the ice, I felt like an astronaut making contact with the surface of the moon. I wandered around the trio of heated research tents and the buzzing generators and the snow tractors. The sky was blue-black; the period of twilight, which seemed to grow smaller each day, would soon begin. By April, Antarctica would be deep into winter and there would be no relief from the dark.

I found all five of the Brazilians in the middle research tent, standing by a long white table covered with black rocks. With the snowsuits and the balaclavas, it was hard to tell who was who, though I always recognized Luiz by his height. Some of the rocks on the table were the size of a fist; others the size of a grapefruit. One was as large as a basketball.

"Meteorites," Luiz said when he saw me looking. Apparently the ice in Antarctica preserved meteorites better than any climate in the world. His team had discovered ones that were thousands of years old.

I touched the basketball-sized rock—it was the color of sand and banded with black—and remembered how much my brother had loved the moon rock collection at MIT.

"So what did you want to ask?" Luiz wore an orange snow suit. His goggles rested on top of his forehead.

I stopped touching the meteorite. Red heat lamps were clamped to the top of the tent. Standing before the other scientists, I suddenly felt like the one about to be questioned. It was hard to breathe through the balaclava.

"What do you remember about him?"

Not much, it turned out. One scientist volunteered that he often ate alone; another said he never participated in group activities like evening card games and Ping-Pong. He sang in the shower on occasion, an American song no one recognized. He had a stutter, though sometimes it was barely noticeable.

"What about the other times?" I asked.

"He could barely say his own name," Luiz said.

"How much longer was he supposed to stay with you?" I wished I had a notepad. I would remember everything, of course, but writing it down would have made me feel official and organized, like I was asking questions that might lead us somewhere.

"Two more weeks," Luiz said.

"And when did you last see him?"

There was silence, the shaking of heads. Someone thought they saw him the morning of the explosion, pouring a cup of coffee in the break room.

"Nothing else?" These weren't the questions I came with, not really, but maybe if we kept talking a door would open and I could ask something like, *Did you know he had a sister?* or, *Did he seem happy?* or, *What did he love about being here?*

"I crawled out of the station." The words came from the woman in a sharp burst, like a gunshot. The hood of her parka was down and auburn hair peeked through the top of her balaclava. Bianca, that was her name.

"On my stomach, through fire, smoke. This is what I remember." She swept her hand toward the group. "No one was thinking about your brother. We barely knew him. We can't understand what you're doing here."

She pulled up her hood and walked out of the research tent. The other three scientists looked at Luiz, who shrugged and said something in Spanish, before following her.

I watched them go. The tent flapped open, revealing a pale wedge of sky. Already I was failing as a detective.

"I didn't mean for it to go like that," I said.

"You want to know the truth?" Luiz said. "Your brother was a beaker."

"A what?"

"A beaker. A scientist who can't get along with the others. It wasn't a privilege for him to be at our station. They were tired of him at McMurdo."

At breakfast, Annabelle had bragged that she could teach me to say "asshole" in any language. If you spent enough time in Antarctica, you learned a little of everything.

"*Ojete.*" I picked up a meteorite the size of a grape and threw it at his feet. "*Ojete, Ojete.*"

Luiz looked down at the rock, unfazed. I left the tent and walked away from the station. I tried to run but kept slipping on the ice. When I finally stopped and looked back, the U-shaped building was minuscule against the vastness of the land. It was like standing in the middle of a white sea—ice in all directions, stretching into infinity. I pulled at the balaclava. I wanted to take it off, but couldn't figure out how. The thought of venturing any farther was suddenly terrifying.

Annabelle had explained that most researchers came for short stints, a handful of months. Few stayed as long as a year, like my brother had. There was the feeling that nothing but the elements could touch you out here, and I understood that was something he would have appreciated. Since we had been close, I could make these kinds of calculations.

I turned in a circle, still looking. I imagined my brother trekking across the ice, fascinated by the world that existed beneath. My throat ached from the cold. My breath made white ghosts in the air. It was impossible to distinguish land from sky.

II.

It happened right after Eve's seventeenth birthday, in Concord, where she had grown up. She had been reading Jane Austen in a park and was just starting home. She remembered the soft yellow blanket rolled under her arm, the page she had dog-eared, the streaks of gold in the sky. She was on the edge of the park when she felt an arm wrap around her chest. For a moment, she thought someone was giving her a hug, a classmate or a cousin. She had lots of cousins in Concord. But then there was the knife at her throat and the gray sedan with the passenger door flung open. She dropped the Jane Austen and the blanket on the sidewalk. Somewhere, she imagined, those things were in a collection of crime scene photos.

At The Burren, she'd stopped there. Her martini glass was empty. The band was playing a Bruce Springsteen cover. She balled up her cocktail napkin and asked if I wanted to dance. She was wearing a silk turquoise dress and T-strap heels. Her bracelet shone on her wrist. She took my hand and we dipped and twirled. Men watched us. One even tried to cut in.

Two days later, I woke to the sound of my bedroom door opening. It was midnight. Eve stood in the doorway in a white nightgown. She got into bed with me and started telling me the rest, or most of the rest. She lay on her back. I watched her lips move in the darkness and wondered if my brother had noticed that his wife was no longer next to him. Soon he would be departing for a month-long research trip to study the Juan de Fuca Plate in Vancouver, leaving us in each other's care.

The man was a stranger. He was fat around the middle. He had a brown beard and a straight white scar under his right eye. In the car, he turned the radio to a sports station. He told her that if she did anything—scream, jump out—he would stab her in the heart. He drove them to a little house on a dirt road in Acton, where she stayed for three days.

Her parents had money. She told herself that he was just going to hold her for ransom; she didn't allow herself to consider that maybe he had other things in mind. The thing she remembered most vividly from the car ride was the radio, the sound of a crowd cheering in a stadium.

"That and one of those green, tree-shaped things you hang from the rearview mirror," she said. "To freshen the air." This explained why she hated Christmas trees, why the scent alone made her lightheaded and queasy. On our first holiday together, she'd told us she was allergic to pine and we'd gotten a plastic tree instead.

"How did you get away?" I asked.

"I didn't." She blinked. Her eyelashes were so pale, they were almost translucent. "I was rescued."

Eve had been half-right about the man's intentions. After holding her for forty-eight hours, he placed a ransom demand; it didn't take long for the authorities to figure out the rest. The police found her in a basement. Her wrists were tied to a radiator with twine. She was wearing a long white T-shirt with a pocket on the front. She had no idea where it had come from or what had happened to her clothes. Right before she was rescued, she remembered tracking the beam of a flashlight as it moved down the wall.

In the months that followed, the man's attorney had him diagnosed with a dissociative disorder, something Eve had never heard of before. He hadn't been himself when he had taken her, hadn't been himself in Acton. That was their claim. He got seven years and was out in five due to overcrowding. Her parents advised her to move on with her life. *He's been punished*, her father once said. *What else do you want to happen?* Now she just spoke to them on the phone every few months. They didn't even know she had gotten married.

"Where is he now?" I asked. "Do you know?"

"I've lost track of him." She tugged at the comforter. Her foot brushed against mine.

This was not a secret Eve had shared with my brother. I should have been thinking about him—how I couldn't believe he did not know about this, how he needed to know about this—but I wasn't. Instead I was trying to understand how anyone ever ventured into this world of head-on collisions and lunatic abductors and all the other things one had little hope of recovering from.

"I never went to therapy, but acting is having a therapeutic effect," she said next.

"How so?" During one of her epic phone conversations, I'd glimpsed her sprawled out on the living room sofa, painting her toenails and speaking in French. I'd picked up the land line in the kitchen, curious to know who she was talking to, but there had just been her voice and the buzz of the line. I'd wondered if it was some kind of acting exercise.

"Getting to disappear into different characters. Getting to not be myself."

I remembered her face on the stage in Medford. She was supposed to be Miranda, but her eyes had never stopped being Eve.

In time, I would learn it was possible to tell a secret, but also keep a piece of it close to yourself. That was what happened with Eve, who never told me what, exactly, went on during those three days in Acton. The floor was damp concrete. He fed her water with a soup spoon. I never got much more than that.

Of course, I could only assume the worst.

The Aurora Australis was Luiz's idea of a peace offering. We met in the observation room after dinner. It had been dark for hours. Despite my studies in astronomy, I couldn't get over how clear the sky was in Antarctica. I'd never seen so many stars, and it was comforting to feel close to something I had once loved. Annabelle and the others had gone back to work. I still hadn't forgiven Luiz for calling my brother a beaker.

"I've had too much ice time," he said. "I've gotten too used to the way this place can swallow people up." In his first month in Antarctica, two of his colleagues hiked to a subglacial lake and fell through the ice, into a cavern. By the time they were rescued, their bodies were eaten up with frostbite. One lost a hand, the other a leg.

"So it's Antarctica's fault you're an asshole?" I said.

"I blame everything on Antarctica," he said. "Just ask my ex-wife."

"Divorced!" I said. "What a surprise."

Luiz had arrived with two folded-up lounge chairs under his arms. They were made of white plastic, the kind of thing you'd expect to see at the beach. In the summer months, when there was no night, the scientists lounged on them in their snow pants and thermal shirts, a kind of Antarctic joke.

"I got them out of storage." He had arranged the chairs so they were side-by-side. "Just for you."

We reclined in our lounge chairs and stared through the glass. Since we were indoors, I was wearing my New Hampshire gear, the tassel hat and the leather gloves. A wisp of green light swirled above us.

"Tell me more about the explosion," I said, keeping my eyes on the sky.

The early word from the inspectors had confirmed his suspicions: a gas leak in the machine room. They were alleging questionable maintenance practices, because it was impossible to have a disaster without a cause. When the explosion happened, the three people working in the machine room were killed, along with two scientists in a nearby hallway. A researcher from Rio de Janeiro died from smoke inhalation; she and Bianca had worked together for many years. Others were hospitalized with third and fourth degree burns. But my brother, he should have made it out. His seismograph was on the opposite end. He'd been sleeping next to it, on a foam mattress, for godsakes. Everyone thought he was crazy.

The green light returned, brighter this time. It was halo-shaped and hovering above the observation room. I hadn't stayed with astronomy long enough to see the auroras in anything other than photos and slides. I thought back to a course in Extragalactic Astronomy, to the lectures on Hubble's law, and the quasars that radiated red light and the tidal pull of super massive black holes, which terrified me. In college, I had imagined myself working in remote observatories and seeing something new in the sky.

"He thought he'd found an undiscovered faultline," Luiz continued. "He was compiling his data. No one believed him. The peninsula isn't known for seismic activity. He was the only one with an office in that part of the building who didn't survive."

"Where were you during the explosion?" I watched the circle of light contract and expand.

"Outside. Scraping ice off our snow tractor."

So that was his guilt: he hadn't been close enough to believe he was going to die. He couldn't share in the trauma of having to save your own life, or the life of someone else; he could only report the facts. My brother had been too close, Luiz not close enough.

"We hadn't spoken in a long time." The halo dissolved and a sheet of luminous green spread across the horizon, at once beautiful and eerie.

"I asked him about family," Luiz said. "He didn't mention a sister."

I closed my eyes and thought about my brother in that hallway. I saw doorways alight with fire and black, curling smoke. His watch felt heavy on my wrist.

"Luiz," I said. "Do you have any secrets?"

"Too many to count." Silence fell over us in a way that made me think this was probably true. I pictured him tallying his secrets like coins. The sky hummed with green.

Later he explained the lights to me, the magnetic fields, the collision of electrons and atoms. I didn't tell him this was information I already knew. He reached for my hand and pulled off one of my gloves. He placed it on his chest and put his hand over it.

I sat up and took the glove back from him. He held on to it for a moment, smiling, before he let go.

"Of course," Luiz said. "You are married."

That afternoon, I'd emailed my husband from the recreation room: *Still getting the lay of the land. Don't worry: polar bears are in the North Pole.* He was a real estate agent and always honest about his properties—what needed renovating; if there were difficult neighbors. He believed the truth was as easy to grasp as a baseball or a glass of water. That was why I had married him.

"Yes," I said. "But it doesn't have anything to do with that."

As it turned out, Eve had lied about losing track of the man who had taken her. After his release from prison, she had kept very careful track, aided by a cousin in Concord, a paralegal who had access to a private investigator. It was February when she came to me with news of him. We were sitting in a window seat and drinking tea and looking out at the snow-covered lawn. A girl passed on the sidewalk, carrying ice skates and a pink helmet.

"He's in a hospital," she said. "Up on the Cape. He might not get out. Something to do with his lungs." She sighed with her whole body.

"And?" I said.

"And I want to see him."

"Oh, Eve. I think that's a terrible idea."

"Probably." She blew on her tea. "Probably it is."

In the weeks that followed, she kept at it. She talked about it while we folded laundry and swept the front steps. She talked about it when I met her for drinks after her rehearsals—she was an understudy for a production of *Buried Child* at the American Repertory Theater—and while we rode the T, the train clacking over the tracks whenever we rose above ground to cross the river. Eve explained that her parents had kept her from the court proceedings. She had wanted to visit him in prison, but that had been forbidden too. Now he was very sick. She was running out of chances.

"Chances for what?" We were waiting for the T in Central Square, on our way home from dinner. On the platform, a man was playing a violin for change. Eve had been in rehearsals earlier and was still wearing the false eyelashes and heavy red lipstick.

"To tell him that I made it." She raised her hands. Her gold bracelet slid down her wrist. "That I'm an actress. That I got married. That he wasn't the end of me. That I won."

"How about a phone call?" I said. "Or a letter?"

The T came through the tunnel and ground to a stop. The doors opened. People spilled onto the platform. A woman carrying a sleeping child slipped between me and Eve. My brother had been in Vancouver for two weeks and called home on Sunday mornings.

"You don't understand," she said as we boarded the train. "It has to be done in person."

I missed the perfect chance to tell my brother everything. The day before he left for Vancouver, I went to see him at MIT. His department was housed in the Green Building, which had been constructed by a famous architect and was the tallest building in all of Cambridge. From the outside, you could see a white radome on the roof. The basement level was connected to the MIT tunnel system. The first time I visited him on campus, he told me you could take the tunnels all the way to Kendall Square.

"How about some air?" I had found him hunched over a microscope. He was surprised to see me. I hadn't told him I was coming.

"I'm gone tomorrow." He gestured to the open laptops and the stacks of notebooks and the empty coffee mugs that surrounded him. Eve had been trimming his hair, and there was an unevenness to the cut that made him look like he was holding his head at a funny angle. The lenses of his glasses were smudged.

"I know," I said. "That's why I'm here."

We left campus and walked along Memorial Drive. By the river it was cold and windy. We pulled up the collars of our coats and tightened our scarves. We turned onto the Longfellow Bridge and kept going, until we were standing between two stone piers with domed roofs and tiny windows. They reminded me of medieval lookout towers. We leaned against the bridge and gazed out at the river and the city skyline beyond it.

I should have had a plan, but I didn't. Rather, the weight of Eve's secret had propelled me toward him, the way I imagined a current tugs at the objects that find their way into its waters.

"The house," my brother said. "Is everything okay there?"

Without him realizing, I felt he had become an anchor for me and Eve; we always knew he was there, in the background, and with his departure, I could feel a shift looming: subtle as a change in the energy, the way the air gets damp and cool before a storm. But this was before Eve had brought up going to the Cape. I didn't know how to explain what I was feeling, or if I should even try. I couldn't imagine what the right words would be.

"Everything's fine."

"Eve says you've been like a sister," he said.

"We'll miss you," I said. "Don't forget to call."

A gust nearly carried away my hat. I pulled it down over my ears. Snow clouds were settling over the brownstones and high rises. My brother put his arm around me and started talking about the Juan de Fuca plate, his voice bright with excitement. I could only detect the slightest trace of a stutter. The plate was bursting with seismic activity, a hotbed of shifts and tremors. I wrapped my arms around his waist and leaned into him. With his free hand, he drew the different kinds of faultlines—listric, ring, strike-slip—in the air.

The near constant darkness of Antarctica made my body confused about when to rest. At three in the morning, I got out of bed and pulled fleece-lined boots over my flannel pajamas. I put on my gloves and hat. Annabelle was babbling in Spanish. At dinner, under the fluorescent lights of the mess hall, I'd noticed a scattering of freckles on her cheekbones and thought of Eve. I had to stop myself from reaching across the table and touching her face.

The station was quiet. The doorways were dark and shuttered. I peered through shadows at the end of hallways and around corners like I was searching for something in particular—what that would be, I didn't know. I drifted to the front of the station. In the mud room, I surveyed the red windbreakers hanging on the wall, the bundles of goggles and gloves, the rows of boots. The entrance was a large steel door with a porthole window. I thought about opening the door, just for a moment, even though the temperature outside would be deep in the negatives; I imagined my hair turning into icicles, my eyes to glass.

Through the window, the station lights illuminated the outbuildings and the ice. The darkness was too thick, too absolute, to see anything more. When Luiz first told me that the rescue crew hadn't found any remains, there had been a moment when I'd thought my brother hadn't died in the explosion at all. Maybe he hadn't even been in the building. Maybe he had seen smoke rising from the land and realized this was his chance to vanish. I could picture him boarding an icebreaker and sailing to Uruguay or Cape Town. Standing on the deck of a ship and watching a new horizon emerge.

For a long time, I kept watch through the window, willing myself to see a figure surface from the night. Who was to say he hadn't sailed to another land? Who was to say he wasn't somewhere in that darkness? For him, I would open the door. For him, I would endure the cold. But, of course, nothing was out there.

In the observation room, after the Aurora Australis had left the sky, I'd turned to Luiz and said: *Here's what I want.* The idea had come suddenly and with force. I wanted to go to the Brazilian station, to the site of the explosion. At first, Luiz said it was impossible; it would involve chartering a helicopter, for one thing. I told him that if he could figure out a way to make this happen, I'd be on the next flight to New Zealand. I didn't care how much it cost. He promised to see what he could do.

I left the window and slipped back into the hallway. A light had been left on in the recreation room. I sat in the armchair next to the phone. I'd tucked my calling card into my pajama pocket, thinking I might phone my husband. Instead I dialed the number of the house in Davis Square, which I still knew by heart. The phone rang five times before someone answered. I'd thought a machine might come on and I could leave whoever lived there now a message about polar bears and green lights in the sky. For a moment, I imagined my sister-in-law picking up. *Où avez-vous été?* she would say. *Where have you been?*

A woman answered. Her voice was high and uncertain, not at all like Eve's. I pressed the phone against my ear. I pulled on the cord and thought about faultlines. I could see a dark streak running down my ribs, a fissure in my sternum.

"Hello?" she said. Static flared on the line. "How can I help you?"

III.

It was a military hospital, just outside Barnstable. The morning we left, Eve talked to my brother on the phone and said we were going to see the glass museum in Sandwich. I drove. She was dressed in jeans and a gray sweatshirt, unadorned by jewelry, the plainest I'd ever seen her. She rested her socked feet on the dashboard and told me what her cousin had discovered about this man. He'd been in the military, dishonorably discharged. Years ago he'd been involved with a real estate scam involving fraudulent mortgages and the elderly, but pleaded out of jail time. He had two restraining orders in his file.

"I'm surprised someone hasn't killed him already." She cracked the window. The air was heavy with moisture and salt.

We drove through Plymouth and Sandwich. From the highway, I saw a billboard ad for the glass museum. At the hospital—a labyrinthine gray building just off the highway—we learned he was in the ICU. We pretended to be family.

He was in a room with two other men. A thin curtain hung between each of the beds. Eve slowly walked from one to the other. The first patient was gazing at the TV bolted to the wall. The second was drinking orange juice from a straw. The third was asleep. He wore a white hospital gown. His gray hair was shorn close to the scalp. One hand rested on his stomach, the other on the mattress. I followed Eve to his bedside. His face was speckled with broken capillaries, his cheekbones sharp, his slender forearms bruised. He was on oxygen and attached to a heart monitor. I smelled something sour.

"Are you sure this is him?" I asked Eve, even though I could see the scar. It was just as she had described: a thin line of white under his eye.

"Don't say it." She walked over to the window and looked out at the parking lot.

"Say what?"

"That's he's old and frail and defenseless." Eve turned from the window. "He's not like that at all. Not on the inside." She pressed her fist against her chest.

She slumped down on the linoleum floor. A nurse was attending to the patient next to us. I watched her shadow through the curtain.

She carried away a tray with an empty glass on it. She told the man who had been drinking the juice to have a nice day.

"So what do we do now?" I asked. "Wake him up?"

"I'm thinking," Eve said. "I'm thinking of what to do."

It took her a long time to do her thinking. I listened to the din of the TV. I thought a game show was on from the way people kept calling out numbers.

Finally Eve jumped up and started digging through her purse. She took out a tube of lipstick, the garish red color she wore on stage, and raised it like a prize.

"Okay," she said. "I have my first idea."

She uncapped the lipstick and went to the sleeping man. She smeared color across his mouth. I stood on the other side of his bed and stared down, trying to see the evil in him. Eve used the lipstick to rouge his cheeks before passing it to me. I drew red half-circles above his eyebrows. We waited for him to wake up, to cry for help, but he only made a faint gurgling sound. His hand twitched on his stomach. That was all.

"Now I have another idea," Eve said.

For this second thing, she wanted to be alone. I looked at the clown's face we had given this man. My stomach felt strange. On the intercom, a doctor was being paged to surgery.

"Five minutes. Three hundred seconds." Her face was free of makeup, her freckles visible. She'd had her teeth bleached recently and they looked unnaturally white. "That's all I'm asking for, Lee."

After what had happened to her, wasn't she owed five minutes alone with him? That was my thinking at the time. On my way out of the ICU, the same nurse who picked up the juice glass asked me if I'd had a pleasant visit.

I waited on the sidewalk. I watched people come and go through the automatic doors. An old man on crutches. An old man in a wheelchair. A nurse in lavender scrubs. What was the worst thing these people had done?

Eve stayed in the hospital for fifty-seven minutes. I couldn't bring myself to go back inside. I paced in the cold. I had forgotten my gloves and my hands were going numb. Even though I'd never smoked in my life, I asked a doctor smoking outside if I could bum a cigarette.

"These things will kill you." The doctor winked and flipped open his cigarette pack.

When Eve emerged from the hospital, she took my hand and pulled me toward the car. We drove in silence. She rested her head against the window. When I tried to turn on the radio, she touched my wrist. Her fingertips were waxy with lipstick.

"Please," she said.

After a half hour on the road, I exited at Sagamore Beach. The silence felt like a pair of hands around my throat. Eve didn't object when I parked in the designated beach lot, empty on account of it being February, or when we climbed over dunes and through sea grass. Cold sand leaked into our shoes. I didn't stop until I reached water.

We were standing on the edge of Cape Cod Bay. The water was still and gray. Clusters of rock extended into the bay like fingers. A white mist hung over us. A freighter was visible in the distance.

"Why didn't you come out when you said you would?" The freighter was moving farther away. When it vanished from sight, it looked like it had gone into a cloud. "What were you doing in there?"

"We were talking." Her face was dewy from the mist. Her pale hair had frizzed. She picked up a white stone and threw it into the water.

"So he woke up?"

"Yes," she said. "He did and then he didn't."

She picked up another stone. It was gray with a black dot in the center. She held on to it for a little while, turning it over in her hands, before it went into the bay.

In Cambridge, she wanted to be dropped at the Repertory Theater. She had to tell the director that she couldn't make rehearsal; she promised to come home soon. Her hair was still curled from being at the beach. Her cheeks and forehead were damp. I tried to determine if anything had shifted in her eyes.

I idled on Brattle Street until Eve had gone into the theater. Her purse swung from her shoulder and somewhere inside it was that lipstick. I kept telling myself that the most dangerous part was over. We were home now. Everything would be the same as before.

But no. Nothing would be the same as before. Eve never talked to her director. She never returned to the house. I had to call my brother and tell him to come home from Vancouver. When I picked him up at the airport, it was late. I waited in baggage claim. Long before he noticed me, I spotted him coming down the escalator, a duffel bag slung over his shoulder. He had lost weight. His hair had grown out. I remembered thinking that I wished I knew him better, that I wished we'd taken the time to learn how to talk to each other. When he finally saw me, he tried to call out, *Lee*, but his stutter was as bad as it had been in childhood. It took him three tries to say my name.

A report was filed. Eve's parents—a frail, bookish couple—came into town from Concord. An investigation went on for weeks. There was no sign of Eve, no sign of foul play. As gently as he could, the detective asked us to consider the possibility that she had run away. Apparently women—young mothers, young wives—did this more frequently than people might think. I told everyone I'd dropped Eve at the theater, but the truth stopped there. Every time I tried to say more, I felt like a stone was lodged in my throat.

Because I was his sister, because we had been close, my brother knew I was holding something back. He pressed me for information. Had she been taking an inordinate amount of calls? Had anything peculiar arrived in the mail? Was she having an affair with a castmate? Had we really gone to the glass museum in Sandwich? I submitted to these questions, even though I didn't—couldn't, I felt at the time—always tell the truth. And I knew he was confronting his own failing, the fact that he hadn't cared to know any of this until after his wife was gone.

We waited months before we packed up her belongings: the silk dresses, the shoes, the jewelry, the plays. Her possessions had always seemed rich and abundant, but only filled three cardboard boxes. My brother kept them stacked at the foot of his bed. When he moved, two boxes went to Eve's parents and he took the other one with him. I don't know what happened to her things after that.

The last time he asked me a question about Eve, we were on the front porch. It was late spring. The trees were blooming green and white. I was in a rocking chair. My brother was leaning against the porch railing, facing the street.

"Do you think you knew her better than I did?" he said.

"No." Once I had come upon them in the upstairs hallway: they were pressed against the wall, kissing, and he was twisting one of Eve's wrists behind her back. It was clear that the pleasure was mutual, which led me to believe that she might enjoy a degree of pain. Only my brother could say how much.

He stared out at the glowing streetlights. I could tell from the way he licked his lips and squeezed the railing that he did not believe me.

By summer, we had moved into separate apartments: his in Beacon Hill, so he could be closer to MIT; mine in the North End, scrunched between a pastry shop and a butcher. I bounced from one entry-level lab job to another, my ambition dulled, while I watched my brother pull his own disappearing act: into his dissertation; into the conference circuit; into one far-flung expedition after another. The Philippines, Australia, Haiti. Antarctica. The phone calls and postcards turned from weekly to monthly to hardly at all.

I got married the year I turned thirty. My brother came, but left before the cake was served. It was too painful, watching the night unfold; I understood this without him ever saying so. I only told my husband that he had been married briefly and, years ago, we'd all lived together in Davis Square. Soon I had a child. I worked part-time as a lab assistant, sorting someone else's data, and cared for him, which was not the life I'd imagined for myself, but it seemed like a fair exchange: I hadn't kept sufficient watch over Eve, hadn't kept her from danger. This was my chance to make it up. I tried to tell myself she was some-place far away and happy. I tried to forget that she might have been in trouble, that she might have needed us. When I looked at my son, I tried not to think about all the things I could never tell him. I tried to shake the feeling that I was living someone else's life.

In the years to come, I would start so many letters to my brother, each one beginning in a different way: *Eve was not who you thought*, and, *I don't know how it all started*, and *how could you not have known?* I never got very far because I knew I was still lying. The letter I finally finished—addressed to the McMurdo station but never mailed—opened with: *None of this was your fault.*

Another thing I never told him: before leaving the house in Davis Square, I cut open one of Eve's boxes and found her gold bracelet in a tiny plastic bag. The chain was tarnished. I popped open the locket; the frames were empty. I took the bracelet and re-sealed the box with packing tape. I held onto it—never wearing it, always hiding it away, even before there were people to hide it from. My husband found it once, and I said it had been a gift from my mother. I imagined other people discovering the bracelet through the years, and telling each one a different story. I would carry it with me to Antarctica, tucked in the side pocket of my suitcase, though I was never able to bring it out into the open.

Not long after Eve's disappearance, I looked up the name of her abductor on a computer: Randall Smith. I'd only heard her say it aloud once, in the hospital. After a little searching, I found an obituary. He had died the day after our visit, survived by no one. The obituary said it was natural causes, which explained nothing.

It was twilight when we flew over Admiralty Bay. Luiz said that if I watched the water carefully, I might see leopard seals. The pilot was from the Netherlands, hired for a price that would horrify my husband when the check posted. Luiz's boss had gotten wind of our expedition and wasn't at all pleased; that morning, he'd called from Brazil and told Luiz that he was not in the business of escorting tourists. Soon I would have to get on the plane to New Zealand, like I had promised, but I wasn't completely out of time.

The landscape was different on the peninsula. The ice was sparser, exposing the rocky peaks of mountains and patches of black soil near the coastline. When the explosion site came into view, it looked like a dark scar on the snow.

The helicopter touched down. Black headsets swallowed our ears, muffling the sound of the propellers. The helicopter swayed as it landed. I could feel the engine rumbling beneath us; it made my skin vibrate inside my many layers of clothes. Luiz got out first, then helped me onto the ice. The pilot shouted something in Dutch, which Luiz translated: soon the twilight would be gone; he didn't want to fly back in the dark.

Together we approached the wreckage. Luiz still had his headset on. I had taken mine off too soon and now my ears buzzed. Up close, the site was smaller than I'd expected: a black rectangle the size of the swimming pool I took my son to in the summer. Nothing of the structure remained except for metal beams jutting from ridges of ash and debris. The sky was a golden haze.

"I told you there wasn't much to see." He slipped off his headset. His face was covered except for his eyes. I was wearing a balaclava too and knew I looked the same.

"Tell me what it was like before."

The station had been shaped like a horseshoe. He pointed to the empty spaces where the mess hall used to be, the dormitories, the bathroom, my brother's seismograph. Their base had been smaller than Belgrano. They didn't have an observation room or heated research tents. Everything had been contained under one roof.

I stepped in the ash and listened to it crunch under my boots. I passed black spears of wood and warped beams. One section of the site was even more charred, the ground scooped in. I stood inside the depression and looked at the bits of metal glinting in the ash. I picked up something the size of a quarter. I wasn't sure what it had been before; the fire had made it glossy and flat. I slipped it into my pocket and kept walking. I told myself it was evidence; I just didn't know what kind.

The wind blew flurries of ash around my legs. On the other end of the site, I looked for some sign of my brother's seismograph. I came across a spoon, the handle melted into a glob of metal, and a lighter. I put those things in my pockets too. More evidence. Luiz was still on the edge of the site. By then I understood he was someone who had no desire to go searching for things. He didn't even collect the meteorites; his only concern was classifying them. The helicopter would be ready for us soon, but the sky still held a dull glow.

There were so many times when I wanted to tell my brother everything—when, in the middle of the night, I wanted to kneel by his
bed and whisper, *I have a secret*. In Cambridge, I'd told myself these
were Eve's secrets to keep or expose; it was her life to walk away from,
if that's what she wanted. And the more time that passed, the more
unimaginable the truth seemed. To admit one lie would mean admitting another and then another.

I imagined myself at home in New Hampshire, arranging everything
on the living room floor. A map of Antarctica, with stars to mark the
bases: McMurdo; here; Belgrano. My brother's watch. Eve's empty
locket. The photo he mailed, without a note, when he first arrived in
Antarctica. He was wearing a yellow snowsuit and standing outside
McMurdo, surrounded by bright white ice. Around these materials, I would place the metals I had collected at the site and try to see
something: a pattern, a sign. Or maybe I would just read aloud the
last letter I wrote to him. Or maybe, in the helicopter, I would turn
to Luiz and tell him everything.

The sky was almost dark. I was back inside the depression. I was sitting down in it and hugging my knees. I had no memory of walking
over there and stepping into the hole; I had just done it automatically.
Luiz was calling to me. The wind carried his voice away.

Maybe it was just an iguana, I heard my brother say.

In Antarctica, I did not know if he had denied himself the chance
to get out of the burning building. I did not know what he believed
I knew, or what would have changed if I'd given him the truth. I did
not know if I would ever see Eve again. I did not know what had
happened in that hospital room, or in Acton. Some of these things I
did not know—not because they were unknowable, but because I had
turned away from the knowledge. In Antarctica, I decided that was the
worst thing I'd ever done, that refusal.

The stars were coming out. Luiz was crossing the site, waving and
calling my name. The temperature was dropping. My eyes watered. I
sunk deeper into the hole.

In Antarctica, I did not know that a month after I left, Luiz would
become trapped in a whiteout and lose two fingers to frostbite. I

did not know that the tibia would turn out to have belonged to my brother, that it would be shipped back to America in a metal box. I did not know if one day I would disappear and no one except a missing woman and a dead man would be able to tell the people who loved me why.

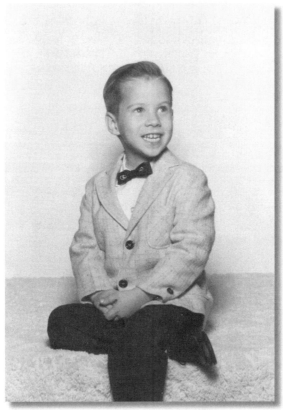

The very picture of Virtue.

Joseph O'Malley was born and raised in Detroit and now lives in New York City. His work has appeared in *Alaska Quarterly Review*, *Santa Monica Review*, and *Iron Horse Literary Review*, among other places.

THE MANLY MAN'S
GUIDE TO VIRTUE

Joseph O'Malley

Almost everyone was dead, and Joe was lost. Two lovers dead—one of AIDS, the other of pancreatic cancer. Both parents dead; brother, sister, all dead. When Joe was young, he did what most Midwestern gay boys did: he moved to New York to get away from his family. When they were all gone, he didn't know what to tell people who asked about them. His siblings, both older than Joe, hadn't died from any horrible accident, but from the slow, steady accumulation of ill health wrought by sedentary Midwestern life lived among the most mundane of murderers: television, cars, food. They'd surrounded themselves with as much flesh as their bodies could bear, and then suddenly collapsed within months of one another. Joe told all of his friends that his family died of heterosexuality. It was a cheap shot, but sometimes it got a laugh.

So, lost and alone, Joe was free to do anything he wanted. He tried not to feel stupid for not realizing until he was almost fifty years old that he had always been free to do what he wanted. Part of the problem was that he had had an idea of himself. He was a funny guy, a guy's guy. A gay guy's guy, but still. He still had his dancer's body, complete with aching joints, a ruined knee, and shoulder pain, but he stayed vigilant and the gym kept him slim. He stopped dancing after age and

Glimmer Train Stories, Issue 88, Fall 2013
©2013 Joseph O'Malley

injuries caught up with him in his thirties, then worked his way up from a variety of café jobs to a position as maitre d' in the Standard Hotel's restaurant, not far from his rent controlled apartment in the West Village, where he had lived for thirty years.

Joe had taken no more than a few days off work during the deaths of his family, and only a week off for each of his two lovers. His friends thought this showed "strength," but Joe knew his ability to power through the tasks of daily living was directly wired to the peculiar engine of his anxiety. His constant activity during times of great stress was the only way to expel his agitation, thus allowing him to appear outwardly "cool" to most of the world.

Both of his lovers had been named Tom. When the shock of the second Tom's death had faded—his cancer was diagnosed two months after moving in with Joe, and he died three months later—Joe felt nothing more than empty. He was bursting with emptiness. Or rather, it was nothing like that, but if it had to be like something, that would be the closest to it. If he'd had to *feel* something, he thought he might just die.

He wasn't glum; he just wasn't interested in anything. He went to work, he came home. He learned to knit, which was an immense comfort. The repetitive movement calmed him; there were only two options—knit and purl—and at the end of it one had a scarf, or a blanket, bath mats, washcloths, big floppy knit bags with which to hold more yarn. When he knit, he didn't have to listen to people talk. At work people talked all night. The bartender talked to everyone, waiters talked to waiters, waiters talked to customers, customers talked to each other, and they all talked to Joe. On the subway, in the street, in lines at the grocery: talk, talk, talk. People had conversations about sandwiches, curtains, the inner workings of a computer, painfully detailed descriptions of their petty little personal dramas. *Should I defriend her on Facebook? It's the best bran muffin in New York! How many gigabytes does it hold? Yes, the film was intellectually stimulating, but I found it indulgently self-referential.*

There was way too much talk in the world.

Joe enjoyed listening to music, but the songs he liked best were those in languages he didn't understand. Then one day on NPR he heard a panel show with comedians, and for the first time in a long time, he was interested. He realized the only time he could stand people talking was when they were funny. And every once in a while he thought: I could do that.

He went to comedy clubs, and again thought: I could do that. He went to drag shows, where the humor was filthy, raw, and sometimes dangerous, if a bit broad. I would never do that, he thought, but I *could*. Perhaps he could write for a drag queen. Drag queens needed writers, didn't they? He bought an unlined notebook, a purple felt-tipped pen. He met the emptiness head on, and it was easy because now the emptiness was limited to eight and a half by eleven inches.

The first time I shit my pants in public I was in an elevator. With twenty other people. On the way to the top of the Empire State Building. It was three o'clock in the afternoon, and two hours earlier I'd thought the all-you-can-eat buffet at the Chinese restaurant was a good idea. One too many helpings of mu gu poo pants. Then there was the Indian restaurant two days later. I got the panty saag. What a week!

Well. It was a start. But one needed a whole routine, didn't one? A beginning, a middle, an end.

"Poop humor." Joe's friend, Oswaldo, wrinkled his face. "Even when it's not funny, it can get a laugh. But that's the problem. It's the pity fuck of jokes. And if it goes wrong, it goes *really* wrong."

Of all his friends, Oswaldo understood him best. He'd had his own battles and desolate moods, and had a sixth sense for when to call Joe and when to leave him be. Oswaldo and Joe had met the week after Joe moved from Detroit to New York, and Oswaldo from Cleveland. Joe was nineteen, Oswaldo twenty. They'd checked one another out from folding chairs stationed directly across from each other at a dance audition for the same company. Joe got in, Oswaldo didn't, but he got into another, better, company. Years later, Oswaldo became a choreographer and formed his own company. Joe and Oswaldo had never slept together, and because there was never any of that confusing sexual tension, they became the best of friends.

After hearing a few more of Joe's jokes, Oswaldo said, "Sometimes things that work on paper don't always translate to the stage. And you have to think about the persona. Jokes should be specific to character. You should be your own drag queen," he said, and left Joe with his empty pad of paper to figure out the rest.

It all clicked at a MOMA exhibit devoted to Ernst Ludwig Kirchner. The Berlin street scene paintings of people in severe poses wearing lush colors reminded Joe alternately of Toulouse Lautrec and of drag queens. And that's when his character's name came to him: Tootight Lautrec.

It was all a joke. Even if he never intended to do anything about it, just considering it cheered Joe up. He made an offhand comment to one of the waiters at work about maybe wanting to do drag; the waiter said he had friend who did makeup on Broadway, and was always up for something kicky. A nudge here, a nudge there. Joe reminded himself he was free. Oswaldo said, *Why not*, and soon Joe was in a panic of preparation, on track for an open mic night at the Stonewall as Tootight Lautrec.

It couldn't have gone worse. It wasn't like a dance crowd, where people sit quietly in their seats and pay attention. Is that what he wanted? Attention? All the discomfort that he'd been avoiding by knitting alone in his apartment had been collected in this barroom, and there stood Joe, all covered up in a short, dark bobbed wig, garish green–yellow makeup, and a tight orange evening gown, with every nerve exposed.

He told his jokes, but what he thought was funny apparently was not funny. Or his delivery was off. Or his charisma lacked the necessary flash.

"In fact," said Oswaldo, "it's the best thing that could have happened. Could you imagine if you had been a huge success? Every time after would have been disappointing in comparison."

"There will be no time after."

Oswaldo laughed and said, "Nonsense."

Two weeks later, Joe tried a new set out on Oswaldo.

"Genital humor." Oswaldo crinkled his nose. "Yes, it's funny enough, and I understand the impulse, but I'm hoping you'll grow beyond it into the subtler, more intelligent humor that you use in your daily life. Or rather, Tootight's daily life. But anyway, go with what you have. Work toward building a real persona. It takes more than tossing a wig on your noggin and flouncing around in a dress to make a character. But this is fine. For now."

During the second performance a band of rowdy, drunk boys grew noisier and noisier as the set wore on, until Joe could no longer hear himself speak, and he unleashed Tootight on them.

"Ladies, ladies, ladies," Tootight said pointing at them with a hand gloved to the elbow with chartreuse satin. She clapped twice, as if calling a classroom to order, and then, in a quiet, elegant voice said, "Ladies, please. We must learn to comport ourselves with a modicum of *éclat* and *élan*." She paused as the room quieted, then looked out at the other patrons. "Do we know what these words mean?" She cocked her head. "Of course not. But we must *act* as if we do."

The crowd responded well, and Joe tucked the technique into a pocket of his mind knowing that along with his standard jokes he'd need a grab bag of witty ripostes for hecklers and ne'er-do-wells.

"How about this," Joe proposed to Oswaldo. "She never purposely talks dirty. The filth slips out in malapropisms. She's uptight—Tootight—well meaning in a schoolmarmish way. She quotes people like Balzac, but mispronounces it as Ball Sack. She throws the audience off by alternating between extreme intellectual rants interspersed among her malapropisms and jokes. She wants to be sophisticated, makes up convoluted stories about her life that are too far-fetched to be true."

"Like what?"

"Like," Joe paused to think. "I don't know." He thought some more, and brightened. "Like, she talks about her days as Mother Superior in a convent on the French border. Alsace-Lorraine. The Asslips-Lorraine region. But she left because she just couldn't stand the smell of all those unwashed virgins." Joe slipped into character, and said, "So I went back to Paris to resume my career in a much, much, much older profession. Of course I mean *teaching*."

Oswaldo chuckled, "Okay."

"It slips out that really she's just a school teacher from Normal, Illinois who was fired after a particularly scandalous photocopier incident. She's a French chanteuse who can neither speak French, nor sing."

Oswaldo approved. "But that floppy thing you call a wig won't do. I picture her with black hair pulled super tight into an abnormally long bun that goes out and up at a forty-five degree angle. Maybe bangs in front."

"Yes!" said Joe. "She'll begin every act by saying, '*Bon soir*, class.'"

"Pronounce it *Bone sore*."

Bone sore, class. I thought it might be fun if tonight we talked about Virtue. By the looks of it, some of you here need a good talking to. In fact, there are seven virtues, but it depends on who you get to do your research for you. Did you know the word "virtue" in Latin means "manly"? Manly with a capital MAN. And who knows more about manly men than those Greeks, with their Ganymedes, and geisha boys, and Roman orgies, and… Well, uh, there's a slight probability I have my geometry a little mixed up, but you know what I'm getting at. Now, my girlfriend, Febreze McQueaf, and I were chatting about this the other day—just a little girl talk, you know—and Febreze asked if I remembered how Aristotle departed from Plato by saying that virtue is a habit of being. Oh, I laughed. Yes, Febreze, I said, everybody knows that. But don't forget that Kant revised Aristotle by saying that virtue is a moral solution to ignorance and weakness. Such a silly girl, that Febreze. Well, for us, tonight, we'll simply consider Virtue as moral character, rather than dealing with the messier deontological or consequentialist approaches. That okay with you?

A man in the front row whistled. Tootight stopped, and said to him, *Quite a mouthful, huh? Don't look so shocked. As if you've never had a mouthful of manliness.*

The rest of the show was light and silly. A manager of a club in the East Village saw the act and invited Joe to bring Tootight Lautrec to perform there for a small chunk of cash, plus tips. Joe decided to develop an entire series of acts surrounding the seven heavenly virtues, one virtue a month to keep him busy through the winter.

Then, on the night of the first installment of his new act, in the bathroom of the club, while affixing an oversized eyelash more securely, Joe's mother walked in. Well, not really his mother. But another queen who was also performing that night drifted past wearing a perfume that thrust Joe back to Detroit, the family bathroom, him as a seven-year-old boy watching his mother powder, rouge, and lipstick herself for a night out with his father while Joe talked about the four o'clock movie he'd seen on TV. There was a French psychiatrist in the movie: hypnosis, past lives, flowers that bloomed at the touch of a lady with long fingernails who sang like nobody Joe had ever heard.

Joe's mother—the seven-year-old Joe's mother—steps back from the mirror to appraise herself fully. She and her husband are young, healthy parents; none of her children are fat yet. She approves of what she sees in the mirror, and smiles at the young Joe. She removes a velvet, black and orange striped cap from a bottle, waves the bottle over head, shoulders, heart, as if she's blessing herself in church, squirts, lets the mist settle. She pulls the blousey front of her dress out with one finger, sprays deep into the cleavage, dabs the spray nozzle under each ear, replaces the striped cap, and when she sets the bottle back down on the vanity, Joe can see that the perfume is called Tigress. Joe's parents are in love. His mother is happy. They are all happy.

The club music from the floor above the bathroom where Joe secured his lash was so loud that it shook the bathroom mirror. Joe inhaled deeply and peered at the drag queen in the other part of the mirror, who was fully made up except that he hadn't yet pulled a wig onto his bald head.

"What are you wearing?" Joe asked. He had seen this queen before, a fat, crass stage hog who mistook vulgarity at high volume for humor, and called himself Muffy McGillicuddy. Joe watched him pull a big red curly wig out of his bag and shake it violently with one hand.

"What?" said Muffy. "This old thing?" He pulled the edges of his tight skirt toward his knees with his free hand. Joe had never liked this queen, and the fact that he answered with the oldest cliché in the book normally would have bothered Joe, but the smell of the perfume eased his annoyance.

"No," said Joe. "Your perfume. What perfume are you wearing? Is it Tigress?"

"It's a mixture of four different perfumes." He leaned forward, pulled on the wig, and jerked back up to adjust. "I don't really know which ones, I just spritz and go. I saw Cher talk about doing it on a talk show once. It's different every time."

The flippancy with which Muffy said this reminded Joe why he hated this queen, and yet he didn't want to leave. He wanted to fall into that smell. Joe didn't say anything. They stood side by side in the mirror adjusting their drag equipment.

"Hey," Muffy said. "Are you okay?"

"It," Joe said. "It's lovely. The perfume." He leaned in to sniff, and Muffy flinched.

"Ooookayyyy," Muffy said, stepping gingerly back a pace. She turned from Joe to inspect herself in the mirror. "Damn," she said. She made a great show of rooting through her bag. When she found what she was looking for, she pressed her face very close to the mirror, tweezed out a long nose hair, sneezed aggressively, and said to Joe in a high, loud, imitation of camaraderie, "Break a leg," and sauntered out.

Tootight's first lesson of the seven virtues was Charity. Joe couldn't think about his mother directly during the act, so he tried to let the memory of her dance around him like a cloud. His mother had been the most charitable person he'd ever known; she never judged other people, always considered the peculiar predicaments of the human condition, always tried to imagine the difficulties other people endure. She would have been ashamed of Joe's meanness of heart with Muffy McGillicuddy.

Muffy had left the crowd frenzied with some sort of raunchy, raucous nonsense, and Joe wanted to bring them back to a more relaxed mood. Tootight walked slowly onto the stage, waving like the Queen of England. She stared out at the audience gesturing for quiet until they fell into a more dignified silence. At first, fear threatened to stop him in his tracks, but Joe had prepared well, and the smell of his mother lent some odd strength he didn't feel on his own.

Bone Sore, class. I beckoned you all here this evening to discuss something of vital import. Charity. Mostly, Charity to me. Buckets in which you can deposit your appreciations are positioned at either end of the stage for your convenience. Tens and twenties are acceptable, but fifties and hundreds are a more exemplary show of charity, aren't they? My philosophy is similar to that gorgeous silver screen icon, Loretta Young, who once said, "Like Charity, I believe Glamour should begin at home."

Joe's mother wafted close and receded, and Joe knew he was loved. His mother had been dead for years, and yet he felt her love. This love was alive, like a young animal. It occurred to him that this ghost of a feeling that was so strong and so real must be why some people still believe in a god. His act went off with a verve and panache it had never before had.

As he neared the end of his material the lights glared and Joe saw Oswaldo gesture to his watch and hold up five outstretched fingers. He was finishing way too early. "Twenty minutes is an eternity when you're alone on stage," Oswaldo had warned, but Joe had dismissed this as poppycock. Joe had wanted Tootight to end on a big joke, but the joke had been told, and still there was more time. He thought that as long as his mother was wafting around, he'd let her help him push toward something more. Joe moved Tootight forward toward the edge of the ragged stage floor. He felt as though he were stepping off into thin air. He had nothing planned.

Now, you're wondering, what's the use of all this talk about Charity? What is the point? What is the point of anything? Only this: Charity is a practice. It's a tool to help you live a more satisfying life. Decency and human kindness require work. I know you have encountered people who hate you for who you are, or what you are, or what they think you are. You will never change their minds. But I want you to try something the next time you're faced with an enemy. This is the most difficult kind of Charity: Imagine your enemies in their purest state, whether it be as a scared child, or the first time they fell in love. Be kind to them, even if you think they don't deserve it. It's those people who need kindness and forgiveness most who are the last to get it. Now, being charitable at heart with your enemies won't stop them from hating you, but it might stop you from hating them, and that's worth a lot. Hate is poison. It kills every good thing. You're going to die someday, but while you're alive for this very short time, don't live with the poison of hatred in your hearts.

Tootight paused, stared down the audience, brought the microphone close, and said quietly, insistently: *I can see you don't believe me. You're young, healthy, invincible, right? Don't be so stupid. Make no mistake. You will all die. You: in the tight red shirt, so young and virile. Fifty or so years hence, perhaps much sooner, you will be as nothing. You, over there. Yes, you with the pretty, unlined face, smooth as a Creamsicle. If you're lucky, and you become very old, all your powers to attract will leave you before you return—Poof—to dust.*

Joe barely knew what he was saying, or where it might lead. Nobody spoke. People stared, some with jaws ajar.

My mother told me when I was just a wee little drag princess, Tootight, she said, remember what that famous philosopher Epididymis said: "Have a little imagination."

It was the funniest feeling. Joe heard himself talk, but he was more observer than performer. It was him, Joe, speaking, but he'd have never uttered these thoughts if he'd had to say them as himself. His voice grew louder, stronger, and took on an edge of anger as he spoke, but he kept going just to see what would happen.

Imagine yourself better than your enemies. Every day, every moment, imagine yourself decent, loving, beautiful. No matter what happens when you leave here tonight, no matter who calls you a filthy fucking faggot, or a dirty dyke, or hetero scum, remember: You are beautiful. You are loved. And not just because I say so. I'm not some fucking Hallmark card up here spouting easy nostrums for your benefit. You're all ugly, too. We're all ugly. But we each have a tiny part of us where beauty and love live. Find it. Cultivate your beauty, inside and out. It takes a lot of work, certainly, but everything worthwhile takes a lot of work. If you've ever known love for even three seconds of your miserable life, then you know love. Mother, father, sister, brother, lover, friend. It doesn't matter who loved you, who showed you your beauty, or how long ago. Once you've found that kernel of love with your name on it, bring it out. Show it to the world. Give it away every chance you have to everyone you meet. It's contagious. Kind of like crabs, but not as itchy. Let everyone in on your secret. You are beautiful. You are strong. You are loved.

He stripped off a glove, threw it into the audience, and walked off stage.

Oswaldo brought the glove back to Joe, hugged him close, and said laughing, "What the hell was that?" Everyone was very kind. Boys and men sent so many drinks over to him that he had to give them away. Even Muffy waltzed over to congratulate him on a fabulous show.

For the next two days Joe couldn't leave his apartment. He told work he had the flu. He didn't answer the phone, didn't return messages, didn't turn on his computer to answer emails. When Oswaldo knocked on his door, Joe said, without getting up from his knitting, "I'm okay, Oswaldo. I just need to be alone for a little while."

"I'm worried," Oswaldo said.

"Don't worry."

Joe heard the soft slump of Oswaldo's body against his door. Oswaldo sighed heavily, probably so that Joe could hear. "I'm not going to have to call the police to break down the door or anything later on, am I?'

"No."

"Or clean up any...big mess, right?"

Joe laughed.

"A laugh. Good. Call me if you need anything."

"Thanks," Joe yelled to Oswaldo's retreating steps.

A host of abstract emotions swarmed Joe. He decided he would sit and knit a big blanket and let the swarm wash over him and try not to think too much. He took cover, the way one might sit out a passing tornado in a cellar. But after two more days of doing not much more than knitting and drinking tea, he ran out of milk, and as he walked to the corner to get more, Joe's father walked slowly, haltingly down Jane Street in his old walker with the tennis balls on the two back legs to keep it from rattling. Of course, when the man smiled at Joe it wasn't his father at all. And then the woman eating ice cream who was so fat she could barely walk wasn't really his dead sister, nor was the sweaty guy with the black plastic framed glasses and ridiculous mustache his dead brother. Suddenly, Joe's ghosts were everywhere. The Tiffany lamp next to Joe's bed was Tom One's lamp, and every time he touched it, Tom was there. Joe danced around the apartment to Nico's manly voice because she was Tom One's favorite singer. Tom Two's favorite Snoopy T-shirts were still in the drawer, and Joe found himself making enough of Tom Two's famous garlic borscht for four people, only to end up eating it alone when he was done. His senses magnetized, gathering his ghosts into his eyes, ears, nose, even brushing against his skin from their former comfortable distances hither and yon. But why? Why now? And why didn't he want it to stop?

Meanwhile, he had to work on the second heavenly virtue for his act, Prudence. How does one make Prudence funny? Tom One used to call Joe "Prudence" because of his relative lack of sexual experience, but they both realized near Tom's end that Joe's delayed awakening had probably prevented him from getting infected. Joe spent the next few years after Tom One's funeral catching up sexually, and while he was always safe, he made sure he could never be called a prude again.

Bone Sore, class! My, my, my, my, my, my. Just look at you all. You're all so young, and ripe, and tight! Mmmm. For tonight's class, I thought we'd have a friendly little discussion about Prudence. Of course, when I say "discussion" I mean I talk and you listen. Now, class, I know you're all at an age when, how shall we say it? Your…juices are flowing. Pointing to a man in front. *Yes, Dear. I mean you. You have juices, don't you? They should call you Minute Maid. Made in a minute.* Snap. Aside to his friend. *I'm right, aren't I? Don't worry, Dear, it's okay. Just sit back and enjoy your martini while I talk, but don't forget to tip your adorable waiters. I'm a very liberal teacher. Très hip. Très cool. You can even eat in my class. Order a little nosh and I'll continue the lesson while you, you know, masticate. Oh, please! It's all right. We all do it. Some of us maybe more than others.*

All of us here are Homosssssapiens, oui? Non? Oui! We all know about… juices. Tootight fixes her eye on an especially attractive man. *Oh, hell-loooo!* Giggling, touching her bun, smoothing her dress. *Sorry. What was I saying? Oh, yes. Prudence. Let's get to it tout de suite.* Smiling at man. *And the tooter,* hip bump, *the sweeter.*

And Tom One was there the whole time as a man who looked nothing like him, but laughed the same laugh, like air squeezed rhythmically from an inner tube. Joe made sure to leave time at the end to walk to the edge with his ghost. It was terrifying to depend on bald improvisation, but it was also thrilling.

Joe summoned his father to walk him to the edge with Fortitude, his brother with Justice, his sister with Hope, and Tom Two with Temperance, and by the end of the winter Joe had worked through all his ghosts. They didn't leave him completely, but now when they arrived, the pang was sweet. He'd no longer mist up into tears at their appearance, when they had brought to mind the total helplessness of his love against their deaths. Tom One transformed from the person he had become at the end—the sunken-eyed emaciated thirty-five-year-old who was so weak that he walked like a newborn fawn. Now he appeared happy, joking, sexy as when they'd first met. Tom Two was still the funniest person Joe had ever met. Joe's sister was again young, vibrant, slim; his brother was patient and funny with Joe's total ignorance about anything mechanical; his father could split wood just like in the old days when they went to the farm in Bad Axe, where Joe's grandparents lived. His mother wasn't shaking and crying for more Xanax in the nursing home. Now when they appeared they enveloped him in the memory of their love, then faded away slowly before he remembered how much he missed them.

The last stop on the Virtue Tour was Faith for Atheists. All his ghosts were there, in the blinking lights, in the coughs from the back of the room, in the hoppy beer smell that rose from the wooden floor, in the glitter and puffs of powder swirling around the other queens, but his ghosts were just there for the show. They didn't help him at all.

He left time at the end of his act as usual, moved to the stage edge to step onto air, but this time there was nothing there except silence, the impatience of a waiting audience, bald faced fear. He scrambled to cobble together old bits from his previous lessons. He couldn't even come up with a funny new name for a philosopher. The sweat rolled out from under his wig. He couldn't see the peeling wallpaper, the chinks in the concrete walls that he'd seen before the lights dimmed to work their magic and drown out all the flaws, but he knew they were there. Joe was finally exposed in the bright light at the edge of the stage, his lipstick bleeding into the craquelure of his makeup, a lost, lonely man pretending to be witty and strong as he fumbled to finish.

Because it was the last performance of the Virtue Tour, and Tootight had acquired a loyal following over the winter, the final act was received warmly by the crowd, who were overly kind. The hoots and applause at the end sickened Joe. He thought about all the times people gave standing ovations in New York theaters for less than mediocre performances. Their sturdy clapping had nothing to do with the quality of the performances. People were basically stupid sheep who needed to convince themselves that they had had a "good time," that they hadn't wasted their money on mediocrity yet again. Every accolade was suspect. Everyone was a fake. Joe knew he had failed. He could be original and scintillating only with help from his ghosts. Alone he was nothing.

The club cleared out after four a.m., and Joe headed home. It was early April, that in-between time when an ice storm was as likely as a day for shorts and T-shirt. Blackened peaks dotted the tops of small clots of snow left from the last storm, which had covered the city with three inches. It had warmed twenty degrees or more over the past few days and, rather than bleeding away in small rivulets, the snow seemed to be rising into steam.

The city looked just as it had the first time Joe visited and fell in love with it. Then as now the buildings charmed him, their shapes, their varying heights, the facades designed with bricks and stones placed at various geometric angles, and the variety continued on down the line. Water towers crowned buildings here and there. Fire escapes zigzagged up toward roofs. It was all merely bricks, stone, plaster, wrought iron, a door painted Spanish red, or Mediterranean blue. He walked alone, and tried to forget about the impermanence of all things. He loved this feeling of dissolving into the night, drifting for a little while, almost disembodied as he walked home.

He tried to conjure his ghosts as he drifted, to no avail. His memory had never done his brother, Paul, justice. Paul had taught Joe how to listen, really listen to music, by making him close his eyes, stand in front of the stereo with his fingers in his ears and feel the beat the music made against his body. Without Paul, Joe would never have sought out dance as his refuge. His sister, Chloe, had treated Joe like her own child. She read him the funny paper so many times when he was three and she eight that he memorized the frames and pretended to neighbors and relatives that he was a genius three-year-old who could read. He'd always spoken cursorily of his family to keep from missing them. In his youth he'd thought that admitting he missed his family was uncool, too sentimental, weak. He couldn't deny it; he loved them. Even now he felt it, if only in flashes, but his love was true; it was a palpable thing.

His happy memories of the Toms tangled with memories of all the dull, dull hours, all the disappointments. Joe had never confessed his irritation at wasting his days sitting at the hospital with Tom Two, even after Tom had slipped into the coma from which he'd never wake. He never told anyone about the joy of knowing he'd no longer have to wipe Tom One's shitty ass, look into the longing, uncommunicative recesses of his lover's eyes not knowing what he wanted, or how to help him. How could he tell anyone about the horrible relief he felt when Tom's long, slow, miserable slide from life was finally complete? But the love he had felt! He had as hard a time explaining that as anything.

He was only halfway home and already he was so tired. As far as Faith was concerned, he'd never been faithful to the memories of his loved ones. He called his lovers Tom One and Tom Two to keep their specificities from tormenting him.

Wet buds barely sprouted on trees. Joe walked home from the East Village to the West, watching fog curl over the backs of rats in the alleyways. He had scoured off his makeup in the bathroom at the club and fit all of Tootight—dress, wig, shoes—into a bag he'd slung over his shoulder. As he'd left the club, people asked what Tootight's next act would be. He simply shook his head in answer. *She's dead,* Joe had wanted to tell them. *It was just something to do.* Couldn't they see how he'd failed by reprising bits from his previous shows? But Oswaldo, who read the gloom in the lines on Joe's forehead, told him he should consider this his Greatest Hits Show. "How many times do you think Barbra Streisand has sung 'Memories,'" he said before he kissed Joe on the cheek, then went home with a comely, younger, prematurely silver-haired banker. Perhaps Oswaldo was right. Perhaps he'd given the crowd exactly what they'd wanted.

A truck rolled past, fluttering skirts of fog in its wake. Joe wondered what a skirt like that would look like in the material world. Crinoline, he supposed. Or strings of fringe like on a flapper's dress, mid-Charleston. How would Tootight have looked in that?

Maybe he'd resurrect her, and counter his Virtue Tour with the obvious. He could see the poster: Tootight with the same outrageous bun, but wearing a 1930s Bonnie Parker style beret, and a beaded deco dress, a machine gun slung over one shoulder. The poster would say: *Tootight Lautrec and the Seven Deadly Sins,* and stamped slantwise in red ink across the picture: *Public Enema Number One.*

Joe laughed, and watched his breath paisley the fog.

It was too warm for the jacket he'd worn earlier. His sweat collected in a dew on his upper lip. He passed signposts ankleted with chains and locks from which bikes had been stolen. The *beep beep* of a produce truck sounded its backing-up warning in front of a Korean grocery. A man hosed down the sidewalk in front of a café.

The temperature had risen steadily during the night, raising a lush mist over the island that softened everything. Fog swaddled the moon, muted the streetlights, and Joe imagined it floating over the drunks in Tompkins Square Park, collecting in the ramparts near the Cloisters where Joe had first met Tom One, beading on the tin horses of the carousel in Central Park, where Joe went on his first date with Tom Two. The fog curled around Joe in eddies, white wisps of it playing around the *suck* and *poomph* of the opening and closing door to his building. After his shower, the mist nuzzled against the windowpane with a faint glow of either moon or morning. The sheets on his bed were smooth, his skin smelled clean, and sounds of traffic whirred softly in the distance, as Joe sank into the deep comfort of his senses, and slept.

My sister Kerri and me, 1971 I think. I'm the one in the hat.

Tom Kealey's short story collection *Thieves I've Known* won the 2012 Flannery O'Connor Award and is forthcoming from the University of Georgia Press. Tom is also the author of *The Creative Writing MFA Handbook*. His fiction and nonfiction have appeared in *Best American NonRequired*, *Glimmer Train*, *Story Quarterly*, *Prairie Schooner*, *Poets & Writers*, and other publications. He received his MFA in creative writing from the University of Massachusetts Amherst, where he won the Distinguished Teaching Award. Tom is currently a Jones Lecturer in the Stanford Creative Writing Program and a volunteer tutor at 826 Valencia.

THE LOST BROTHER

Tom Kealey

Tom Kealey

I went down to the basement in late evening because of a strange, familiar shiver that frightened me. There was water down there, shin deep, and it was filled with silt and sand. My brother Albert and I had been trying to pump it out. I opened the gun cabinet and checked for his pistols, and sure enough there was one of them missing. I'd been worrying over him for a while. I'd felt something similar, years before, and another feeling had set me to motion. Out from school and into home, and when I got there Ma was under the table, eating pills, talking on the phone to nobody. And another time, after a visit to my granddad—a good visit, he'd been feeling better—I woke and knew that he'd died. These were not visions to me, and not ghost whispers in my ear. I was an Atkins, and a good number of us had turned crazy over the years. But I was not yet crazy. I was fifteen and Albert's only brother, and we were friends, he and I, back then.

It was dark outside, and the moon was half, and I could see up for as many stars as I'd like. I listened to the rustle of the dead leaves across the yard, and there was some smell in the air, like a storm might be moving in, though there was no other sign. I had the chills down the spine. Albert had pulled himself up on the engine of the old Jeep, and he was looking down into it, like maybe he'd lost something down there. I could see the night bugs pinging against the gas lamp, and Albert's wheelchair was just outside the glow, leaned against the fender. There were other bugs—lightning—out near the river, as many as I could recall that summer, and they flashed on quick and faded slow, and there was a gray mist creeping up into the yard from below them. Some kids were playing basketball in the dark across the water: I couldn't see the game, but I could hear the ball and the rattle of the chain, the shouts here and there. I went down and sat up on the engine with Albert. He was twelve years older than me and looked it that night. I cleared away some beer bottles to make a space. The oil in the pan made the air seem sweet and sharp, and I tipped the lantern in so he could see.

He was scrubbing something down in the dark with an old toothbrush, and he was really going at it. Like he was almost there, whatever he was working on. He had two fuel pumps, one new, one old, set up on the alternator, and his black hair—waist long—was pulled back, sheened in the light.

"Thought I'd surprise you," he said.

"I don't need any surprises."

He looked up at me. He had eyes the same color as the hair, and they were not yet drunk, like they usually were this time of night.

"You're not sure what you need," he said.

Maybe that was true. He'd sensed my mood, as he often did. I was believing I needed to hold on to whatever I still had, and I told him as much.

"That's a road to ruin," he said. He was smiling. There was always something about me that he found funny.

"I could use one of those," I said.

"I've been working on a joke," he said.

"All right," I said. "I'm ready."

He handed me the new pump and switched the lantern up, traded the toothbrush for a wrench. I squinted in the brightness.

"So the farmer comes back in from the barn," he said. "And he sees all these empty bottles on the table, and one of the cowboys looks up and says to him: 'You got anything else? Seems like we're even more thirsty now.'"

I shook my head, but I laughed a little. I was nervous, I guess. "What was in the bottles?"

"I'm working on that," he said, and he caught what he was looking for with the wrench. I could hear it click into place. "You used to be the joke teller," he said.

"Those were kids' jokes."

He tensed up, trying to get the bolt loose. "Okay, old man," he said.

We got that fuel pump in there eventually. We filled the oil back up, and then I caught him under the arms and eased him down into the chair. He wheeled around in the mud and helped himself into the driver's seat. He'd done it plenty times before. The Jeep was topless and it had hand controls: Ma had found it somewhere in Virginia, and it had gotten him around enough to hold a job delivering the papers. But that hadn't lasted. There was always something breaking down.

When he turned the key it started right up. A plume of blue-white smoke blew out from the back. I took his tools down from the engine and closed the hood. It was almost ten o'clock. The headlights switched on, and the stretch of dead grass was all lit up, and a cat who'd been watching us from the driveway flattened itself against the gravel, then just as quick disappeared into the trees.

So Albert was happy back there, behind the wheel, listening to the engine. Happy as I'd seen him in a while. He turned on the radio, set the seat back a bit. The engine sounded like it was deciding between quitting and staying. I got the broom and set to sweeping out the seats. They were all full of leaves. I wondered if there might be a bird back there. I swept over and around my brother, and he was looking up at the stars.

"Why you trembling?" he said.

I looked down at him. "It's cold."

"It's not cold," he said.

In the house I got myself a jacket, and I packed up some food: a bag of snap beans and what was left of a pizza. I took out a half-case of beer, which seemed to me both dumb and right. I got the quilt from the couch. Then I put it all in the backseat of the Jeep. I folded up Albert's chair, put that in there, and I climbed in next to him.

"Where we going?" I said.

"To see my girl."

I'd tricked her name out of him the previous weekend. He'd been all secretive about her. Merrill.

"Hope she lives close," I said. "We're not going to get ten miles in this piece of shit."

He looked at me for a while, like he was maybe waiting on something else. I thought maybe I shouldn't call his Jeep that. It had meant something to him. We listened to the engine idle, and I was thinking of something to say. But he reached back into the seat behind and brought up the quilt. He folded it out and set it over me.

"Hold tight of that, old man."

We went out from the city, on the state highway. There was nobody much out that night. We passed the paper mill and its ammonia smell and the stretch of farms beyond that, the bales of hay set in rows up over the hills. In the blue they looked like a line of long, strange caterpillars to me, and the barns with their doors open like giant heads, their mouths toothless and hungry. I remembered, then, a broad sky, daylight, and me and Albert and Granddad stretched out in a sunflower field. We'd been in Indiana. It warmed me up a little, thinking about that, though I'd lowered my sights since then. I closed my eyes, listened to the wind, and I could picture Albert's face in that field and Granddad next to him. But I couldn't see myself. It was like it was me, but with somebody else's body; my name, but somebody in my place.

"Sit up on the seat," said Albert.

I looked at him, his hair tossed every way with the wind. He looked wild and ancient to me. I had this feeling that there was something in the Jeep that shouldn't be there. I don't know why. I got up, tossed the quilt back, sat on the back of the seat. I could see some horses behind a fenceline, shadows milling about. We were going fast down the road, and I held on tight to the seat, bouncing a bit with the Jeep. I let the wind blow my hair around, though I didn't have the length of Albert's—when I'd grown it out Ma was always yanking at it.

"Put your hands up," he said.

I did that. I held them up like I was on a roller coaster. The wind was whipping in my ears. I looked at what I could see of the road stretched out before us, flat and straight. I couldn't make out much in the distance.

"Scream or something," said Albert. He was looking up at me, looking back at the road. He punched my leg. "You're a crazy Atkins. Act like one."

I didn't scream. I took my hands down. We were moving fast. There was a long line of electric towers past the farms, and I watched the red lights flashing on and off. I watched and watched them till they were long past. Then I took hold of the windshield and stepped up on the dash. I set one leg over to the hood.

Albert grabbed hold of my other leg. "What the hell are you doing?"

The wind was all in my face then. "Let go," I said.

"Get back in here."

"I'm going to fall," I said.

"Daniel," he said. He was shouting at me.

"I'm going to fall if you slow down."

He couldn't do that though. He had one hand at my leg, one on the steering wheel.

"I'm falling, Albert," I said.

He let go of my leg and put his hand on the brake switch, though he didn't pull on it. I went out onto the hood and held on to the windshield, my back toward the road. We were flying down the road. My jacket was all filled up with air, like it might lift me away, and what hair I had was in my eyes. I looked at Albert through the glass.

"I'm crazier than hell," I said. I had to yell it above the wind.

"Don't let go," he said.

"I won't. You want me to scream?"

We hit a dip in the road, and I lost my footing for a second. When I looked down I was crushing one of the windshield wipers with my shoe.

"Don't let go," he said.

"You want me to scream?"

"Whatever you want. Don't let go."

I screamed. I screamed as loud as I could. I took my foot off the wiper and set it on the hood again. I could feel the metal popping under my weight and the cold of the wind all down my spine. The farmland was flying past us. I screamed some more and looked back on the road. There was a car back there, way back. The headlights seemed like one headlight. I held one of my fists in the air.

"Don't slow down," I shouted at Albert.

"I won't," he said. "Get your hand back down."

So I did that. I wasn't scared at all. I wanted to dance up there on the hood.

"How crazy are you?" said Albert.

"Crazier than hell."

"Everybody knows that."

"Damn straight they know."

"Tell them," he said.

"I'm crazy," I yelled out. "I'm crazier than hell."

"Nobody crazier," he said. "Now get back in here."

I looked behind me, into the wind. It about lifted me off of there. I watched the tobacco fields coming toward us in the dark.

"I can't ever fall," I shouted at Albert.

"That's right, don't do that."

I looked at him through the glass again. "I'm not ever going to."

"Okay," he said. "I hear you."

I looked as clear at him through that glass as I could manage. We hit another dip in the road, and my feet came off the hood for just a second. I grabbed on to the busted wiper.

"You can slow down then," I said.

And when he did, I climbed back over the windshield and into the seat. The car behind us passed us on the left side, and we watched it go, an old farmer it looked like. I took up the quilt again. I hadn't lost the shivers.

"Where's she live?" I said.

"Farther on."

"Near Jake?"

"No."

And he didn't say anything more. He'd been in the Gulf War, Albert, and I thought maybe we might see one of his friends tonight. They were scattered all about these parts. I came up every weekend from

Raleigh on the bus, spent Friday and Saturday nights with him. With his veteran's check we bought groceries for the week, worked on the car. Whatever there was to do. We had a canoe, and we'd take that out in the river when we felt like it, if the water was still enough to get back upstream. We read the newspaper to each other. We watched TV. We drank. In the spring and summers we had a vegetable garden, though we didn't have much success with that. We went bowling sometimes. Albert had been a combat engineer in the war. They found and disabled landmines. They called themselves a British word that I'd always liked. Sappers. He'd had a friend who'd missed a wire. The man's helmet had snapped Albert's spine. I'd heard this story only a few times. There was a pop and then the other pop and then silence. Stateside, I'd lived with him for a while in the hospital, sneaking around, after Ma went under the table.

"How about some beers?" said Albert.

I reached back, pulled two from the twelve. I opened them, passed one over.

He took a long swig and then another. He looked out on the road for a while and we didn't say anything. We watched the farmhouses every few miles, some standing, some fallen, some looking to. I drank my beer. I didn't want the cold of the drink, but I kept sipping at it. By the time it was empty, Albert turned to look at me.

"That was fun as hell," he said.

I was feeling the buzz already. "Damn right. That was fun as all get out."

"You're not that crazy," he said.

"No," I said. "That was above me."

"No need to do that again."

"No," I said. "That's it for now."

We took a turnoff from the highway and moved along next to a long gully filled with dark water. The moon had reached its height and was beginning to dip, and I watched it, the strange patches of gray and blue. I tried to see a face in the moon, but I couldn't quite make it out. That storm smell was in the air again, and there were clouds, not dark but white-gray, off toward the north, and I watched them, waiting for lightning. The road turned to gravel, and we could hear the rocks and pebbles kick up from the tires, clattering in the chambers and popping against the chassis. I took out the beans as we rode along, and I snapped a few in half, chewed them down. I handed a couple to Albert, and he studied them, set them on the dashboard, and I watched them rattle with the movement of the Jeep till they became lodged against the windshield. I pulled my hands from beneath the quilt. Unsteady. I was still trembling. They looked like mad hands to me.

We pulled off into a trailer park, and a couple dogs came out and chased along beside us. We passed empty clotheslines and a yard full of tires and bicycles. An old steel barrel filled with wood, burn marks down the side. Lights inside the trailers were blue and shifting, televisions likely, but maybe ghosts, said Albert, and he made some creepy voice and I rolled my eyes. I wasn't sure how, but he was making fun of me. There were chairs tossed here and there, sideways, like no one would be sitting out soon, and the dogs gave up as we pulled past a small lake in which I could see the moon, and on the near end I could make out a school bus, half sunk in the dark water. I put my hands into fists, thought that might help some. We pulled up next to a yellow trailer with Christmas lights—white, red, and green. Though it was the wrong season, they were strung all along the roof and the windows.

When Albert cut the engine, we could hear some music from inside, something slow and strange, and beyond that the crickets ticking together out by the lake. He switched off the headlights and we sat and listened to the music. We finished our beers—my second, Albert's third—and watched for movement in the trailer. I put my fingers up to my neck, to feel my pulse and what my heart was pushing through.

A light came on above us, and we both held our hands up to block the shine. In that light Albert looked as old as I'd ever seen him. He looked as old as Ma. Older.

Somebody came out on the steps, and Albert reached over and opened the glove box, and there in the light I could see one of his pistols. The one missing from the gun cabinet. The long black handle was sticking out from the papers and maps. But he left the pistol there and took out a roll of money. He closed the box and I got out and got his chair.

Merrill came down from the steps. She was wearing a black dress and a thin rope necklace, and boots. When I'd gotten Albert settled, she took his head in her hands, gentle, like she was trying to find his ears in all that hair of his. We were just outside the light, but I could see that she was a little older than Albert. Her hair was tied back with a band and she had a slight smile, though it seemed to me that there was maybe another face behind the first, one that was sad and not smiling. She bent down and kissed him at the bridge of his nose, and then she just held his head for a while, but she was looking over at me.

"Daniel," I said, though she hadn't asked.

"The brother," she said.

"I told you I would," said Albert.

She nodded and took her hands from his head, slowly, like maybe she might put them back there again.

"Can I touch you?" she said.

I looked at Albert, and he just shrugged. I felt like there was maybe a joke being put on me.

"Where?" I said.

She smiled. "Right here."

I shrugged. "All right."

She stepped over and put one of her boots on my shoe, then she pushed back my hair with the tips of her fingers. I looked away.

"Can I turn you into the light?" she said.

"Not too much," I said.

"Just a little."

When she turned me, she pushed my hair back again and lifted my chin up. I had to squint in the brightness.

"You all right?" she said.

"It's strange," I said.

"You're shaking."

"I'm cold."

"You don't feel cold," she said. "You're a beautiful child."

"I'm not a child."

"No," she said.

I wanted to get out of that light then, and maybe she sensed this, because she took me out. She let go of me.

"Let's say we go inside," she said.

So we went up into the trailer. I leaned Albert and his chair back and pulled him up the steps. I'd done this many places before. I knew the trick of it. He stared up at me.

"You're spooking," he said.

"Says you."

There was a couch inside, two chairs, lampshades. Drapes on the windows. Merrill turned off the spotlight outside, and there was a white candle on a small table, lit, and the red and green lights shining through the glass. I liked the music on the radio. Still slow, but no longer strange. Something familiar, though I could not quite place it. Merrill was in the kitchen, and she seemed to move to the music as she walked about. A big map of the country was pinned up on the wall, opposite the couch, and I examined it for a moment. Little stars drawn here and there: Fresno and Grand Junction, Boston and Sioux Falls. Portland, both of them. Below, on a shelf, were about a dozen porcelain mice, each of them the same it seemed. Each of them standing with the same hopeful expression—big eyes—but dressed different, in little felt outfits. A hippie and a surgeon, a nurse and a fisherman. One of them held a butterfly net.

Merrill called from the kitchen. "Don't make fun of my mice, Daniel Atkins."

"I thought they were rats," I said.

She looked at me from over the counter. "You can wait outside in the Jeep if you want."

I looked at Albert, and he gave me a look I couldn't read. He took a swig off a beer.

"I didn't mean nothing by it," I said.

"Then have a seat," she said.

I sat down in a chair next to Albert, and he closed his eyes and listened to the music. He started moving his shoulders, his neck. He seemed to be whispering some words, though there weren't any voices on the radio. I crossed my arms over my chest. I was shivering something terrible.

"I've got a whole box of donuts here," said Merrill. "I think these are going to be good. You'll have some donuts?"

"Sure," said Albert. He opened his eyes then and reached into his pocket. He took out the roll of money—twenties—and handed it over to me. He nodded at Merrill.

"Give it to her?" I said.

He nodded.

So I got up and leaned over the counter. I looked at her for a moment. I was scared of her, though I didn't want to show it. I handed over the money.

"Those are steep donuts," I said.

Something young came over her face then. Some sort of pleasant tremor it seemed to me. She had the same expression as when she'd tipped me into the light. She reached for the money, but took hold of my wrist. Her grip was tight, and I didn't know if I could pull free.

"Did you hear that, Albert?" she said.

He was laughing. "I heard him."

"Steep donuts."

"You sending him out?" said Albert.

She was laughing now, and she began to move again to the music. "I was never to send Daniel Atkins out," she said.

And then she put the money away and let go of me. She handed over the donuts.

So, we had some donuts and some beer, and I was feeling all right. Merrill helped my brother out of his chair, helped set him on the couch. She leaned him back till his head was lying on a pillow. Then she slipped his shirt off, turned him over. In the hospitals I'd seen the nurses do this a hundred times. He had his eyes closed, and it seemed that his face held some troubled thought. I could barely make it out in the candlelight. It sent a chill down my shoulders. He reached back, and she took his hand.

"There's a blanket," said Merrill. "On the bed in the room. When you get it, bring me the brush on the nightstand."

"Me?" I said.

"Yes, you, Daniel Atkins."

So I went in there and got the blanket, and I got the brush. On the stand there was a picture of a boy. He looked about three. He was set up against a fence, and he was looking at a toy in his hand. It looked like it was a truck or something. He was looking at it like it was the most curious thing. I picked up the picture and checked the hallway. I studied that toy in the picture. I was wondering what was so curious about it. I was getting pretty drunk. A minute, and I set the picture back as best as I could.

In the den, I gave Merrill the brush, and she looked at the blanket and said, "Go on," So I sat back in the chair and pulled the blanket over me. I took the last swig of a beer and put my feet up on the table.

"Where do you live during the week?" said Merrill.

"Me?" I said.

"Yes you. I don't want to talk to this fool brother of yours."

"Hey," said Albert.

"Hey," said Merrill.

"With my ma," I said. "Up in Raleigh."

"Are you in high school yet?"

"Next year," I said. "If some things start to go right. I've missed some time lately."

She nodded. "We've all got things to take care of. Albert has told me some about you."

"A little," said Albert.

"What does he say?" I said.

Merrill was sitting next to him, and she took out some oil and poured it on his back. "You're a hell of a bowler," she said. "That's him talking. What else? Bowling's a good start. Someone takes something up, they should be good at it. You're a swimmer, and you work nights at a restaurant. Dishes, right?"

"Boring," I said.

She rubbed the oil into his shoulders, down his spine. "Well, he didn't tell me that part. Here's one. You order your clothes on hangers, light to dark."

I smiled at that. "Which way?"

She considered. "Light on the left."

"Wrong."

"I've got to keep closer attention," she said. "Now I've got to make up for it. When you were younger, you had a duck who you thought was your girlfriend."

I sat up at that. I looked at my brother. "Albert!" I said.

He opened his eyes and looked up at me. They were both laughing.

"Be careful what you ask," said Merrill.

I tucked the blanket up to my neck. "She was just my friend."

And that set them to laughing more. I let them ride that out. I wasn't going to say another word. I looked over at the mice, and for some reason I started thinking about that picture in Merrill's room. I listened to the music, and I was buzzing pretty good. I thought I might just close my eyes if I could get warm enough.

"I had a mule when I was a kid," said Merrill. "An old blind mule. His name was Albert."

"No it wasn't," said Albert.

"Think what you like," she said. "But I used to take care of him. He'd follow me around in the fields. We were picking apples. And he'd eat the hell out of those apples. I'd have to keep them from him, or else he'd get sick if he ate too many. I had him for years. When I first got him, they were like, 'He won't last a year,' but he just went on and on."

"What was his real name?" I said.

"Oh, I don't know. What was your duck's name?"

I didn't say anything.

"Good," she said. "That's yours to keep."

She took up the brush, and she took up Albert's hair and began pulling it back. She worked out the tangles. He curled his arm under his cheek.

She brushed his hair straight. She hummed to the radio while she was working, and I watched her. She took a lot of care with it, I thought. I was about ready to close my eyes.

When she was done with the brush, she reached over to a drawer and took out a pair of scissors. She ran her thumb down the blade.

"You sure about this?" she said.

"Yes," said Albert, a whisper.

I sat up from the chair. "No."

He opened one eye and looked at me. "I've been thinking about it. This isn't spur of the moment."

"It'll take you years to grow back," I said.

"It's time to let go of things," he said.

He closed the eye and set his head against the pillow. Merrill watched me for a while, and then she slipped some hair between her fingers and cut off a few strands. She set them across his face.

"Last chance," she said.

"I told you," Albert said.

She looked at me and waited. She snipped the scissors a few times in the air, waited for something from either of us. I was drunk. I looked over at Albert, and he didn't move. I decided I wouldn't say anything else. He seemed to me at peace there, as much as I'd seen him. Merrill moved to the music again, and she began to cut his hair. "It's a long, long way to the moon," she sang, though there weren't any voices on the radio.

Merrill brought the candle over and pulled a chair up next to me. She had Albert's hair in her fist, and we sat there for a while and watched him sleep. His face was slack and silent, and it seemed to me that he was without dreams. It put me in mind of my grandfather again, and I could see us, all three this time, down in the sunflowers in Indiana. There were grasshoppers popping over us. Just a few at first, then more, then a hundred it seemed. Like they'd arrived just behind us. We were picking them off our shirts, or we'd flick them at each other, and they'd leave some spit behind. There wasn't any shade, and the sun was warm and it dried our clothes. We'd been caught out in the rain, in the back of a stranger's pickup that morning. We were on our way to St. Louis, to see about a basketball scholarship for Albert, though that hadn't worked out. We could just reach up and grab as many grasshoppers as we liked. They'd sit on the tips of your fingers if you let them, their legs poking at you. I caught the most, and my granddad looked at my hands and said, "These flowers'll be gone in a week now."

Merrill had brought out some spools of thread, and she set those on the table between us. She had a needle between her teeth, and she was digging around in a sewing kit for something.

"Would you hold this for me?" she said, a mumble.

I took Albert's hair. I held it tight so it wouldn't slip out from me. It was soft and heavy and I brought it down near the candlelight. There were all different colors in there. Black mostly, but auburn and even some gray. Brown hair like mine, but I'd never seen this before in Albert. It seemed like it might be a few people's hair, all mixed together.

Merrill found what she was looking for, and I handed the hair back. She made a knot of it at the end, held it together that way. I still had some strands stuck to my fist, and I took those and set them on my knee. She threaded the needle in the candlelight.

"What happened to your duck?" she said.

I shrugged. "Christmas dinner."

She looked over at me. "You're lying."

"Maybe."

"You got another girl now?"

"Maybe," I said.

"Well, you either do or you don't."

"I don't, I guess."

She got that needle threaded. "You got your eye on one?"

"Maybe."

"I know parrots that have more words than you," she said.

"I guess."

She smiled a little, set a fancy clip on Albert's hair. She started sewing the knot to the clip. "What's her name?"

"Amy."

"That's a pretty name," she said.

"I made it up."

I tried to take deep breaths. I was trying to get warmer. I looked around the room. There wasn't much to it. Just the furniture, a TV. The mice. I looked up at the map on the wall.

"You been to those places you marked?" I said.

"When I was younger."

"What were they like?"

She considered that, though she didn't take her eyes from what she was doing. "They weren't too good, I guess."

"Did you get those mice there?"

"No."

"Did you make those little outfits for them?"

"I know better than to answer that," she said. She pulled the thread tight. "You're getting ahead with your questions. Time for me to ask one."

"All right."

"Go get us some beers first."

"Was that a statement or a question?"

"That was a statement," she said. "And yours was a question. So now you're down two."

I got up and got the beers. When I settled back, I nodded at the hair. "What are you making?"

"Not your turn," she said. "What's your mom like?"

"She's tall."

"Tall, huh? She look like you?"

"A little."

"What does she do?"

I shrugged. "Albert's told you about her."

"No," she said. "He hasn't."

I thought about Ma. I tried to picture her in my mind. "She takes care of herself. She's getting better at that. She tries to stay in this world as much as she can."

"And you're close to her?"

"No," I said. "She's not someone to get close to. That's not in her. But I spend a lot of time with her. Weekends she's at her sister's. My turn?"

Merrill finished a stitch in the clip, took up the scissors. "Okay."

"You got other boyfriends besides Albert?"

She nodded. "I do."

"What are their names?"

"A name is a powerful thing," she said.

"One of them, then."

She thought about that. She looked up at the map. "Hank."

"Did you make that up?"

"Yes," she said. "My turn. Why are you shivering all the time?"

"Cause I'm drinking cold beer."

"Is that it?"

"I guess."

"You ever kissed a girl?"

I pulled down the blanket a bit. I didn't like that question much, but I didn't want to show it. I thought about it for a while, though there wasn't much to think on.

"No," I said.

"Why not?"

"I suppose the opportunity hasn't come along."

"I doubt that," she said. "Do you want to kiss me?"

I thought about that, and there was plenty to think on. "I guess not."

"Why not?"

I blinked. "Because you're my brother's girlfriend."

"He said it'd be all right."

I looked over at my brother. "Did he?"

"Yes," she said. "And it would quit you of your shivers."

"Is that right?" I said. "You got magic lips?"

"That's right. Magic lips," she said. She pulled another stitch tight but didn't cut it yet. She looked over at me. "I'm going to ask you again, and that's going to be the last time. You're not going to get this kind of courtesy from other women. You understand?"

"Maybe I should take some notes."

"Maybe," she said. "Would you like to kiss me?"

I thought about that. "All right."

"Well," she said. "I don't think so. You had your chance."

I settled back in the chair. I pulled the blanket up. I wanted to pull it over my head.

She set the hair aside and got up and leaned over me. "I don't want you to touch me this time, all right?"

"Okay," I said.

She kissed me then. She turned her head to the side and ran her fingers at the back of my scalp. "Close your eyes, dummy," she said.

So I closed my eyes, and she kissed me some more. She pinched one of my ears with a fingernail and pushed my head back against the chair. I could feel her weight against my knees. I listened to the music and felt her sway with and, it seemed to me, within it. She pulled my lip with her teeth, and her kiss was warm and it made me warm. I slid down into the chair. We were done before I wanted us to be. She sat back and took up Albert's hair again.

"Don't say anything," she said.

"Okay."

"Some day you'll figure what to say after, but it's got to be the right thing. If you don't know, then keep quiet. Got it?"

I closed my eyes. "This is complicated."

"No, it's not," she said. "Can I ask you something?"

"Sure."

"Did you see that picture in my room?"

I opened my eyes again. "I think you put it out there for me to see."

She nodded. "Well, bully for you. I did. I was scared of you coming here tonight."

"Why?"

"That's my brother in the picture. He and I were close once. That's a picture I had that'd fit the frame."

"He's older than that now," I said.

"He died when he was eighteen," she said. "He was working a ferry down at Ocracoke. He tried to jump from the dock in a storm. He hit his head and went straight down. I miss him a lot. He and I were as close as you and Albert."

I didn't say anything to that.

"You remind me of him," she said.

"I do?"

"Well, I suppose if you had three eyes, you'd still remind me of him."

"What do you mean?"

She didn't say anything.

I thought about something. I thought it through twice before I said it.

"Did you teach him how to kiss?"

"My brother?" she said.

"Yes."

She laughed a little at that. She didn't take her eyes from the stitching. "No," she said. "But I guess you won't believe me."

"I believe you," I said.

"You want to know his name?"

"Yes," I said.

She studied me for a moment. I couldn't read her face in the candlelight. She set the hair aside. Then she leaned over to my ear and whispered his name.

We went out back, the three of us. A big stretch of clouds had moved in, and the stars were all gone. There was lightning in the distance, and the clouds would flash up every minute or so, dull and sudden. A warm breeze from the north pushed across the lake. We took Albert down to the water's edge. He was wide awake now, though he was yawning. He couldn't seem to stop. His eyes were all wet, and it was like I couldn't recognize him with all that hair gone. He looked like something young had come over him. There were frogs making all kinds of sounds—low, then high—along the shore. "Peepers," Merrill said to us, nodding out into the dark. We got Albert down there, then we pushed his chair a ways into the water. Not too far. It sent a couple ducks flying out from the reeds, honking and complaining. We watched them skim across the water and then disappear into a mist in the center of the lake.

We got Albert a beer and a donut. "This water's cold," he said. But it wasn't all that cold. Me and Merrill took off our clothes, and we waded out into the water, the scum and rocks against our feet.

"There's brambles in here," she said. "Watch where you go."

I went under and I couldn't see anything, but as I settled, I could hear the blood in my head, bouncing through the water it seemed. I was warm down there. I came up and wiped my eyes. I let my sight adjust. I looked back at Albert, and he pointed with his beer.

"What's that out there?" he said.

I turned where he was looking, and I saw the school bus. I waited for the next flash of lightning.

"That's been there for years," said Merrill.

"How'd it get there?"

"Somebody was very drunk, I suppose."

When the lightning came I could see that all the windows were smashed out. There were cattails growing up all around it, and it rested low against the bank. Somebody had popped the tires a long time ago.

"How come no one's pulled it out?" I said.

"It's junk," said Merrill. "I know what you're thinking. There's no kids in there."

"How do you know?"

"You're spooking again," said Albert.

And I was. I didn't like that bus in there. There were all sorts of things floating around my legs. I'd swallowed some water.

"I want to get out there with you," said Albert.

I looked at him. "Out in the water?"

"Hell, yeah, out in the water. I never get to do anything fun."

He dropped his bottle in the water and took off his shirt again. We swam up to him. I got him under an arm and Merrill got him under the other arm, and we eased him out of the chair and turned him. He settled back with us, and he tensed a bit as he went into the water. His face was pointing up at the clouds. The darkness of the water was bobbing at his neck. "That's good," he said. I had my arm across his chest, my ribs at his back. Merrill took him from the other side.

"Don't let go now," said Albert.

"No," we said.

"I'll drop for sure."

"We won't," we said.

"Then go out some."

We pushed past the reeds, and out a little ways from shore, out where the water was colder. We moved away from the bus, and I was glad of that. And then I got to thinking about Merrill's brother. We went out till I couldn't feel the mud at my feet. We paddled out. I looked over at her.

"You all right with this?" I said. I couldn't see much of her face in the dark. Our chins were dipping under, and we could hear some thunder off in the distance.

"She's all right," said Albert.

"I can take the weight," said Merrill.

We went out toward the mist, and the water became very cold. I set my hip against Albert to keep him up. It took me and Merrill a while to keep our legs from tangling, but we got the trick of it.

The air smelled flat and green, and we could hear the nightbugs and the peepers clicking all along the shore. I looked out toward the mist. It was not too far out now. I thought we might could make it there and then turn back. I was feeling all right. I felt like I could take my brother across the ocean if it needed doing. And I was glad to have Merrill there with us. It seemed to me like we were the only three people left in the world. Like all but near us was empty space. I looked at the two of them in the flash of lightning.

"Daniel," said Albert. He had his eyes closed. He was just a face and two shoulders in the water. "Do you remember a scarecrow?"

I kicked under the water. "No."

"Ma's," he said.

"No."

"I told you about it though."

"No," I said. "I don't know anything about that."

There was another flash of lightning, close I thought, and I said so. We listened to the thunder after.

"It ain't that close," said Albert. Then he looked over at Merrill. "Did I tell you?"

"What?"

"The scarecrow."

"I don't think so," she said.

"I'm drunk," he said. "It was somebody close to me, but I can't remember now."

"Who?" I said.

"The person I told."

"Well tell us."

"There's nothing to tell," he said.

"We're going to dunk you under."

He laughed at that, clutched onto my arm. "Don't."

"Tell it," I said. "Then we'll turn around."

We were into the mist now, and the air was warmer, though I could hear a breeze moving up along the shore and the fields. I took a tighter grip across my brother's chest.

"It had a face of corn," he said. "She had this box for a head. The scarecrow I mean. It was just a couple sticks and some old clothes, and the box for a head, and Ma spent all night at the table, gluing this corn to the box. She made the eyes and a mouth. I don't know. She just put the corn all over the head. Different shades of corn. She stayed up like she would. No sleep. Just gluing this face on the box. A kernel at a time."

"Why'd she do that?" said Merrill.

"Cause she's crazier than hell," said Albert.

I laughed. "She's crazier than all get out."

But Albert wasn't laughing. "You know what happened."

"What happened?" I said.

He reached up and swatted at the mist. "I can't see the sky through all this," he said. "We could be under the water for all I know. The birds came and ate all the corn off. It was gone by the afternoon. There were so many of them, they ripped the box right off the sticks. You could see them out there fighting over the head."

I thought it might be good to turn back now. I started to turn us, but they wouldn't come.

"My mom had a garden just like that," said Merrill.

"We're not talking about your mom," said Albert.

"What are we talking about then?"

"I didn't say anything about any fucking garden. Why don't you listen?"

"You're drunk," I said.

"So?"

"So, you're being rude."

"I'm trying to tell a fucking story, but I've lost it now."

"Sorry," said Merrill.

"Drop me if you want," he said.

"No one said anything about dropping you," she said.

"I can get drunk if I want. I've been through enough."

"Nobody said you haven't," she said.

"I haven't been through shit," he said.

He laughed, and I had this feeling he was going to try to slip from us then. I thought about how crazy a drowning person can get.

"Let's go back," I said.

"You hear that wind?" he said.

We listened, and it was thunder we heard, from the west, not the north. When it faded, I listened to the trees, and sure enough there was a wind coming down on us. I could feel my legs starting to cramp up.

"Why'd y'all bring me out in the water?" said Albert. "It's lightning out."

I looked around, and the mist was spinning in every direction with the wind. I held tight to Albert, and I turned us around. I pulled hard. We could see the rain off in the distance. A gray, it seemed, against the blue.

"Y'all are stupid," said Albert.

"You're stupid," Merrill said.

"What was in your garden?"

"There wasn't anything in there," she said.

"Did y'all have corn?" he said.

"Snap at me," she said.

The shore seemed like a long ways off. I was thinking of pulling Merrill's hand away. I thought I'd take hold of my brother and make some time.

"Man, did y'all have corn or not?" he said.

"Yes," said Merrill.

"What kind?"

"Why you asking?"

"It's important to me," he said.

"Well, I don't remember."

He settled back then. He'd been all tight. There was a lightning flash, and I could see that bus then. I was glad to see it now. I made for that end of shore.

"It don't matter, I guess," he said. He closed his eyes and set his head back in the water. "Can y'all hear that wind?"

We said we could. We could hardly hear anything else by then.

"I once had a friend blown right off the road."

"By the wind?" said Merrill.

"No," he said.

I was driving on the way back. It was just the two of us. I wasn't going to let him behind the wheel. The rain was coming down not straight but sideways with the wind, and I was soaking wet and had to wipe the water from my eyes. We listened to it fall, slap against the pavement, and tin-tap against the Jeep. The wiper I'd busted on the passenger side didn't work, and we went slow down into the dark. I was feeling sober and feeling bad. The rain and the swim had sobered me up. I was getting a feeling then, but I couldn't place it. Albert sat next to me holding his hair in his hand, running his fingers through it.

"I wanted you to have this," he said.

"I didn't ask for it."

"I know," he said. "I was hoping you'd clip it on and feel it behind you."

I didn't say anything to that.

"It's all wet now."

"That's all right," I said. "I'm going to grow mine out. We got the same length now. We'll have us a race with it. Down to our butts."

"First one gets this Jeep," he said.

I looked at him. "This is yours."

"That's the deal," he said. "Can't have a race without a bet."

"All right," I said.

He looked down at his chest. "Your butt's closer to your head than mine is."

"I guess."

"I'm getting screwed."

We drove on for a while, and I kept watch at what the headlights would show. We listened to the thunder, and the lightning turned the road like day in front of us. We passed those horses behind the fence, and they were all worked up with the storm. Milling about the field, some were shaking their heads. They kind of looked like they were ready to break loose. I wiped the rain from my eyes.

"Why you shaking?" he said.

"It's cold out."

"It's not that cold," he said. "You've been shaking all night." He looked in the backseat. "Where's the quilt?"

"We left it at Merrill's," I said. "You were the one that wanted to go."

He looked out into the dark. His clothes were all soaked through.

"Why you climbing on hoods and shit?" he said. "That was damn stupid."

"I couldn't help it," I said.

"That's bullshit. That's something Ma would say. I got no one to rely on but you. Understand? Look at me. I'm all fucked up."

"You're not all fucked up," I said.

He held up his hair, studying it. It seemed like it was the first time he'd seen it.

"You're not like you used to be," he said.

He kept looking at the hair in his hand. He played for a while with the clip that Merrill had sewn on. We were moving past the farmhouses now, and he looked out at them, out at the rain. Then he reached back and tossed his hair out into the dark.

I pulled on the brake switch and pulled the Jeep over to the shoulder. I had to take it slow because of the rain. When we came to a stop I put the switch into park. We sat there in the rain for a while.

"Go get it," I said.

"I can't fucking walk. You go get it."

"It's your hair," I said.

"It's your hair," he said. "Leave it there if you want."

I took the key out of the ignition and got out. "Don't go anywhere."

"Where am I to go?" he said.

I went back on the road. I couldn't hardly see anything in the rain. There were some shapes: the fenceline down below the hill, a long stretch of treeline that we'd passed. I tried to figure how far we'd gone. I searched all down on the shoulder of the road, waiting for the lightning to see anything. There were some old tire treads, an old shirt. Some bottles and a ball of aluminum foil. I walked along for a while, and then I walked some more. A car was coming, and I looked back toward the Jeep. I could barely make out the red lights in all that rain, and the car went on by. I walked a ways past where Albert had thrown the hair. I'd thought all night that I was moving into crazy. I thought the shivers might be a sign of it. Part of me wanted it to come on. I was hoping to trade away lonely.

There was a farmhouse off in the fields, and I recognized it, I thought. I thought maybe we'd just passed it before he threw his hair out. They all looked alike. I headed back. I looked along in the mud and peered down the slope. If it'd gone that far, I wouldn't find it tonight. Another car was rushing down the road, and I waited for the head-lights. I looked down at my feet, holding my hand to shield my eyes from the rain. I reached down and took hold. It was then I heard the gunshot. I thought first it was thunder, but it'd come from the Jeep. The car went rushing by.

I looked up, and I couldn't see much in the rain, just that car trailing off toward the Jeep. I took off running. I was a long ways it seemed. The car passed my brother's Jeep and kept going. I ran past all the trash I'd seen, all the farmhouses. A flash of lightning lit up the road, and I kept running. I ran as fast as I ever did. When I closed the distance some, I could see him up there, his head leaned back in the seat. I ran through the rain.

When I got up to him, the pistol was sitting in his lap. He was look-ing up into the rain.

"Sorry," he said.

"Are you hit?"

He looked down at his body. "I guess not," he said.

I took up the pistol and threw it out into the fields. It disappeared into the dark and the rain.

"That was my best pistol," he said.

"Tough shit."

"I brought that back with me. It belonged to my friend."

I looked at him. I kicked the side of the Jeep. "I don't want to hear about your fucking friend."

I walked around for a while, on the shoulder of the road. Up then back, and I wouldn't look at my brother. The rain came down on me. There was a farmhouse across the field, and I could see a man standing there. On the porch, standing in shadow. He had his hands in his pockets and was looking out across the way.

It was necessary to hold on to what I still had. This is what I would've told that man. I wouldn't have meant Albert or Ma, though I wanted to hold on to them. I'd have meant my head. The insides. I wanted to hold on to my insides. I wondered if there was any hope in it. I walked around in the headlights so maybe the man or Albert could take a good look at me.

I went and checked my brother out. He was dripping wet, and in his face, I could see my mom. His hair was all short, stuck to his head.

"Are you going to hit me?" he said.

"I'm thinking it."

"Don't fuck up my nose," he said. I didn't say anything to that. I wasn't going to hit Albert. I stood there in the rain and watched him. I was waiting on something, I suppose. Though I felt like it was on me. I wiped the rain from my eyes, and I dropped his hair into his lap. We both looked down at it. We couldn't see any colors but dark in it. He sat and I stood. In the rain we studied that hair. I was young back then. And I was hoping maybe he could help me out.

Me with my father at the Philadelphia Zoo, circa 1991.

Michael Deagler is a writer living in Philadelphia. He has a BA in English from Temple University and is currently pursuing an MFA in creative writing at Rutgers University Camden.

ETYMOLOGY

Michael Deagler

Michael Deagler

Cocktail, for example. They don't know its exact provenance, but I read somewhere something about it being the last drink guys would have at the pub, just at dawn, when the rooster was crowing. Hence the name. Or half of it. But it would be mostly non-alcoholic to sharpen you up for the walk home, only a little spirit to keep the hangover from setting in. Or something like that. And that was way back in, like, pre-industrial times. Rooster times. I mean, meanings change, obviously.

Because now it just means mixture. Like tonight, Shane procured a cocktail of ketamine, MDMA, Valium, and NyQuil, which we supplemented with a bump of cocaine in the car. And another in the bathroom. And another, just now, in the alley here. I'm feeling sharp. I think I could sprint home, but the night is not over. The cocktail has made Shane quite angry. He came to me this evening with the pills and NyQuil and said, *This is what killed Lester Bangs!* and I said I didn't know who that was. Lester is one of those given names that started as a surname, Lister, which was occupational, back in the day. They dyed wool. Bangs is onomatopoetic. I can hear my blood flowing. Shane has become very angry, but I've mostly just been experiencing these not-unpleasant pulses that feel a bit purple.

He was fine in the car, Shane was, and fine in the bathroom, I think, though I can't quite remember what exactly it was he was saying. He was definitely angry at the back bar, with the vodka Red Bulls, and also when we were shoving this man into the alley. I think, actually, that most of Shane's anger is directed toward this man, kneeling here, which is why my Glock 22 is in his mouth.

This man—*this Albanian*, as Shane called him—is shortish, portly, pug-faced, pie-eyed, and sweaty. He has translucent blond hair. He can't be much older than us, maybe twenty-five, but he's dressed a lot better. His shirt is torn, but that was probably us: it has a silky, greeny, smoothy softness. It's probably organdy or cambric or some other fabric from a Simon & Garfunkel song. I reach down to feel its collar between my fingers while Shane sifts through the Albanian's wallet. It feels like floral clay, like it's rubbing off into the grooves of my fingerprints. The Albanian is looking at me. I stop pinching at his collar. I don't like how scared he is looking at me.

And technically the Glock belongs to John O, and he didn't exactly give me permission to borrow it, and I can say with certainty he would definitely be very angry if he knew I was holding it in this Albanian's mouth. When we brought him out into the alley, Shane sort of knocked his head on the brick wall and then kicked him for a bit while I took a bump. And then Shane asked me to kick him while Shane took a bump. The Albanian made a lot of noise during all this, shouting and such, so Shane said, *Let's show him our guns*; so we did that, but it actually just made him shout more, so Shane said, *Shut him up!* and I stuck my gun in his mouth. And the Albanian has mostly shut up since then, though now he is kind of drooling all down the Glock's barrel, which I know would also make John O very angry, but it can't really be helped now. I take full responsibility, anyway.

John O calls me Spacey Jones, 'cause my last name is Jones. Jones is a Welsh name. Shane's last name is Welsh, but that's an Irish name. My dad said Jones was a good name because it makes you like everyone else. I'm feeling very Jones right now. This whole alley is feeling very Jones.

He's got no ID, says Shane. He spikes the wallet on the wet asphalt with a slap. Shane is under the impression that this Albanian is friends with another Albanian, called Tirana Gjon, who did, according to Shane, testify against our mutual friend John W, resulting in the latter's incarceration. He told me as much when he spotted this Albanian at the back bar. *Who's John W?* I had asked. *John Wollard,* said Shane. *John Wollard's in jail?* I asked. *For seven years,* said Shane, *'cause of this Albanian fuck's fucking Albanian friend.* We finished our vodka Red Bulls angrily, though Shane more so than me, because I don't think I know a John Wollard, and then we dragged the man out into the alley.

What's your name? Shane is shouting at the man now. The man is kneeling in a puddle, which seems unnecessary. We could have let him kneel somewhere else. I shiver at the thought of my knees being wet. How inconceivably uncomfortable. *What's your name?* Shane shouts again, his face contorted, bat-wing eyebrows beating above a sand-worm mouth. He's very angry, and all the Albanian can do is sputter and gurgle around the barrel of the Glock.

Did you know the Glock's inventor was named Gaston? That was his name: Gaston Glock. Like a supervillain. He was from Austria.

Evan, take the goddamn gun out of his mouth! Shane bellows. I pull it out sharply. I hear the steel click against his front teeth and wince apologetically. The man gags and chokes a glob of phlegm out onto the ground. He pants a little. *What's your name?* Shane shouts.

Donald, the man gasps. He is turning his head as far to his left as he can, forcing his chin almost over his shoulder, trying not to look at us. He looks like a goose. Not a Canada goose, but like a Christmas goose, like they have in England. A lot of people say Canadian goose, but that's incorrect. Shane is admonishing him with his own gun, a squat Ruger LCR. It's not as slick as the 22, but Shane actually owns it. I don't know what LCR stands for. L-C-R. Lando-Cal-Rissian. It's got a rubber-coated butt that looks like it'd be good for sneaking up on a storm trooper and clubbing him in the back of the head.

Shane is shouting, *Donald? Donald? Albanians aren't fucking named fucking Donald!* which is a fair position to take, Donald being the Anglicization of the Irish/Scottish Dónall, so you would expect the name to remain fairly exclusive to the Anglosphere. But then the prime minister of Poland's name is Donald Tusk, which just goes to show you that you can never know with names. They're global now, just like Guinness and dubstep, though I don't point this out right now to

Shane. The name Shane is an Anglicization of the Irish name Seán, as is Sean and Shawn and Shaun. It seems like half my friends are named Shane or Sean. And Seán just means John, so about three-quarters of all my friends are named John. That's weird to think about.

My name's Donald, man, cries Donald. *I don't know what you want. I'm Donald.*

You're a liar, shouts Shane. *Put the gun back in his mouth.* I put it in more carefully this time so I don't clack it against his teeth. He still makes an unpleasant choking sound. *I know your name's not Donald*, says Shane. *And I know you know Tirana Gjon. Now tell us where to find him or we're gonna shoot you in the face.*

Donald makes a particularly terrified squeal at this. He is tearing at the eyes. He's sad like a plump Christmas goose who knows he's going to be eaten. *Don't worry*, I want to tell him, *we're probably not going to shoot you in the face.* I smile at him soothingly. He does not look soothed. He needs the catharsis of these purple pulses. They're traveling through him, the same as me, but he doesn't seem to be feeling them. The only class I ever enjoyed during my sojourn in college was Introduction to Linguistics with Professor Jacques Johanneson. I went to his classes straight. He said, the first day, that something can't exist if there isn't a word for it. And in English, where we have five words for everything, everything exists with five times the potency. That's why Donald is especially shivery right now, why the pulses are especially calming. Why the Glock is especially heavy like a magnet and shaky like a collapsing star. I tell him through the pulses, *I will not shoot you, Donald. You will be okay.*

Shane decides we need to regroup and have another bump each. I have to snort it off Shane's knuckle because I'm holding the gun. My mind curls like a drill bit and fires up into my skull. Whew. I think of offering one to Donald, but he has all this weepy snot flowing out of his nostrils and I don't think it's feasible. He's clearly uncomfortable from kneeling on the asphalt. He shifts his weight and scrapes the toes of his boots across the ground. They're the elasticky leather kind without laces. I like boots like that. I could never pull them off. *I like your boots, Donald*, I try to say. *Boots*, I say.

Boots! says Shane. He scurries behind Donald and begins jerking off the boots. This causes Donald to teeter back and forth and I have to pivot on my ankles to keep the gun safely in his mouth. Shane upends a boot and a plastic booklet slips out onto the ground. *That's a fucking passport*, he says. He snatches it up and examines it closely. *I don't see any Donald in here.* He holds it out to me. *Which one's his name?*

Donald's photograph, in which he looks far calmer than we've know him to be, is surrounded by recognizable if festively accented characters. I point with my non-gun hand. Gjin Lika, it says, Tiranë, Republika e Shqipërisë. Shqipërisë. That's silly. Do you know Greeks call Greece Ellada, and Egyptians call Egypt Miṣr? Shane is smacking Donald in the forehead with the passport. *Your name is Gjin Lika, Donald. Gjin fucking Lika.*

Albanian, the language, is an Indo-European isolate. It has its own branch in the language tree. We had a dictionary when I was a little kid, a sort of heirloom, with all the names written in the inner cover like some families do in a bible, and also on the inner cover was a diagram of the Indo-European language tree. It was a literal tree, curvy and sort of impressionistic. I remember Albanian had its own little runt of a branch. And I know, not from that but from later, that there are two smaller twigs off the Albanian branch, Gheg and Tosk. Not Tusk, like the Polish prime minister. Tosk. I know this about Albanian. I tell Donald. *Tusk Tosk*, I say.

Take the gun out, says Shane. I do. Donald gurgles like a garbage disposal. *What the fuck, Gjin?* Shane demands. *You lied to us.*

I have dual citizenship, says Donald. He is weeping. *We came here when I was twelve. I've been Donald here since I was twelve, to be normal.*

I know you know Tirana Gjon! shouts Shane. *I know you know him! Where is he?*

I don't know! cries Donald. He is begging somehow. His entire body is occupied in the act of begging. *I don' know! I don' know! I don' know! I don' know!*

You're a fucking liar, Gjin! shouts Shane, and smacks Donald with his Ruger. It cuts him minutely to the left of his left eyebrow. *Put it back in his mouth.*

Donald opens his mouth to receive it this time. I hope he is not afraid of me. This is the longest I've ever held a gun. This is the most times I've ever put something in someone's mouth. There's a Freudian subtext here. I will not hurt you, Donald. I want to be friends, Donald. We can go have vodka Red Bulls, Donald. *Donald*, I say.

All right! Shane is saying. He is pacing. *All right! All right! I gotta think!* He sits down against the brick wall of the alley, scrunching his legs against his chest and resting his chin on his kneecaps. *I gotta think! I gotta think!*

My father was named John Jones and he came from a long line of fathers named John Jones. Their names were in the dictionary. He was an all right sort of man. He drank only occasionally and never took ketamine, MDMA, Valium, NyQuil, and cocaine in front of me. He named me Evan Jones to let me be a person who was different but still the same as everyone else.

Donald is jittering like a secondhand percolator, inhaling twice for every exhale. By the wall, Shane has taken a clairvoyant interest in his own hands.

He was interested in language, my father. He told me the story of a word, once, a word he couldn't say, a word that everyone had forgotten, that originally was the name of a certain seed for a certain type of plant; then, because it became a kind of metaphor, it changed to mean an act of birth, and then a tribe, and then a god, and then the whole world, and then everything after the whole world, and then a sort of fear that no one wanted to think about. And that's why they forgot the word. They had to. I used to try to make the sound I thought the word would sound like. It would end in a velarized *L*, the dark *L*, a sound I could hold forever if I didn't have to breathe.

What time is it? Shane appears to be shudder-sleeping along the wall, stuffed into the corner where it meets the ground like a hiding millipede. How long have I had my gun in Donald's mouth?

At first any illicit substance shuts off language. They all do it a little differently. One muffles it like a fog. One snags it like flecks in tar. One drowns it out like an airplane engine. One shatters it like light through a prism. One chokes it like a breath in an immense sky.

But just at first. Then it comes back, roaring, multiplied, and you hear all five words at once, all fifteen, all fifty. And it becomes nearly impossible to say any one of them, just once, one time.

And you know, I bet Gjin means John. Shane is trying to tell me something, but his words seem to foam up as they leave his mouth and roll down his chin. I'm fading. What time is it?

There's a great sharp shattery black barking shock.

I have shot him, I think. Donald is pulsing—dark red pulses—and still.

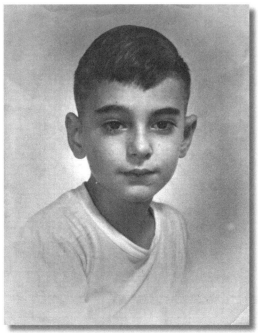

Time's arrow, reversed.

Louis Gallo was born in New Orleans and now teaches at Radford University in Virginia. His poetry volumes include *Omens, Halloween, The Truth Changes, Witness, Shadows,* and *The Private Confessions of Diablo Amoricus Wishbone.* He has published work in numerous journals, such as *Glimmer Train, Berkeley Fiction Review,* the *Pennsylvania Literary Review, Texas Review, storySouth, New Orleans Review, American Literary Review,* the *Southern Quarterly, Raving Dove, Bartleby-Snopes, Baltimore Review, Portland Review, Tampa Review,* and *Missouri Review.* He is founding editor of the now defunct journals *Barataria Review* and *Books: A New Orleans Review.*

STOOGES IN PARADISE

Louis Gallo

For Cathy

May your hair ever blaze
in the sun, in the sun,
When I am undone,
when I am no one.

— Theodore Roethke

Once again we nestle in a luxurious oceanfront condo not one hundred yards from the beach. In the past it was always Destin, Florida and the Gulf, but since BP's ravage, we worry about pockets of crude oil and the even more toxic dispersants. Apparently, sharks have fled the Gulf and the coral has died, neither of which bodes well. So we changed our itinerary for the last three summers and now camp on Myrtle Beach. The waves rush forth and break more ferociously here, which we love, but no more ultramarine water or bone-china white sand; Myrtle water is murky and gritty, the sand dirty, smudge-like. But neither must we contend with the vast colonies of algae and seaweed always plaguing Destin. All in all, it's worked out.

The CDC warns that E. coli and MRSA contaminate beach sand and the ocean itself. Mothers scour children who build sandcastles with Germ-X.

Only five years ago Lea and I sat on the condo balcony and spotted at least four UFOs. Renee and Bee dismissed our sightings as experimental aircraft, but Lea and I steadfastly cling to our instincts. We *know* we saw UFOs, and we know they contained extraterrestrial aliens. Seems so long ago and nothing has come of it, but still...

This time my younger daughter Bee sits with me on another balcony overlooking the Atlantic. I tell her stories about her ancestors, especially my father and grandfather, both dead before her birth. Dusk stumbles in as we try to relax. I say *try* because no one in this family has ever achieved pure, easy relaxation, a primordial state I associate with sponges and mollusks lurking at the bottom of the sea. Must be nice. But somewhere along the genomic line, worry and anxiety and foreboding tainted our ganglia cells. We co-exist in low-grade panic most of the time, which occasionally accrues and explodes into full-blown hysteria. Not healthy, of course, but how to override genetics? We have feebly tried yoga and meditation and visualization techniques, but they seem paltry, like trying to slay a dragon with spears constructed of crepe paper. These seizures are no joking matter, but I often do in fact joke about them: "Hey, girls, Renee, when do you think the voltage will scorch us again?"

Bee usually shakes a puny fist at me; Lea just laughs; Renee, who prefers to sweep the notion under some pristine Sarouk carpet, gives me the evil eye.

We scramble for horoscopes in the newspapers, women's magazines, wherever we can find them. We know full well they are bogus and invented by underpaid staff. Nevertheless. We scrutinize often-ungrammatical messages in the Chinese fortune cookies we crack open every night when commencing supper. We seek omens and portents in every insect and bird we come across when on walks; we relate our dreams to each other in ancient tribal fashion, hoping for collective insight. When it comes to dreams, I'm partial to Jung, maybe Freud, whereas Lea, Bee, and Renee prefer the dozens of dream interpretation manuals strewn about the house. Renee still dreams of monks disguised as sharks and alligators, and these dreams disturb her as profoundly as when they started nearly a decade ago. I am always dreaming about visitations from the dead. The other night I waltzed with my great-aunt Du, who passed on a few years ago, my favorite of the four great aunts. An elegant affair, the *Blue Danube* rendered by a full tuxedoed orchestra, yet choreographed in a seedy warehouse. That one woke me up with night sweats. The girls' dreams are more idiosyncratic and novel, though Bee's are always epic in scope. Lea specializes in snippets; she might, for instance, dream about retrieving envelopes from the mailbox.

We have ordered miracle cures from the varied tabloids. Holy water from Jerusalem. Splinters of the cross. Lockets of the Buddha's hair. Did the Buddha have hair?

At random moments each of us smells the urgent scent of gasoline. Olfactory hallucinations?

And yet, even as I think on these things, as Krishnamurti advises, even as a modicum of blessed peace seems to envelop us, Bee shoots up from her slouch in instant alertness. "Daddy, look!" She must have noticed that my eyes were closed and I had begun to drift into rare, sweet reverie. Instantly they click open, and lo... right before us, hovering within the architectural frame of our balcony, hovering, yes, but impossible...three extraordinary pelicans so close we could, with a hint of effort, reach out and touch. Their wings seem stationary, tacked into place, riveted by invisible spikes to the very air. Three pelicans! Neither of us have beheld pelicans this close before, though I've seen my share when driving around Lake Pontchartrain in my hometown of New Orleans. And all I had wanted at the moment was an iota of the peace that surpasseth human understanding (which I know, if taken literally, probably means death).

So we're into death? Buddhism at its best: prepare every waking moment for your final demise. Dismiss the entire external world as samsara, illusion. Well, I'd prefer a new Jaguar, the return of youth, unlimited sensual pleasure, and the wisdom of either Solomon or Faust.

But pelicans! The instant seemed eternal. Now they're gone, swept up with the currents. Bee rushes to the rail to watch them ascend.

But they have vanished. How can it be? She sweeps into the condo to inform Renee and Lea, who are attempting to assemble some sort of complicated high-tech beach chair.

"Pelican?" Renee stops her wrench work for a moment and puts on her thinking face. "Pelican," she repeats. "Christian symbol." And of course she rises from her crouching position on the carpet and makes her way toward the room where we store our luggage, no doubt to return with one of our directories of symbols. Renee may take symbols even more seriously than I, though I doubt it. We simply react in different ways. She does research; I rely upon my reservoir of memory, reading, and mostly good old hunch and intuition. Lea whips out her laptop.

Renee looks supple and voluptuous in her one-piece black bathing suit; she flips through pages as she returns to the room. "The pelican," she reads, "will feed her young with her own blood and is therefore an icon of ultimate sacrifice." She gazes thoughtfully at the ceiling. "Hmm, like Jesus and the Eucharist."

"Sacrifice," I say stonily. "Who among us is going down?"

"And *three* of them," Renee quips.

"Barabbas and that other guy."

It does not matter that we are neither Christians by decree nor temperament. We draw wisdom and nuggets of enlightenment from whatever source seems most apropos, be it Taoism, Hinduism, Sufism, witchcraft, the Delphic oracle, Christianity too, Indian sutras, Jung, quantum physics, or Dr. Sanjay Gupta.

"A portent of sacrifice," I mutter. "Who's the sacrifice?"

"You, Dad," Lea laughs. As does Bee, who still remains in awe of the pelicans. "*I* saw them first," she has said a number of times. Balboa, first to spot the Pacific—among his kind at any rate.

"Not funny, Lea," I snarl. "Though I guess you're right. I'm the old man of this tribe."

"But it's probably a good omen," Rene says. "Resurrection and all that."

"Resurrection implies being dead," I say. And think…there are four of us, but *three* pelicans. "Numerology counts."

A mighty fine bird is the pelican
His beak holds more than his belican
And I wonder how in the helican

In our devotion to the hidden significances of quotidian events and spectacles, our family has become its own isolated fiefdom, a close-knit band of wary food gatherers who monitor symptoms and symbologies and have thereby lost touch with the bustling world of mercantilism, portfolios, corporate mergers and shenanigans, and politics (is Obama still president? After enduring Bush for eight years, who can possibly care any longer what happens?). Renee and I know that our children have grown, that they need to start distancing themselves from their parents, which they say is normal; but this other tug, you could call it the claws of the supernatural, ever welds us together. Did not Gautama say that the most difficult affection to extinguish is the love for a child? And yet suffering entails clinging to affections. This is what pisses me off about Buddhism. Chucking the wondrous world.

"Well at least it wasn't ospreys," Renee half laughs. The ospreys have bothered her a great deal during the last few days. On the very balcony where Bee and I encountered the pelicans, Renee says she saw not one but three—the infernal trinity again!—ospreys, which at first she mistook for hawks. Renee reveres hawks in totemic fashion, but these looked slightly odd. She assigned Lea to look them up on the laptop, and Lea dutifully obliged and informed Renee that what she described were ospreys, not typical hawks. Osprey, a new portent for Renee. She commandeered the laptop only to discover that ospreys betoken imminent death and destruction. And to spot *three* in so brief a span thus seemed horrendous indeed. The ospreys so upset Renee that I myself Googled "osprey" on Lea's laptop (I, who otherwise refuse to go near a laptop) and found dozens of references to ospreys as symbols of abundance and good tidings. I reported this to Renee, but she still insists that the most reliable sources spelled out mayhem, desolation, and *imminent* devastation. I tried again. I cannot locate Renee's sources. She says the claim is Hebraic in origin. Or has the laptop acquired some seditious component that alters information user by user? Information theory be damned! It was Szilárd who discovered that the mathematical equations for information theory and entropy are one and the same. How demonic is that?

North Carolina is on fire. Smoke from the blazes sometimes cascades our way; yesterday it was so turgid and noxious we had difficulty breathing.

And yesterday morning as we frolicked in the surf (yes, we are still capable of frolicking!) Bee reached into the water for what she thought was a shell. The girls, hell, all four of us, still collect beach shells, and we like those best that come straight from the sea, barring those still beslimed with living protoplasm. These we toss back into their oceanic womb. Bee's shell turned out to be, we later realized (thanks to Lea's laptop), a mushroom jellyfish. She tossed it away but not before it had sunk one of its talons (spikes? teeth? what do jellyfish have?) into the skin of her thumb. That thumb, by nightfall, had swollen to twice its size, and we lathered it with Benadryl and gave her an Advil. Oh, the perils that beset even modest frolickers! Luckily, the mushroom varieties of jellyfish, however frightful (yet eerily beautiful), are not extremely toxic. Another night, with our flashlights, we found dozens of dead ones stranded on the sand. Bee, the most gentle and compassionate of our clan, wept a salt tear for them, despite her wound. Bee has just made fifteen. Just yesterday I pushed her to sleep in a little blue swing for toddlers that I found on sale at Sears.

Last week, when still at home, my Chinese fortune slip informed me that I would soon embark upon a long journey. Journeys…every third or fourth fortune, right? I could not get the "long journey" out of my mind; it still adheres to my gray matter like a barnacle. See here, see here! I request no long journey. I must consult Confucius about how to reverse fortunes.

In Golden Corral, one of the few places Lea can eat because of her food allergies, we found a vending machine full of voodoo effigies. We slipped in the two quarters and out popped this little straw voodoo doll, which I fastened to my rearview mirror. Just in case. Pierce it with a few needles, incant some Latin, ward off evil. Or do evil.

During the trip down from the Blue Ridge we noticed that Little Debbie trucks saturated the highways. Why? No direct routes to Myrtle Beach exist; Googled directions are complex and labyrinthine and one gets inevitably lost in varied little Carolina towns still encapsulated in the nineteenth century. Yet Little Debbie travels the interstates and state roads and some old fashioned mud roads, her cheerful face plastered on all the trucks. Happy, wholesome American goodwill, optimism, peachy-keenness, fun, Good Ship Lollipopism? Americans have little tolerance for sour speculation, cynicism, Armenian desolation. Pass the Prozac. Bite another potato chip.

The days blur together as we engineer ocean time, restaurant suppers, and touristy mall jaunts. I love not knowing what day it is or the date; timelessness is ultimate liberation for me, and I assume for everyone else, though who am I to hypothesize? On either the first or second day after arrival I commenced my duty to seek out a rubber float boat at one of the many garish, fluorescent beach shops along the main highway. The boat must be an exact replica of the model we have used for the last three years or else the girls will sink into petulant sorrow. Ritual and repetition are important, nay, necessities for any family mired in nostalgia and semi-autistic tradition (to conquer time, you repeat it). We christen this rubber boat/float The Stooge each year. The next one, Stooge III.

So as the early riser (I don't sleep well on vacations and will harmonize the early rising with a delicious afternoon nap), I take it upon myself to make the drive and fetch a boat. I do so with loving urgency, for this particular Stooge is often hard to come by. Indeed, I've already searched four shops, including Wings (our favorite Florida store), without luck. I saunter into the fifth shop, Paradise, and am greeted at the desk by one of the most beautiful blond, blue-eyed Russian girls I have ever seen on the entire southeastern coast of America. You probably already know that beautiful blond Russian girls have replaced native whites, Hispanics, and blacks as the clerks and waitresses and motel workers in just about every business establishment from at least South Carolina to Florida. Perhaps on all coasts of this country for all I know. Exchange students or work programmers, whatever. I noticed this trend about eight or so years ago and must say I don't mind at all.

Paradise seems empty save for this exceptional beauty and her momentous smile, aside that is from the bounteous shelves and display units full of conches, sunscreen, T-shirts, baseball caps, beach chairs and umbrellas, jewelry, postcards…the trivial surfeit of America. I scan the glass counter case since I'm also on the lookout for a pair of brass knuckles. I bought a pair last year and feel compelled to purchase another…you know, for added protection, however illegal they may be in my home state. I point out the pair I want to Nadya, as her nameplate reads, and she, giggling and smiling, inserts her own fingers into the holes. Then she audaciously pretends she will smack me in the face! Laughing flirtatiously, I might add, as she sizzles with radiant hormones.

What a moment! Nadya, surely no older than twenty-two years. I could be her grandfather, I instantly and forlornly note.

"Don't do it," I laugh. "It's for defense, you know, in case I'm attacked by terrorists or deranged tourists. And I'm looking for a rubber boat for my daughters. Yellow, black, and red, a two-seater. Do you have those?"

Nadya holds up a finger as if in thought. "Ah," she says. "Follow me."

How can I describe Nadya's scandalous shorts that I do indeed follow to the back of the store? Surely I must *not* think on such things. Sorry, Krishnamurti. How young I suddenly feel! I could leap and yelp. Young, flirtatious women, alas, have this effect on aging male hominids, since usually such young ones look right through aging male hominids as if they were invisible and kaput or just plain grotesque. I have stared into my mirror often enough trying to determine exactly when I began to morph into Nosferatu.

We come to a display of the boats still packaged tightly in bright boxes, and sure enough, Stooge III beckons. "This is it," I say, "must be this one. Can you blow it up for me? The valves on gas station machines won't fit. Do you have an air machine here?"

Nadya looks at me and nods. She gazes straight into my eyes, and I must describe this gaze as passionate. "Your face is very handsome," she says in highly Slavic-scented English. What ho? What is happening here? For a moment it crosses my mind that sweet Nadya might be a hooker. But if so, why would she spend time clerking in a junky souvenir shop? Little Debbie, where art thou? I'm a married man; I love, adore my wife, twenty years my junior and sexy and hot and wondrously beautiful. My two daughters are approaching Nadya's age at the speed of light. Bee and Lea dwell in a different dimension altogether. Neither dreams of escaping the condo to seek out boys roaming the night beach; neither has any desire to storm the nightclubs, get drunk, tattoo or pierce themselves, or leave town for Moscow or Kiev as exchange students; to flirt with boys their own age much less geezers; to become Nadyas. They still love to stay home and play board games with their parents! Which the norm, Bee and Lea or Nadya? When I was Bee's age I couldn't wait to speed away in a fast, dark car with my chums and cruise into the Vieux Carre, where anyone twelve years or older could buy beer by the gallon.

Which the norm? I feel disturbed, conflicted, as if a little personal Katrina has swept through my pores. I thank God my girls are as they are; I thank God for the Nadyas of the world. And I am absolutely certain that every man who has ever lived would agree with me. What, *my* daughters...? No, no, no—I will crush your eyeballs with my brass knuckles; some other schmuck's, fair game.

Nadya unhooks an air hose from the wall and squats forward slightly as if to pretend she will aim the air gun at my face. Playful, of course. "Don't do it," I laugh. "You'll finish off my dry eye," I laugh, flattered, amazed. She inserts the contraption into the nozzle of the Stooge and it begins rapidly to bloat with air, as if coming alive, freed from imprisonment inside its package. Within seconds Stooge III is alive and well. Nadya shifts it aside to refasten the air hose to its hook. I'm still squatting near the base of the Stooge. She turns, and I cannot help but gaze not at her smiling face but the sleek, svelte, Coppertoned contours of her long legs. Eye level. All is well in the universe at this moment. Referred pleasure. Innocent, nothing will come of it.

But all is not well. Nadya's body begins to twitch and lose balance, and before I know it I'm holding a beautiful albeit unconscious young Russian beauty in my arms, while still squatting! She has simply passed out and I happened to catch her to break the fall. I cry for help, but no one else is in the store, no other clerks, no customers, no managers. What the hell? Too early for other people? I must now decide whether to lower her onto a filthy floor—she smells clean and soapy as lavender—or attempt to rise with her and risk destroying what's left of my lower chakras. Sacrifice? I refuse to sully the girl by depositing her on a really scummy floor; so slowly, cautiously, I begin to bear her weight (no more than 120 pounds, surely), lifting, as instructed by my chiropractor, with the legs only, not the backbone, holding the weight close to my chest and stomach. And while ascending in such afflicted fashion I see that Nadya's skimpy blouse, unhooked down to the second button, has pulled apart by the angle of her descent, and an exposed breast positions itself a mere head nod away from my, yegads, face! And I, sinful, egregious I, become instantly aroused! What a salacious cad I am. The poor girl remains unconscious, her head dangling over the crook of my lower arm, and I, bad Samaritan, leer at her naked, exposed breast. This was in no set of cards, no horoscope, no fortune cookie. They should exile me to Siberia in a Little Debbie truck. Along with the three ospreys. The long journey?

On the other hand, *Am I not a man*? Thanks for that one, Zorba.

I also note that Nadya wears studded pelican earrings.

Omit the *y* and Nadya become *nada*.

Jung said there are no coincidences. Everything is connected. Déjà vu, synchronicities. The entire tableau presents itself instantly in all its cornucopian wholeness to the eye that dares perceive it. The fully flared peacock's tail. Another mighty fine bird. Lots of birds on this venture, birds, the headgear of shamans worldwide. Something going on here; something going on everywhere all the time.

I carry stricken Nadya toward the front counter and plan to slide her onto it between the cash register and a display of sand-dollar jewelry. Once I have secured the buttocks onto a thick plate of glass, I gently nudge the errant breast back into place within her blouse. Braless, of course. How to explain such firm softness? A material oxymoron—no wordplay this. Soon a heavyset, short Dravidian who vaguely resembles Deepak Chopra walks in and cries, "What is happening here?" He carries a box of Krispy Kremes. The manager, I assume, off on an errand to secure breakfast for himself and his employee. I of course want no trouble. "She passed out," I say. "I didn't want to leave her on the floor. She blew up my Stooge."

He nods, a dark, lowbrowed man, and therefore serious and hopefully intelligent. "Oh yes, she does that," he waves the free hand. "Some sort of low blood sugar, but not dangerous form. Yes, just rest her onto the counter. That will be fine. A lovely, lovely girl."

(Told you!)

"It's already been a few minutes. Should I call 911?"

"Give it few more," he says, and I realize he knows the routine with Nadya.

"Will she be all right?"

"Certainly. She always is all right. Just some dazed at first. She will not remember fainting or anything about an hour before. Have a glazed?" He holds forth the box.

"No thanks, but let me pay you for a pair of brass knuckles and that rubber boat Nadya blew up for me. Then I'm on my way."

He looks puzzled. "Oh, Stooge?"

"Right, that's my daughters' name for the boat."

As he makes his way behind the counter, Nadya begins to moan a bit and shift her body toward me. Slowly her eyes open and she blinks rapidly as if trying to focus.

She mumbles in Russian but I don't understand.

"Are you okay?" I ask, figuring it will take a while for her to regain full consciousness.

I give the manager a hundred dollar bill and he rings me up.

"You came back to see me," Nadya whispers sweetly. This time it's clear, in English, and I don't know what to make of it. I came back? Has she mistaken me for some other aging dude? Whatever... according to the manager, she's tabula rasa for a while.

"I did," I say, wink, and retrace my steps to find the Stooge. My lower back feels terrific! No damage. I am proud to have rescued a damsel in distress, the stuff of myth and fairy tales. I'm a freaking hero of olde!

• • •

When I return to the condo Renee and the girls are still asleep, so I sit out on the balcony and drink some coffee and wish I'd taken that Krispy Kreme. Not many people on the beach yet, some early joggers, some guys pitching sand tents. No signs or omens to speak of, nor do I wish to encounter any. What I really want is more sleep, so I head for the bedroom and slide in and embrace Renee's supple body. She stirs gently and I feel her breath on my wrist. Ah, two unconscious women in one morning. Maybe that's a sign! But I quickly fall off and by the time I awake the troop is up and eager to sail. I had lugged the Stooge up an elevator into the condo and rested it against the entrance wall. I faintly hear giggles and whoops of delight. Stooge time! History has repeated itself. The Stooge will launch again. I stagger onto the balcony, my favorite spot, and clutch its railing, and out of nowhere a miasma of enormous black remorse assails me. In a hundred years none of this will make any difference; almost everyone alive on the planet will be dead. But this ocean, this sand, will remain. Back to Buddhism and Taoism: live for the moment, savor the *now*, time is an illusion. I stare down at the pool five stories below and behold a splendid sight. A young, shapely bikinied woman floating on her back, arms and legs outstretched, her hair sweeping over the water like golden seaweed. *She* could be dead for all I know; she doesn't move. But of course she is very much alive. Schrödinger's cat—dead and alive at once.

I must distract myself from perilous thoughts. I must buy a box of Krispy Kremes and devour them one by one. Or even a Little Debbie sugar concoction. Anything sweet.

A commercial on the inside television proclaims: *Good news for catheter users!*

So launch we do, but the waves tumble in violently this morning and the girls capsize with every bout. Then it's all four of us lifting the blasted boat full of heavy water and draining it. And this goes on for about an hour before I inform them that I need a break. So does Renee.

"Okay, girls, you're on your own with the Stooge for a while, so stay close to shore. Not much of a riptide yet but it's there, it's always there, like evil—ubiquitous. Never have too much fun."

Renee and I make our way back to the chairs and umbrellas and take turns keeping an eye on the girls. It's so peaceful and pleasant when it's not your turn. Must parenthood mean relentless paranoia? Sharks, mushroom jellyfish, typhoons, mere drowning, aquatic serial killers. When one or the other of us fails to spot the girls as they gambol in the surf our hearts sputter and lurch. Got to keep them in sight. And thus vacationing means hard work. But how wondrous it feels to close your eyes and feel the sun rain down on you—and empty your head, if only for the nonce.

Didn't Hamlet say that conscience makes cowards of us all? He meant *consciousness*, not conscience, though either suffices.

Floaters wriggle across my close-eyed and thus obfuscated vision. Bits of retina defecting. Myopic pressure in the old vitreous humor. Why not vitreous tragedy?

The image of Nadya's breast crowds out the floaters. I have resisted thinking about it, I don't want to think about it; thinking on such things means suffering, for me anyway, though in some alternate world of possibility it could have meant supreme joy. Why always these polarities? Who thought up this tormented, convoluted scheme of things?

Renee raps me on the knee, my bad one. My turn to climb the crow's nest of observation. Life guarding. I open up to her sumptuous smile. "Nodding off, Paw?" she asks. "Your watch."

"Close your eyes, babe, feels good. We'll soon be out there again navigating the wretched Stooge in deeper waters."

She does close her eyes, but murmurs, "We're the stooges, Paw, all of us, haven't you figured it out yet?"

I want to raise a finger, proclaim to the contrary, but it requires too much energy.

It's about eight o'clock and the girls want us to take them to a 1950s-style amusement park in the thick of Myrtle Beach. Parking costs fifteen bucks. We have just eaten at the Golden Corral *again*, our main source of food on this trip aside from Bob Evans and the snacks we pick up at BI-LO. Vacations cost a fortune these days, unlike back when my parents took my sister Lisa and me to Destin, before it was Destin. Same ocean, same sand, no Holiday Inns, no McDonald's, no condos, just pure beach and a pleasant stay in a motel that cost twelve dollars a week! St. Francis Courts, I believe that motel was called, and you can still find remnants of this early chain along Highway 11, from the Blue Ridge to down south. They have converted one in our area into a stone and mulch company.

Lea begins to sulk because the trip is largely over: three or so days to go. It does seem as if we just arrived, I agree. But Lea lives for our trips, so it will be rough going for a while. Bee too laments the swift passage of time, but in her own quiet, melancholic way. Renee and I just want to get home so we can take a vacation from the vacation. Since when have vacations become onerous labor? Is it merely aging? If so, why do I hear many complaints along the same lines from both codgers *and* young people? What has happened to simple fun? Did it ever exist? Do we merely imagine we once had it?

I begrudgingly pay the attendant fifteen and follow Renee and the girls into this really dumpy amusement park. No sidewalks or walkways, only mud, which at the moment is dry and powdery and coats our sandals and exposed feet. A few watermelon rinds and gnawed corncobs bespot the trails. The owners have billed it as a retro park reminiscent of the 1950s, and I grant it does have that aura. And the same types of rides: swirling teacups, Bump-a-Cars, little crafts shaped like airplanes that swing their passengers out into ever-widening arcs. But the girls mostly want to ride the Ferris wheel, mainly because they have never ridden one before. No Ferris wheels in our neck of the woods. On previous expeditions to Williamsburg, they were too little to ride alone, and neither Renee nor I can go near a Ferris wheel without violent retching and nausea. Thus this ride would become an historic event for Bee and Lea, a first.

So they stand in line while Renee and I perch on the nearest bench, so hot we pant and long to lick ice cubes.

And once again blond Russian girls everywhere, taking tickets, selling lemonade and dripping buttery corn at the stands, emptying trash cans, hawking necklaces and T-shirts. And every one of them, gorgeous, though not of Nadya's ilk. One of the prerequisites for coming to America on exchange programs must be beauty. The crafty old Soviets have defeated us not with an atom bomb, but splendid young women!

When Bee and Lea have finished numerous revolutions, they head straight for our bench. Lea looks green and ill. "I'm going to throw up," she mumbles, and does indeed vomit out her entire supper from Golden Corral. We had steered her behind a large, rusted waste bin to avoid a scene. She moans and cries, "I feel terrible," and we, of course, hurry her back to the van and head straight to BI-LO for Dramamine. I have often suggested ginger as an natural alternative, but the females complain it tastes like soapy water. I love the zing of ginger, and treat myself to several slices every night. I have even brought my own supply to the beach. Gingerol inside each crystallized wedge reduces inflammation during arthritic flare-ups. And certain Asians claim that ginger revs up lust, yearning, desire—an aphrodisiac, in other words. Does this explain my retrograde, inordinate concupiscence? Why not? A favorite Chinese wedding gift is a ginger bowl decorated with images of peacocks.

I will no longer recommend ginger to my daughters.

It's our final day, a crestfallen Lea informs us. On the balcony last night, and several previously, I had spent a good portion of time with each of my daughters, and sometimes both at once, chatting, joking, "relating," as sociologists would say. How I despise sociologists for presuming to know what is best for all of us. Generalized schematics, that's all they're good for. The essence of each sovereign individual remains a mystery, and I hope it stays that way. Anyway, the girls now appreciate me from a new angle; previously, I was good ole Da, a father who bought toys by the bundle, who ate supper with them and hustled them to emergency rooms, who told bedtime stories, a regular mythic figure. Now they have become genuinely interested in conversing, in listening to what I have to say and joshing around in not merely a babyish way, but intellectually. We can discuss history, science, literature, for much of it they have already learned in school. I had no idea Bee had read

Poe's "Cask of Amontillado" in one of her classes, so when I casually intoned, "For the love of God, Montressor!" she replied, "Yes, for the love of God." I was stunned and fascinated. How much have they learned without me? How much do they know that I don't know? Why have the years sped by so treacherously?

Yet I can now speak with children as adults! A geological epoch has passed, another arrives. It may have commenced earlier, but I missed it, perhaps refused to acknowledge that it would ever happen. The babies are gone forever—which breaks my heart. Though now there are these two "new" people, no longer babies, but real people whom I adore and who adore me, people who are actually people. (Let's face it, babies are not real people; they are pre-people.)

On this trip then I have crossed a Rubicon of revelation. And all revelation costs. No free rides in the universe.

And yes, it is our last day. We plan to spend most of it in and beside the sea, and by twilight set Stooge III adrift forever—or at least until some shark tears it to shreds in open water. No room in the van for both the Stooge and our luggage. Deflate a Stooge and it dries up and cracks within months. I know, tried it with Stooge I. Stooge I, an eternity ago, and yet an eyewink.

Someone with supernal powers walks up to you. I'll give you all you desire—eternal youth, unlimited sensual pleasure, the knowledge of Solomon and Faust and, what the hell, throw in Socrates and Aristotle—you can have it all in exchange for your past.

What about the Jaguar?

Hmm, my past? Polio and A-bomb terrors, witnessing the deterioration and deaths of many I loved, teenage pimples, rejection by certain girls of my dreams, an hegemony of embarrassing, excruciating moments, spying the first gray hair, then the defection of hair altogether, two ex-wives with machetes in the wings…but hold on, that past would include Renee, Lea, and Bee! Perhaps they represent a sliver of my life, but a fairly good sized and the best sliver. Get thee behind me, supernal power. Let me wither on the vine. Come near me again, it's brass knuckles pummeling your gaseous vertebrae.

• • •

Once again Renee and I take a break as the girls fiddle with Stooge III in the surf. They drift out a bit farther than we would like, but we remind ourselves, after all, they can handle it. Before I lower myself into the beach chair I inform Renee that I must return to the condo to, er, relieve myself. Ordinarily the ocean itself makes a wondrous bathroom, but ever since that Discovery Channel special about hideous parasites that just wait for some unsuspecting male to pee in a body of water so they can zip up the old nozzle, embed and cause untold mayhem and pain, I rely upon modern plumbing. Some splendid perks to modern life after all. Plumbing!

It's so hot I take my time returning to the fifth floor. I plod, in fact. We have forgotten to close the balcony doors, and the main door *whooshes* open with much effort on my part, and the blinds rattle like wild aboriginal musicians clacking bamboo tubes. I take care of the business at hand, but before heading back I step onto the balcony and zoom in on the girls with my new Canon digital, click a perfect shot as if they were ten feet away. I turn my gaze toward Renee, and… whoa! I must have the wrong umbrella and chairs. But no, Renee's flamboyant copper hair is unmistakable. And, yes, our ragged towels and crooked umbrella. A *man* sits in my chair beside Renee! I zoom to full magnification and steady the camera on the railing. A man! He and Renee seem to be chatting amiably. He pokes her upper arm gently and cannot stop touching her. At one point she clasps his wrist as she slouches over in laughter! What ho, what ho! She's having a grand old time… my wife and this stranger. And within sighting distance of our daughters. I must retrieve the voodoo doll from my windshield and impale its groin with needles. I gauge that he's about her age, maybe even somewhat younger! There are many young guys who prefer older women, but for me Renee remains very young. It's all relative and your personal kink.

I can make out profiles—alas, the man has a full set of tawny, curly hair and a rugged jaw, and I estimate about twenty-nine or thirty. Seems moderately muscular with a small tattoo on the neck, some sort of bird…yikes! A freaking osprey! *Imminent devastation?* Am I being cuckolded by a whippersnapper who has followed us to Myrtle Beach to be near Renee? How long has this been going on? Who is this unknown despoiler? Why is Renee having what looks like uproarious fun? I shoot Mr. Curly's head about twenty-five times with my Canon. I had planned to tell Renee about my escapade with Nadya, but perhaps she intuited it, as women do. Perhaps this is revenge. But revenge for what? Nadya, when she was conscious, merely flirted with me, and I must confess that I flirted back. Harmless, right? Or is the grand joy of flirting now off limits as well as everything else regulated by the myriad hyena committees charged with suppressing human nature? Can't even say "Eskimo" now without someone, somewhere accusing you of crimes against humanity. It certainly looks as if Renee is flirting with this osprey dude, but what's strange is that while my initial reaction was rage, hurt, shock, fear…it dawns on me within minutes, why not? Why should Renee too not have the right to flirt? Flirting is an upper! Just as long as he doesn't pass out and she must tuck his wayward schlong back into the Speedo. Well, what of that too? As long as he's unconscious, so what? Just don't make a field day out of it.

I shuffle out the condo and make my way down the halls, across the wooden planks that pass as a pier of sorts, and cross the scorching sand. I suppose I must meet this usurper, and truly I have no idea how I will react when he offers his hand to shake. My brass knuckles are positioned firmly in place and he will shake a hand that is partly metal if I deign to shake at all. Metal means business. Amazingly, when I approach our beach setup, my chair is empty. The malefactor has vanished. Has he absconded into the sea? Have I imagined the entire scenario? I have photographs, evidence. Renee must confess or I shall…I shall do nothing. Not even spill the beans about Nadya. We'll have secrets, minor, trivial, piddling secrets. Who doesn't savor a good secret? Or maybe the girls saw the whole thing and will expose Renee's assignation. Or maybe I can *choose* to believe I hallucinated the incident despite digital evidence stored within my memory card. Choose to believe I am crazy rather than cozy up to the rugged, scrawny truth.

And exactly where are the girls? I spot Stooge III on the sand at water's edge, but no Lea, no Bee.

"Hello," Renee turns languidly as I ease myself in the chair. Her smile ignites me, and the sunlight splashing her face brings out the freckles that I love. She looks wondrously gorgeous. Is it me or has her encounter with Mr. Curly brightened her up? She takes my free hand and squeezes it. I wriggle the knucks off the other, twist them into the sand and bury them.

"Hi," I say, "where are the girls? I don't see them. I see the Stooge but not Lea or Bee."

"They're old enough to venture out a bit on their own," Renee says, and I agree. I don't want to agree, but I—we—must agree. They aren't babies anymore, sad to say.

I scan the water in the Stooge vicinity, and sure enough, see Lea and Bee leaping up as the waves crash over them. I'm terrified, of course, but know that Renee is right. Every so often our daughters gaze our way and wave; they too know that something has changed, some major tectonic plate shift of the psyche.

Renee squeezes my hand tighter and sighs dreamily. "I love you, Paw, you know that, don't you?"

I'm tempted to retort with, "Yeah, well then who was the bozo whose wrist you grabbed while I was taking a leak?" But no, I restrain myself. Instead: "I love you too, babe. You're the best thing that's ever happened to me. And right now, at this very instant, here we are on the beach again. The ocean lulls. The sun feels good. The girls are having a merry old time without us, though we're right here, right here in case they need us—and they know it. What could be better?"

"Stooges in paradise," Renee laughs. "Who would have thought?"

Yep, that's about it. A paradise that ends tomorrow. Back to the grind, to the mountains, landlocked. Back to foreboding and apprehension. Will I tell Renee about Nadya? Probably at some point. What is there to tell? Will she tell me about Mr. Curly? Probably not. And what of it? Who cares? *I* care, but not enough to detonate an explosive. Too many explosions already coming along of their own accord. Every so often I'll think on these things as the eon shrivels, but right now no abstractions, no assessments, no apprehension…only this, being here, absorbed in the moment, the fabulous, eternal, joyous moment that crests and ebbs with the waves, which while it lasts is more than good, more than enough.

Lots of time to brood tomorrow and tomorrow and tomorrow.

A pelican swoops over our daughters, who seem absurdly far away even as they begin to make their way back toward us with smiles and shells and infinite expectations.

SILENCED VOICES:
Eskinder Nega

by Cathal Sheerin

Eskinder Nega, the prize-winning Ethiopian journalist and dissident blogger, is serving an eighteen-year prison sentence for terrorism-related offenses. But Nega is not a terrorist—he is a victim of one of the world's harshest, but least talked about, crackdowns on free expression.

Based in Addis Ababa, Nega has for decades been a leading voice in the call for democratic reform and freedom of the press in Ethiopia.

Eskinder Nega

Since 1993, when he opened his first newspaper, *Ethiopis*, Nega has openly and frequently criticized the government, including Ethiopia's autocratic (now late) Prime Minister Meles Zenawi. There is no better introduction to Nega's defiant style than his article "Open Letter to PM Meles Zenawi," published in March 2011:

"[Ethiopia is] a nation outraged by soaring inflation, a public scandalized by unprecedented corruption, rampant unemployment, political oppression, and chronic shortage of land in rural areas. In sum, the nation is desperate for change. You have essentially wasted the two decades with which you were blessed to effect change. In place of pragmatism, dogma has prevailed; in place of transparency, secrecy has taken root; in place of democracy, oppression has intensified; and in place of merit, patronage has been rewarded. Ato Meles Zenawi: the people want—no, need—you to leave office."

In Ethiopia, this kind of outspokenness does not go unpunished. Nega was arrested on September 14, 2011, following the publication of another article in which he cast doubt on official claims that a number of recently arrested journalists were "terrorists." In the same article he also criticized the September 2011 arrest of the Ethiopian actor and critic of the government, Debebe Eshetu. In an attempt to discredit him, Nega was accused of having connections to Ginbot 7, a banned political group. State television portrayed him as a "spy for foreign forces."

Nega was charged alongside twenty-three other defendants on November 10, 2011, accused of receiving weapons from Eritrea with the intention of carrying out terrorist attacks in Ethiopia. Human rights groups around the world condemned the charges as fabrications.

It was not the first time that Nega had been targeted by the authorities. He had previously been detained at least six times. In February 2011, he was briefly detained for "attempts to incite Egyptian and Tunisian-like protests in Ethiopia." In 2005, following their reports on the government's extremely violent crackdown on protesters, Nega and his wife Serkalem Fasil were jailed along with twelve other journalists on charges of treason. Fasil gave birth to the couple's son in prison in 2006. The couple was acquitted and released in 2007, but their newspapers were shut down.

Ethiopia has been widely criticized by human rights groups for the over-zealous application of its draconian anti-terrorism legislation. Under these laws, any reporting that the authorities regard as "encouragement" to opposition groups is considered terrorism. The law has been used to imprison a number of high-profile Ethiopian journalists. A number of journalists who fled into exile have been convicted in absentia on similar charges and handed life sentences.

The Ethiopian government's clampdown on free speech is so fierce that it is now an accepted fact of life that journalists will be arrested. As the exiled Ethiopian satirist Abebe Tolla says, "Whenever anyone is arrested under anti-terrorism law now, people ask, 'Was he/she a journalist?'" Ethiopia is riddled with security agents and informants, some of whom travel to neighboring countries in order to spy on exiles there. "We even have a saying: one spy for every person," says Tolla.

Nega's trial began on March 6, 2012. The prosecution's evidence against him and the twenty-three other defendants consisted of poor-quality recordings of telephone conversations and a video of a town hall meeting in which Nega discusses the differences between Arab countries and Ethiopia. Nega took the stand on March 28 and denied all charges, maintaining that he had never plotted against the government, and admitting only that—in the wake of the Arab Spring—he had speculated on the possibility of a similar movement in Ethiopia.

But trials in Ethiopia are rarely fair, and when the authorities have publicly painted you as a threat to state security, there is only one outcome. On June 27, 2012, Nega was found guilty of all the charges, and on July 13, 2012, he was sentenced to eighteen years in prison. He is currently being held at Kaliti Prison in Addis Ababa, where political prisoners are housed with criminals. Family visits are extremely limited and torture is commonplace.

Despite his dire situation, Eskinder Nega remains a defiant champion of free speech and peaceful social change. He is a resilient man, and, as he wrote in this article written from July 2011, still optimistic about Ethiopia's future:

"As to our colleagues in prison, Woubshet and Reeyot, we testify to their commitment to non-violence. No independent journalist has given the charges the benefit of the doubt. And we reaffirm our commitment to peacefully serve the causes of truth, justice, and democracy with our writings. We will not be intimidated. Democracy is humanity's common destiny. There is no avoiding it, whether you are an Eskimo or a Zulu, a Christian or a Muslim, white or black, developed or developing. It is truly universal. And after a long journey, Ethiopia's encounter with destiny is right around the corner. We are almost there. We shall be free!"

Appeals calling for the release of Eskinder Nega and all journalists imprisoned for practicing their right to free expression may be sent to:

Minister of Justice Berhanu Hailu
Ministry of Justice
PO Box 1370, Addis Ababa, Ethiopia
Fax + 251 11 551 7775

Cathal Sheerin works for the Writers in Prison Committee of PEN International.

My grandparents, Hyman and Belle Brooks, circa 1941.

Kim Brooks is an Iowa Writers' Workshop graduate, a Michener–Copernicus Fellow, and a Yaddo Corporation Fellow. Her short fiction has appeared in *One Story*, the *Missouri Review*, *Epoch*, *Alaska Quarterly Review*, *Meridian*, *New Stories from the Midwest*, and other journals. It has also received honorable mention in *Best American Short Stories* and the Pushcart Prize anthology. Her nonfiction appears frequently on Salon.com. She lives in Chicago with her family and has just finished her first novel.

YEAR'S TIME

Kim Brooke (signature)

Kim Brooks

Rabbi Stephen Smith was sitting at his desk well after midnight, reading letters from strangers pleading to be saved. This was how he spent his nights. It had been that way for three years now. It was not a great sacrifice; he was an old man and needed little sleep, but it was a sacrifice he took seriously.

Every night he read letters written by the Jews of Germany, Austria, the Western Caucasus, Eastern Poland, the Baltic States, the Western Soviet Union—Jews who had come to the realization in the past month or season or year that if they did not get out of Europe, they were going to die. They'd been writing to him for years, but this summer, with the German invasion of Poland and the British issuance of the White Paper (a padlock on the door of a burning house), the situation had become untenable. He read and he read and he read; for every letter he finished, five more appeared the following day, all of them phantoms to him, all of them writing under the tragic misconception that he, as a member of America's Jewish leadership, could help them.

It had taken him years to accept the fact that he could not. At a luncheon the week earlier, a luncheon he himself convened in his role as a director of the Zionist Organization of America, he confided to Louis Brandeis that he no longer believed there was much that could be done. Two, three years ago—maybe. Now, with the German war machine grinding ahead and the British squeezing off the Mandate, it was all but hopeless. Certainly some could still be saved. A million maybe: the youth, the ones who were strong and resilient with their lives still before them. But the old ones and weak ones would pass. They were, as he himself had declared before the delegates in Zurich, "economic and moral dust in a cruel world, *She'erith hapley-tah*." When he'd recounted this to the old justice from Louisville, Brandeis had smiled at him, a smile Smith recognized as one that was used to hide the process of judgment. Very few people were interested in Smith's discovery of his own helplessness. But what could he say? After years and years of struggling, he had given up.

It dawned on him one morning that if he kept up the fight, he was going to fail, and he was going to die a miserable, bitter husk of a man, whereas if he let go now there were other worthy causes to which he could turn his attention. The decision lay before him, and he'd made it, and now all he could do for the Jews of Europe was read their letters and pluck a few of them, one or two a month, from the pyre. He could do it personally with his own money, his own connections.

Now, he was reading the plea of a fourteen-year-old girl in Vienna. Her father was Polish but had been living there for twenty years when the Nazis occupied Austria and the Gestapo deported him to the Sachsenhausen camp. The girl was left to wander the streets, filthy and half-frozen, for most of December. He picked up the letter and placed it in the thin pile to the right of the large one. He would do his best to find a family for her, to call in a favor with the Austrian consul, create some personal connection. And if it worked, she would live, while all the others died. That he, Stephen Smith, the son of a Brooklyn dry goods store owner, should hold such power—it filled him with equal parts wonder and disgust.

He had just put down the letter when the phone rang. It was Howard Kaplan, the synagogue's treasurer, his personal secretary.

"A fire. There's a fire at the synagogue. I just got the call and I'm on my way. I know it's late but I thought you'd want to know."

"A fire," he said. "Is anyone…?"

"I have no idea. I don't know any more than I'm telling you right now. That's why I thought we should go down there, both of us. Can you get your driver?"

Smith closed his eyes. So, he thought, at long last, it's happening here. He said, "I'm on my way."

He could see the glare of the flames as he rounded the corner onto 68th Street, the sky above the building a lighter shade of black than up and down the block. He'd expected fire, but most of what he saw was smoke, a geyser of smoke pouring out the sanctuary's dome and also out the windows of his office.

As his car drew closer, he rolled down his window and could smell the stench. The smoke stung his throat and his nostrils and he lifted his handkerchief to his face. There was steam in the air from all the spent hydrant water. Three engines on the scene. Dozens of firefighters. One perched on the edge of a ladder extended toward the crown of the blaze. The flames had wrapped around the back of the building now, engulfed not only the sanctuary but the Hebrew school and kosher kitchen. The stained glass windows at the front of the building had all been blown out and smoke poured from the openings. When his driver pulled up to the police barricade, Smith stepped out of the car and felt the heat, dry and crackling and itchy on his face. He stepped forward and a hand came out to stop him. "You can't go any closer."

"It's my temple," he said. "I built it. I run it. Let me pass."

The man looked at him, then at the fire. "The best way to help is to let us work."

"I need information. I need answers. I need to know how this started."

"There will be time for that later." He pointed up and down the street. "Right now we're more worried about keeping the whole damned block from burning down. You see that building next door.

That's a residential building—forty, fifty units. Sleeping kids. You get it?"

Smith nodded.

"So, I'll tell you again, 'Step back.'"

Smith stood there and watched the smoke billowing out. All along the street people had come to look. He knew he should be thinking only about the people in those neighboring brownstones, or about the people—his congregants—who were losing their place of worship, or of his own place in the world—was he going to build a new temple, start again at the age of eighty-four?—but instead he stood there thinking about what would be lost: the *bimah* from which he'd spoken on the High Holidays for thirty years, the beautiful brass pipe organ, the Ark of the Covenant and the *parochet* concealing it, the five-hundred-year-old menorah inside the ark and the chair for Elijah donated by the head rabbi of Palestine, and even the torah scroll itself.

An hour before dawn he walked over to Broadway, then south to a cafeteria on 63rd. He bought himself a hard-boiled egg and a piece of toast and a cup of coffee, ate it alone at a table in the middle so he wouldn't have to look out the windows. He and Rebecca had come to places like this two or three mornings a week for most of the forty-six years of their marriage. How he missed her, that wise smile, the tidy efficiency with which she cracked her egg and peeled her orange, the way in moments of crisis she'd cover his hands with her own and look directly into his eyes and say, "We're still here."

They'd had four children, four human beings they'd fashioned out of nothing, long grown up now with their own children nearly grown, but he remembered, he remembered. There was no time to sit and write old friends. There were days when there was hardly time to tie his shoes. He wasn't even the one doing most of the work, and there was never time. They were angels, though. He remembered that, too. All the sweetness of life was in their children, the love he felt for them. He remembered how he used to come home from work, absolutely exhausted, and he'd lean back in his armchair, and they'd climb all over him like wild monkeys, all four

116

at once. Rebecca'd come in with his evening schnapps, and she'd find him with a girl on his shoulder, a boy on his chest, the other two swinging from his legs. He'd be trapped beneath them all, but he loved it—how he loved it—even if it never seemed there was enough time.

The days passed, the months and seasons, not quickly at first but with a certain driving cadence. And then, in his forties, something shifted in that regard—a sudden acceleration in the passage of time; he and Rebecca had both noticed it. The children had left them one by one, and in the end, Rebecca had left him, too. That was how he thought of it, not that she had died but that she had *left* him. This was due in part to the quickness with which the cancer had ravaged her, but also to the fact that she'd been so angry with him at the very end. It was in '39, right after the *Anschluss*. She read all the news coming through the Yiddish wire; she read it with an urgency he'd never seen her show before, as though in not reading it she'd somehow be aiding the Nazis in their barbaric march. She read it aloud to him sometimes, all the bloody details of the beatings and fires, the arrests, the families torn apart, the children orphaned, the suicides and murders, and she said to him, again and again, "Stephen, you must do something. You must act." She said it when she hardly had enough breath to say anything, when her voice was hardly more than a whisper.

And in response, he had humored her; he'd ignored her. He'd told her the important thing was that she rest, and try to eat a bit, and think about how pleasant it would be in the Berkshires when they went in March (a trip she'd surely known she'd never make). He'd loved her so much and he hadn't wanted her last months to be filled with thoughts of suffering and evil, but the closer she'd gotten to the end, the less afraid she'd seemed.

"Go to Europe," she'd told him. "Go to Palestine. To London. You know people, Stephen. Write letters. Make phone calls." She'd begged him. He'd told her he was doing everything he could. He'd insisted on it. And then she'd died, and the last thing left on earth of their kinship was this lie, this half-truth, this artifact of his own fear and failure that would never go away, that just sat and grew colder and harder, a hard-boiled egg lilting on the counter, an empty closet.

He ate and paid his bill and returned to the synagogue as quickly as he could. Dawn was breaking over the tops of the buildings. The crowd around the temple was sparser than it had been. Only one of the engines remained. There was still a glare in the air that gave the neighboring apartments a brassy tint. If he didn't know better, it would have seemed a fine morning.

The fire marshal, a large man with pink cheeks and pale hair matted and wet from water or sweat, put his hand on Smith's shoulder. "You're the head of this church?" he asked.

"This temple, yes. I'm the rabbi here."

"We need to ask you some questions."

"Go ahead. Any way I can help."

He asked if there had been any candles left burning.

"Of course," the rabbi answered. "The *yahrzeit* candles."

"Yahrzeit?"

"Year's time. The candles commemorating the dead."

"That's our best guess then, as of now."

"Not arson."

"There's no indication."

The rabbi nodded. What a wondrous world it was. All across Europe, temples were burning, and here was his own house of worship smoldering not from the rage of a Jew-hating mob, but from devotion itself; not evil, but luck. The marshal talked on, but Smith hardly heard a word the man said; and even if he had heard him, he would't have been able to answer. A God-like loneliness pressed down on his frail bones. He could feel his ribs straining beneath it. They felt as slight as birdcage wire, as brittle as a winter wreath. He couldn't move. He could barely swallow. He couldn't remember what it was that had once made him believe in God, or in himself, or in anything at all. A veil of smoke rose up in the distance, spread out until it was thin as breath, then vanished into the blush of dawn above Central Park. All of creation was too lovely and too pitiful to behold. He couldn't do a thing besides stand there and watch the younger, stronger men scramble to subdue the flames.

INTERVIEW WITH PETER LaSALLE

by D. Seth Horton

Peter LaSalle is the author of several books of fiction, including the highly praised short story collection Tell Borges If You See Him: Tales of Contemporary Somnambulism, *which was published by University of Georgia Press as the winner of the Flannery O'Connor Award in 2007, and reissued in a paperback edition in 2012.* Bomb *magazine called these stories "masterful and*

Peter LaSalle

idiosyncratic," and Kristin Latina writing in the Providence Sunday Journal *said, "Peter LaSalle may not be a household literary name, but if you read his latest collection of short stories, you may just wonder why not." A new novel,* Mariposa's Song, *was published in 2012 in the Americas Series from Texas Tech University Press, and a new short story collection,* What I Found Out About Her, *is forthcoming from University of Notre Dame Press. His stories have appeared in many magazines and anthologies, such as* Tin House, Zoetrope, Paris Review, Antioch Review, Virginia Quarterly Review, Best American Short Stories, Best of the West, Best American Mystery Stories, Best Sports Short Stories, *and* Prize Stories: The O. Henry Awards. *He has taught at universities in this country and France, and currently teaches creative writing at the University of Texas at Austin, both in the Department of English and the Michener Center for Writers graduate program.*

I would like to begin with Mariposa's Song, *your new novel.*

Yes, seems to me like the best place to start.

The entire novel is delivered as a single sentence, although it is broken up in places through the use of ellipses and section breaks, and it centers around the character of Mariposa, a young woman from Honduras who works as a bar girl in Austin. Could you discuss the genesis of this project, specifically why you became interested in developing Mariposa's character through the medium of a novel-length sentence?

Well, over the years I've relied on this motif, a single free-flowing sentence, in several short stories that have appeared in magazines. But this is the first time I've used it for a narrative of this length, a novel.

It seemed particularly right for telling this story of one Saturday night in the life of the twenty-year-old Honduran bar girl, Mariposa. She's cheerful and pretty, but, as it turns out, also maybe dangerously naive, and that leads to the serious trouble for her. On one level, the flow of uninterrupted prose somehow reflected the tempo of the nightclub she's working in, a rough place in East Austin called El Pájaro Verde, where the entire scene in the course of a night can take on a certain rhythm established as the DJ plays one song after another, *norteño* and *cumbia* and *ranchera*, always continuous, no breaks. More important, the single ongoing sentence, like a meandering song, seemed to get at the dreamlike, half-unreal quality of Mariposa's life, being the undocumented worker she is, somebody forced to live in the shadows due to the absurdity of current immigration laws. It's maybe the way that any of us, when feeling somewhat alone, isolated even in a crowd, does have a certain private song about oneself playing in the head, to ward off the strangeness that seems to surround us, if nothing else.

Interview by D. Seth Horton

Why didn't you use first person, if it was intimacy you were after?

I used third person rather than first to give some latitude in tapping into her consciousness, as well as maybe a larger, eerily metaphysical consciousness of the all-seeing night itself. It worked so well for me that way. Actually, in the course of the writing, the prose just started to accumulate, almost with an energy of its own. I guess I got thoroughly caught up in the freedom of a narration not bound by the confines of terminal punctuation, went into a strange zone with it, as Mariposa's presence and that of those around her in the club came more and more alive for me. To be honest, sometimes it felt that all I had to do was sit at my Mac keyboard and watch my fingers on the silvery keys rhythmically working on their own, with the writing process bypassing logical thought completely and the narrative coming from who knows where. It's something I suspect can happen in any sort of rather automatic writing, if that makes any sense.

Which it probably doesn't, right? And which, now that I think more on this, is what I really like about such writing. Of course, that was only for the first draft, and there was considerable—and I mean considerable—shaping of the arc of the story and polishing the prose later.

It seems as if this notion of a "strange zone," as you put it, could be a germane method of approaching Mariposa's Song. *Not only does it allude to your compositional process and the single-sentence structure of the novel, but it also describes the shadowy nightclub where Mariposa's story unfolds. Perhaps most important, it also highlights the ways in which the narrative breaks through traditional boundaries in point of view. Drawing on modernist techniques, the narrative moves fluidly into and out of Mariposa's consciousness and thereby seems to blur the distinction between her private self and public image. Would you agree that these "strange zones" are ubiquitous throughout* Mariposa's Song, *and if so, do they mark a relatively new development in your writing, or have they always characterized aspects of your fiction?*

That's an interesting idea, the different ways "strange zones" might be applied to the novel. And while I sure didn't consciously see all that going on when I was writing *Mariposa's Song*, I guess it could be true. You know, sometimes my whole life—my time itself on this planet—feels like it's been spent entirely in sort of a "strange zone," though that's another story altogether, as they say.

But concerning the technique in *Mariposa's Song*, trying to find an application of point of view that has, as I just mentioned, the intense personal perception of an individual character, and can also tap into a larger transcendent something to portray the life of a bar girl like Mariposa, I was very aware of aiming for that. It does build on modernist technique, I suppose, even postmodernist technique. Of course, I'd like to be able to say that this is a recent development in my writing, because a writer, especially one at my stage of the game, always wants to think he or she is still developing. But in truth I've been experimenting with things like this ever since I first started writing short stories for creative writing classes way back in college at Harvard, even though much of what I've published since then, including my one previous novel, *Strange Sunlight*, often sticks to a more traditional realism.

Does that mean you have always felt a degree of friction in your work between realist and experimental fiction?

I used to see the two as somewhat at odds, but not anymore, and now it's more a matter of always opening myself up to the options afforded by each, sometimes blending both. I think I was lucky to have been a young, aspiring writer coming of age in the late sixties and early seventies. It was an exciting time when Borges, García Márquez, Beckett, and company were our contemporary heroes. They were all brave experimenters and quite unlike the tame and even comfortably hidebound writers loudly touted nowadays by the commercially oriented major review outlets, or given large-scale exposure, let's say, in a venue such as the essentially mainstream *New Yorker*—those being the kind of writers that some of my grad students in creative writing today often see as important, maybe because we are, in fact, living in an age of the triumph of the publicity/pseudo-celebrity machine as much as anything else. My ultimate hero remains Faulkner. In his greatest works—*The Sound and the Fury*, *Go Down, Moses*, and *Absalom, Absalom!* probably tops—he set the standard, with no apologizing for his indisputable *art*. He showed how you can have a viscerally moving fiction based on solid characterization and effective plotting, also with historical and philosophical weight—which in his case meant having plenty to say about a subject as huge as the Original Sin of slavery in the South—yet at the same time produce artistically challenging work that's always striving to discover new ways of expressing all of it, using a full range of the powerful effects of innovative structure and the limitless, wildly wonderful possibilities of language itself to get at it.

No doubt, it might be pretty presumptuous—actually it's *ridiculously* presumptuous—for me to think this, but I hope *Mariposa's Song* is one work I've written where I'm at least attempting to answer some of that call. And I really hope that while the novel is perhaps daring in presentation, it also has something to say about a social condition and the plight of undocumented workers in our country that surely needs to be said right now, in the midst of so much loud right-wing noise we constantly hear barking against immigration reform.

I do notice that Faulkner turns up often in your stories, references to him.

One can never speak of Faulkner enough, that's always been my slogan.

Setting is an important element in the work of Faulkner and some of the other innovative writers you mentioned. Yet, in American literature, the linkage between place and formal innovation seems to have been severed in the 1960s with writers such as John Barth, Donald Barthelme, and Robert Coover. One of the aspects I find most interesting about your recent work—I'm not only thinking here of Mariposa's Song, *but also your story, "A Dream of Falling Asleep: IX-XVII," which appeared in the magazine* Zoetrope—*is that you seem to be refastening the relationship between place and experimentalism. However, even in your more traditionally realist work, setting seems to have been an important element for you. Your novel* Strange Sunlight *examined the underbelly of the Sun Belt economic boom in Texas during the early 1980s, and the stories in* Hockey Sur Glace *intimately and even nostalgically explored life in New England and Canada by way of the sport of ice hockey. It seems setting has always played such an important role in your fiction.*

Maybe too much so.

But why is setting so important to you?

Basically enough, I think that I still am—and always have been since a kid—dazzled by everything I simply see around me in the physical trappings of life, constantly amazed that it's all here, feeling lucky to be alive and experience the show.

I've got a maybe deep rooted painterly need to recreate as much as I can of it on the page, including not only those places where I've lived—like New England and Texas and Paris, where the story "A Dream of Falling Asleep" that you mentioned unfolds, and where I've also lived on several occasions while teaching there—but also the many places where I've spent time while traveling. A lot of my short fiction is set in such foreign spots, like India and Africa and all over the Caribbean and Latin America. Hemingway once said something along the lines of how good prose writing maybe boils down to two things—writing prose as if it's poetry, with music to the language, and writing prose as if it's painting; and in addressing the latter here, I think I know what he means. It's how words can become the brush strokes, the writer using the techniques learned from painting, such as perspective, shadowing, color contrast, and the rest. Actually, I suspect that I've been almost as inspired and influenced in my writing by art as by other literature.

As for setting apparently being given short shrift in some American innovative writing in the 1960s, with the fiction of those you pointed out, that's probably true, and it's a good observation, something I never really considered before. In fact, I myself have published quite a few stories that work that way, avoiding specific place and relying more on sort of a purposeful nowhere for effect, an outright netherworld, which I think that most of those writers, and I, too, most likely did get from Beckett, and also Kafka, of course. But as you suggest, there's plenty of setting, even a cascading abundance of it, in other innovative writers I just spoke of, including Faulkner and García Márquez and—to add another—Malcolm Lowry, though Borges to a much lesser degree. Whether or not I'm the citizen who is attempting to singlehandedly "refasten the relationship," as you say, here in the U.S. between experimentation and the use of extensive setting in fiction, which seems a rather big task to assign to a writer like me, with the quite limited readership that seems to be mine, admittedly.

In comparing literary settings with painting, you've touched on an aspect of your work that strikes me as quite visual. How would you characterize the unique use of imagery in Mariposa's Song?

I know that setting in much of my own work lately is not simply a matter of precise reproduction, which seems the mission of an amazingly gifted ultra-realist like John Updike. For me, in recent work, my use of description, while pretty detailed, can add a dimension well beyond reproduction, one where the real does become tellingly unreal.

For instance, in *Mariposa's Song* I have the bar girl Mariposa envisioning all the Western Union money telegrams that undocumented workers in the U.S. send back home to their families in Latin America as fluttering through the moonlit night over deserts and mountains and villages like a wave of ever-migrating yellow butterflies—I'm being very careful in the detail there, true to the actual realistic geography, but letting everything serve to trigger a wilder idea as well.

That's a striking image, that of the migrating telegrams, and it sticks with me.
Then I guess it worked.

I remembered thinking at the time I first read it how nicely it fit with the dreamlike atmosphere of the novel. It also gestures toward what I read as a productive tension in your work between landscape and, let's say, dreamscapes. For all of our talk thus far about setting, much of your work also explores the role of dreams and dreaming on character development, perhaps nowhere more prominently than your recently published short story collection, Tell Borges If You See Him: Tales of Contemporary Somnambulism. *In the title story, which also consists of a single sentence, your protagonist says that Borges has taught him the meaninglessness of space and time, an insight that occurs as he is thinking through the differences between dreams and reality. There is a degree of postmodernist play here, because your character after all exists solely in a fictional dream. Yet something else more profound appears to be at stake in this story. Would you discuss how you see dreams functioning throughout your work? Do they, for example, solely deepen the fictional worlds you create, or might they perhaps also challenge them?*

I think I'll vote for the latter. That means I don't consider dreams—which definitely often are a large part of my fiction and have been since my first collection of stories, *The Graves of Famous Writers*—as any deepening of the real worlds of the fiction, but rather creating a window to another more revealing world that could actually be the *real* world, where living often feels like dreaming and dreaming like living, to the point that the distinction between the two doesn't matter that much anymore.

In the recent story collection *Tell Borges If You See Him*, the emphasis on this was probably stronger than ever, so I did use the subtitle *Tales of Contemporary Somnambulism*. I hoped it would give a good thematic unity to the book and announce the state I was after. Not sleepwalking in the old cartoon-cliché sense of somebody moving along in pajamas with eyes closed and arms held out straight, but getting at a straddling of the line between sleeping and waking, with characters in the waking world having the vivid, heightened perception of surroundings and events that we do experience in dreams—life as a richly realized and highly symbolic peregrination, possibly. Again, it's a metaphysical thing.

You seem to like the word metaphysical.

You noticed. Anyway, regarding the protagonist in that title story, "Tell Borges If You See Him," he's a divorced, out-of-work American businessman during the recession, an everyday guy who gets caught up in a small-time money laundering scheme that has him travel to Buenos Aires as a courier. While there he embarks on an affair with a lovely Australian woman, who's on one of those package tours for tango aficionados they have in Argentina. Eventually all of it more or less evanesces for him, and later, looking back on it from where he lives in suburban Houston, it does seem more akin to the stuff of a dream than anything else, which he comes to accept in terms of a new way of thinking he's learned from reading the Borges books that his son, an undergrad literature major at the University of Texas, has recommended to him.

Would you say a little more about what you and your protagonist have specifically learned from reading Borges?

If Borges's stories taught this guy, as he says, everything he knows about shedding common assumptions concerning time and space, they didn't quite do that for me, teach me *everything*, but they taught me in awful lot. Or at least the work of Borges confirmed for me some things that I'd maybe been after all along, especially when I started to read Borges more carefully and very studiously in later life, a different experience than when younger.

That can happen with reading a writer at different stages of one's life.

It definitely can. I even went as far as traveling the five thousand miles via a long overnight American Airlines flight to Buenos Aires myself for a couple of crazy weeks in 2002 to learn more about Borges's work. There's an intriguing book called *Unthinking Thinking*, in which the author, Floyd Merrell, a professor at Purdue University, if I remember right, gives a reading of Borges in terms of the "new" mathematics and physics. One of the points he makes is that Borges might have been scientifically on the money way before most everybody else, undeniably prescient. Today, according to recent ideas like string theory and quantum theory, there is in science more reliance on the kind of so-called dream logic that you do find in Borges—where scenes metamorphose into other scenes, and where time can involve juxtaposition, not chronology, and the rest—rather than on the old clunkily deductive logic taken for granted for so long. Much of Merrell's book contains complicated graphs and numerical formulas that are way beyond me, the sort of thing that, in truth, frightened me when I barely survived a year of high school calculus. Nevertheless, the specific and valuable observation about the validity of dream logic is one point that does sink in.

I have a new collection of short stories, called *What I Found Out About Her*, containing my very recent work from the literary magazines, coming out with University of Notre Dame Press sometime in the future. I think it explores still further the dreamlike territory I was trying to develop in *Tell Borges If You See Him*. I originally gave it a subtitle, too, *Stories of Dreaming Americans*, but the editor has asked me to drop it, and I think that I will eventually go along with his suggestion. Subtitling the *Tell Borges* collection as *Tales of Contemporary Somnambulism* backfired in some ways and resulted in no small amount of confusion when it came to putting the book in a category, as booksellers like to do. On a few online store websites I still see it listed as "fantasy" rather than the admittedly snootier, yet fully intended, "literary fiction" that it is, categorized as such simply because of the subtitle, I suspect. But it could be that the confusion is also because of the nicely weird bookjacket image with a computer-enhanced original sculpture by Brad Michael Bourgoyne showing two heads that look like solid bookends whispering, all bathed in what I, for one, like to think is a lovely bluish moonlight glow, spooky.

Throughout your career, your writing has oscillated between short stories and novels. Many contemporary authors who work in both genres, including T. C. Boyle and Steven Millhauser, have argued that they constitute very different creatures. Other than length, which is rather obvious, what do you see as the distinguishing characteristics between the novel and the short story?

I'll go further than saying the two genres are merely very different and emphasize that for me, as one writer producing both, they sometimes seem to have extremely little to do with each other altogether, are ever-expanding dark universes apart, well beyond just saying they're different creatures.

But exactly why are they different?

It's essentially the poetic element that makes a short story what it is, inarguably unique in the way that it can make mysterious mind jumps in the narrative—or maybe dizzying, high-flying leaps is a better way of putting it—and doesn't have to rely too much on the kind of cause-and-effect, well reasoned out movement that's often needed, understandably, to propel the extended plot of a novel for its couple of hundred pages or so. It's not that one genre is better than the other, and it's not to dismiss or fail to acknowledge the sheer labor involved in committing to and finally producing a novel, which usually is a matter of months and years, not days and weeks, and which William Styron once accurately likened to going from Paris to Vladivostok on your knees. I realize that for better or worse

I personally am a short story writer first and a novelist after that, if judged only by the amount I've published in each genre. I mean, after all, this new novel is only my second one to see print in the many years I've been writing, while I've published what sometimes seem like tons of short stories in magazines.

Also, I might stress that there's always the particular high to a short story that's so very alluring.

A high?

Sorry, and being a child of the sixties I guess I'm forever geologically dated by the jargon of that day. But what I mean is that there's intense transport for both the writer while writing a short story, and ideally the reader while reading one. I really don't want to make it sound as if I'm talking about a purer drug—but there you are, and it is a purer drug, I'd say, for me, anyway. I suppose I wrote the new novel *Mariposa's Song* with a certain decidedly feverish intensity as well in the course of composition, as I spoke of earlier, and it is pretty short by novel standards, so those facts perhaps provide additional evidence of where my true writerly heart lies.

One other thing that I always like to emphasize concerning the short story in a cultural context is how absolutely lucky we are that we have such a vibrant literary magazine scene in America. There are so many places that publish so many short stories, a great situation that seems chiefly responsible for why we have the bumper crop of fine, if not amazing, story writers we do have in this country. I often find myself dazzled, and occasionally very intimidated, by the wonderful work of such younger writers, the raw talent I see. Having lived in France, I have writer friends there and they tell me, bemoaningly, that not many French writers turn out stories anymore, basically because they have few outlets to publish them. Which surely makes me both proud and extremely glad to be an American.

Very patriotic.

Thanks, and, you know, it's maybe the first time I've actually been labeled as such. And thanks, too, for your solid questions. They've gotten me to thinking a lot about the craft and planning in writing, which I really haven't thought about before, or haven't for a long while, anyway.

Now I just hope that with all this thinking about *how* I write, I won't totally jinx myself, and actually go on to write some more fiction—possibly stuff much better than what I've turned out so far, which is what this writing thing is always and ultimately all about, no?

D. Seth Horton is editor of the anthology series, *New Stories from the Southwest*. He also co-edits the series, *Best of the West: New Stories from the Wide Side of the Missouri*. He holds an MFA in fiction from the University of Arizona and is currently a doctoral candidate in literature at the University of Maryland. His fiction and criticism have appeared in various publications.

My mom really liked doing the side ponytail on my hair.
I really liked my stuffed animals. It was a fair trade.

Aja Gabel's fiction can be found in the *New England Review*, *New Ohio Review*, *Bat City Review*, and elsewhere. She holds a BA from Wesleyan University, an MFA from the University of Virginia, and is currently a PhD student at the University of Houston, where she edits the literary journal *Gulf Coast*.

IN THE TIME OF ADONIS

Aja Gabel

"You're too sweet to be in Panama City," says the man selling us ice cream after Hilary hands him a twenty her mom stuffed in her pocket that morning. He smiles when he says it, and I think he looks mostly at me. The beach sun bakes the boardwalk, crowded with girls in shorts and boys without shirts, none of them noticing us being noticed by the ice cream man.

He gives us our cones—mine mint chip, peach sherbet for Hilary—and his damp thumb lingers on my fingers around the wafer. I wipe off the ice cream bits and I don't think much of this until we make our way back to the cabana and Hilary's mom asks, "What did that man say to you?"

Hilary ignores her mother, but I tell her what he said, that we were too sweet. She picks up a purple silk sarong from the ground and calls Hilary over, to cover her with it. Hilary, laid out on a plastic chair, skin already browning, continues to ignore her.

"Beth, you come here," she says to me. I walk over, and Kelly Hulling, Mrs. Hulling, wife of Mr. Patrick Hulling, mother of Hilary Hulling, who is captain of the junior varsity girls' swim team, takes the sarong and wraps it around my body twice, knotting it at my chest, in a place that makes me uncomfortable. Mrs. Hulling's hair, a used-to-be blond, gets in my face when she leans in close to me.

Glimmer Train Stories, Issue 88, Fall 2013
©2013 Aja Gabel

"Don't talk to him again," she says, her eyes so close to mine I can make out the peacock flecks in her irises.

"He touched my finger," I say. My cone is melting.

"He touched your finger?" Mrs. Hulling looks down at her own fingers, then quickly back up again. She moves like a bird, or she tries to.

"I won't talk to him again."

"You either, Hil," Mrs. Hulling warns.

But Hilary is already in a sun daze, the skin on her stomach and legs the color of a rubber band, and elastic like one too. She'll be fifteen on Friday, our last day in Florida, and wants her shoulders to be tanned against the white strapless dress she bought at Dillard's on her father's credit card. I feel stirred, like I'm a thick milkshake and someone's got hold of a straw, slowly whipping me around inside, but Hilary's practically asleep. I think that she's calm because she's older than I am by three months. Or because her mother isn't gripping her arm, squeezing a too-tight knot over her chest, breathing daiquiri breath on her cheek. Or, she just doesn't care. It's the last reason that makes me jealous, just a little.

I'm scared of the ice cream man now, but Hilary is already dreaming about birthday presents, cork heels, the homecoming dance, her arms spinning in time to a line dance, bronzed limbs and a white corsage, wheeling like a carousel, elated like a beauty queen, in the music video of our lives.

"Don't you miss Luke?" Hilary asks. She's going through the drawers in our hotel room, making a pile on the floor next to her of the possible outfits she'll wear to dinner tonight.

"I do," I say, even though I don't think it's true. Even though Luke is my first real boyfriend, a swimmer, I don't think we are the sort of people who sit around missing each other's company. Here, in Florida, I go from the pool to the beach, the cabana to the restaurant, all with Hilary's family, and I'm pretty happy. Or at least, I've never thought I was less than happy.

"When my family and me went to Aspen after I first got together with Sam, I called him every single day." Hilary's hair is dirty blond—

lowlighted strawberry, she will say if you ask—and she grabs a twisted strand to examine it as she relates her story. Her bare knee knocks over a pile of strappy halter tops.

"Every single day," I repeat, because I'm not sure what the equal and opposite response is. I'm the only sophomore in my physics class, and Mr. Dedham is obsessed with the rule of equal and opposite reaction. But a lot of the time there just isn't one for Hilary. Sometimes she's talking and it's like a tractor coming my way, and all I can do is wave to make sure she doesn't run me over.

The thing is, Hilary has had sex with Sam. That's her never-ending tractor. They did it just once, in Sam's parents' bed when they were away for the weekend. Hilary sneaked over to my house in the middle of the night and cried because she said afterwards she woke up to hear Sam throwing up all the tequila they'd stolen out of his parents' liquor cabinet. That was the night, if you ask me, that it became clear to me that Hilary and I would be best friends forever.

I'm wearing my favorite jeans even though it's too humid to be wearing jeans. They're expensive and they are the first pair I own not from the juniors section. The Hullings are taking us out to Mahi Funa, which is supposedly the best open-air restaurant on the beach. I don't really like fish, but Mrs. Hulling smiled so widely when she announced our plans and Mr. Hulling put his hand on my back, and so I acted excited.

Hilary says, "Do you think my parents will let us go to the board-walk tonight after dinner?"

"Alone?" I ask.

She nods. The piles of clothes next to her are all floral and frayed denim. She's looking at me for the response she already knows will come, but wants me to say out loud, the one that will be one rung closer to a later curfew, her own car, a tattoo, no curfew at all.

"Sure," I tell her. "They should let us go all the way to the Ferris wheel and back. We can get churros, and you can see everything from that Ferris wheel."

Then something happens that I couldn't even predict. Luke calls me. On the phone. In my hotel room. In Panama City. When it rings, Hilary lunges for it, bellyflops across the bedspread.

"It's Luke," she whispers, her thin fingers covering the mouthpiece. When I pick it up I can still feel her fingerprints all over it, greasy with Banana Boat lotion and nail polish remover.

"Hi, Beth!" Luke says, a little too dramatically, and then I know it—he's just as nervous as I am. "How's your Hulling holiday?"

Hilary is folding her clothes, but I know she's only pretending. She's listening. She's recording everything I say inside her brain. We, at fifteen, always remember to notice and remember everything.

"It's really cool," I say. "You know, ice cream, Ferris wheels, beach. Stuff like that."

"Sounds awesome. Better than here, I guess."

My turn to talk. For a moment, the way my mouth waters, I think I might be sick. Is this what missing him feels like? "What are you doing for break?"

"My mom is making me study for the PSATs. It's basically like I'm in school."

"Oh. Well, yeah, then I'm having a better time than you."

He laughs, genuinely, and frantic excitement settles into a lump in my stomach. We pass a couple minutes like that, checking questions off our lists and providing light, funny answers to each one. I fidget and by the time the conversation starts to wind down, I'm on the floor between the two beds, rolling back and forth, scooting underneath the low bed frame. The phone cord is wrapped twice around my thigh, and it's starting to hurt, in a good way.

"Well," I say.

"Beth," he says, before I say goodbye. My name holding court in someone else's mouth like that, it's thrilling.

"Still here."

"I miss you."

I yank the cord one last time. If I tie it tight enough, will my leg bleed? Will I lose it? Does that ever happen? Can you tourniquet your beating heart?

"You too," I say. It's the most brilliant answer I've ever given. I hang up, and I'm stuck under the bed, though I feel like I left myself inside the phone. Hilary crawls over. She lifts up the floral dust ruffle.

"Bethany," she says. My full name is Elizabeth and she knows this, but she says Bethany is prettier. "He can't see you, you know."

Of course he can't see me, physically, but just the potential that he might, or the fact that he has, the idea that he wants to, is enough to push me under the bed, in the dark. Hilary's looking at me, though, the length of my body on the floor, her own hair and jewelry and body over there, in the light, and she won't come under the bed to get me, and the distance feels like a swimming pool between us.

Mrs. Hulling smells like white musk tonight instead of daiquiri. She's a woman who is always smelling like something. She's got these collarbones that poke out under her dresses, and tonight her halter straps are stretched tight over them. It makes me lift up my tank top straps and touch my own collarbones, which don't seem to do much of anything but sit there under my neck. They're very subtle, I think. Nothing about Mrs. Hulling is subtle. She is pretty in that way where you can tell she was once prettier, her face now lined like linen in noticeable places, her hair stick-straight at the end, her clothes taut, as if she were wearing the skin of someone younger.

Mrs. Hulling and Mr. Hulling sit on the same side of the booth. Mr. Hulling does that thing again, putting his hand on the small of my back to guide me to my side of the booth. His hand is almost exactly the size of the small of my back, his fingers just cupping the edge of the hollow. He's wearing a white linen button-down and sunshine-yellow suit. I think I would be embarrassed by it in any other place except the Mahi Funa, where there are dinner plate–sized leaves and dried grass that canopy the booth, and the waiters wear ties and vests and flip-flops. This whole place, Panama City, is like a cut-out, neon diorama of itself.

"Tell us about Luke," Mrs. Hulling says. "Hilary tells us you've liked him for a while."

I'm always shocked at the boldness of my friends' mothers. My own mother, too. It's as if they've forgotten what embarrassment is, in the sameness of their family lives. Or maybe they want revenge, on the embarrassment wrought by their own mothers. Mrs. Hulling looks at me, expectant, as if I'm going to tell her right there about the first time Luke kissed me, and about my menstrual cycle while I'm at it. I start to play with my fork and my napkin slides off my lap, under the booth. I do anything but look at Mr. Hulling, who sits across from me with his head cocked, tan skin blending into the graying edges of his hairline.

"He's my boyfriend," I say. "We've only been going out a couple weeks." I take a sip of water and overshoot—it dribbles down my chin. Mrs. Hulling clearly already knows all of this.

"She's being shy," Hilary says. "Luke is on boys' swim. He's completely in love with Beth."

"Is he the young man I saw last week who won the butterfly?" And then, eyes wide, "The Adonis?"

"Yeah, the junior," Hilary confirms.

"What a catch for you," Mrs. Hulling says to me, and she says it warmly, because she really means it, and she doesn't mean for me to feel bad.

But I think, yes, what a catch. For me. What a catch for plain Beth. Plain, dark-haired, bird-armed Beth. What I should tell Mrs. Hulling is that Luke asked *me* out. Luke sat next to *me* in Physics and thinks *I'm* a catch. Luke told me I'm different from most of the juniors, and even though he's only kissed me three times, he used his tongue. I want to say, Mrs. Hulling, it wasn't awkward at all.

But Mrs. Hulling was never like me in high school. She looked like Hilary, and Hilary will look like her when she's older, and I think both of them are just fine with that. What's at stake is whether Hilary will actually become her mother when she's older. I hope not. Because you can tell just looking at Mrs. Hulling that she wishes she was still like Hilary, buoyant and well liked, and I don't want Hilary to wish to be like something else ever.

Just like that, the feelings of despair are replaced with sympathy and guilt, one slides out, the others fill me up, and I say, "Mrs. Hulling, your collarbones are so—pretty."

Mr. Hulling tells me what to order, and when it comes, it's an entire fish with the head still on. The eyes are there too, all cakey and glazed over. They look like my grandfather's eyes. I'm horrified.

"Come on, Beth," Mr. Hulling says, winking at me so quickly I don't think anyone else sees. "Try something new."

But I don't want to try this. I've never been that girl who felt like she was missing out on something if she didn't jump off the tallest cliff at the South Platte River, even though it was dangerous. I've always been the girl who keeps an eye on everyone's things on the picnic blanket. Of course, I can't tell Mr. Hulling any of this. He was the boy who jumped off the cliff first and broke his arm, and everyone celebrated him for it at school the next day. I would have been the girl who signed his cast, but all I would have written was my name, and when he looked at it later, he would have thought, "Who the hell is Beth?"

I tear off some meat so white it's almost transparent. It's translucent, I think. I keep trying to remember the difference between the two. I tear it off from near the tail. I tell myself I won't eat anything within two inches of the face. Hilary is telling her parents about the movie we saw last night. She's taking dramatic pauses and she's telling the story of the romance like she's made it up herself, just now. Her parents are soaking it up, Mr. Hulling occasionally glancing at me to measure my reaction.

"And then, Dad, the guy in the movie, he takes the girl to China!" she says. "Like they were going around the freaking block or something."

Everyone laughs. Hilary's performing adulthood and her parents are her perfect audience, because they think it's an assurance of her childishness, their own authority. But I know what she's really doing. She's buttering them to up to let us go out alone tonight, and it's working.

Mr. Hulling ordered the same thing as I did. I watch him eat it. He doesn't even look at the plate—he's looking at me—when he spears the head of the fish.

The thing that's bothering me is that the Hullings have had sex. Probably even here in Florida. I can't decide if I should let this thought invade my dinner or not, if it makes me feel uncomfortable in a bad way or uncomfortable in a good way, like when the phone cord wrapped my thigh. I have impulses toward both. They're more touchy than other parents, than my own. Like just now, sitting across from me, Mr. Hulling has his hands on Mrs. Hulling's legs. The reason I know this is because I saw it when I dipped under the table to pick up my napkin. There was the yellow cuff of his yellow suit and his hand cupping her knee. Her hand, her nails the color of coral, laced with his hand. Their fingers alternated. Thin and coral, thick and yellow, thin and coral, thick and yellow. I must have stayed under the table forever.

"Honey, do you like it?" Mrs. Hulling asks me, gesturing to the fish with her fork.

I nod. "It's okay." And actually, it is.

"You eat all of it, then. Don't be afraid."

I'm not sure what I should be afraid of. I look at her plate. She's picking at a salmon salad. Hilary's eating the same thing. I suddenly wish I hadn't ordered the entire body of a fish. I feel like an alien. But I didn't know.

Mrs. Hulling is talking about her own homecoming dance. "We didn't even know each other until senior year," she says, leaning into her husband.

"I went to two homecomings with Jane what's-her-name."

"Jane Fletcherman. I hated her because she was your first."

I try my best to ignore this, but nearly choke on my fish.

"She means first girlfriend," Mr. Hulling clarifies. "No one ever marries their first girlfriend, though."

"Don't say that, Patrick. Beth could still marry Luke."

"I don't want to marry Luke." I say it before I even know it. "I hardly know him."

"Come on, Beth," Hilary says. "What are you, a robot?"

"Oh she's just quirky," Mrs. Hulling says. "I mean that in a good way. Like Winona Ryder. Beautifully quirky."

"Better than Winona Ryder," Mr. Hulling says. "Quirky means there's something underneath there."

I think he's just saying this because I have dark hair, round dark eyes, and mostly I smile reluctantly. Then Mrs. Hulling leans her free hand across the table and grabs my wrist. She looks me in the eye. "Don't believe what they say. Sometimes first love can last forever."

I need to recite something louder in my head to drown this out. I keep playing, on a loop, Luke: "I miss you." Me: "You too." Is that grammatically correct? You too what? I play it louder and louder and soon Mrs. Hulling's mouth is forming the words, *I miss you*. But I do miss you, Luke. I miss the way you make me bend over and hold my stomach when we're talking on the phone. I miss the way your own awkwardness makes me feel like a person, instead of someone who's only on the brink of entering personhood. I'm forcing Mrs. Hulling to say these things.

"Besides, Beth," Mrs. Hulling says finally, her fingers still around my wrist. "It sounds like Luke is worth holding on to."

Dear Mrs. Hulling: I don't even think Adonis did the butterfly. What I mean is that the butterfly stroke didn't exist in Adonis's time, in 600 BC. I know this because we just did our Greek unit in World History. But you wouldn't know what I'm talking about if I said it aloud. You would call me quirky again. Zany. You think Luke is handsome, and he is, for a sixteen-year-old, but that's all you know about him. That he does a mean butterfly stroke, and you think I should marry him, because for you, marrying is a reward. I wish you hadn't said it.

Mr. Hulling tells Mrs. Hulling that she can't have another Captain and Coke. Mrs. Hulling takes her hand up from under the table and orders one anyway.

"It's vacation, honey," she says to him.

"I would like it to be a *nice* vacation," Mr. Hulling says, and suddenly all the air at the booth is sucked out and Hilary and I freeze. Mrs. Hulling taps her nails on the table and for a small moment, no one says anything.

Then Mrs. Hulling says, "Anyway, what happened was your father was with Jane at the homecoming, but he saw me across the room."

Mr. Hulling looks over at her, and down at the dips and swells of her bust line. "Kelly commanded me from across the room."

"Oh please, I was with my own date too, you know."

"She was a dream. What was that, 1977? I was wearing a powder blue tux. I'm not joking."

"I'm not going to lie," Mrs. Hulling says. She's only talking to Mr. Hulling now. "You were the man I wanted from the very beginning."

While they're telling the story, Mr. Hulling has reached across the table to my plate. I've made a mess of the tiny fish bones and stringy meat. "Here, like this," he says to me quietly, when Hilary and Mrs. Hulling are talking about prom. He takes the tip of his knife and cuts shallowly down the spine, and then pulls away a big piece of meat with the curved backend of a spoon.

"Tell me what he looked like," Hilary says. She wants to imagine her dad as the prom king. She wants to join in the chorus.

"Like now but with longer hair. Long hair like a rock star. Patrick Hulling. Everyone wanted to be with him."

"But you got him," Hilary says, as if reminding her mother of her prize.

"I did," Mrs. Hulling says, brushing some of Mr. Hulling's short hair behind his ear.

Hilary and I both watch her brush back the hair that is too short to be played with. The action seems desperate, her long nails grazing his razor-burned cheek. He flinches, slightly, her chest rises. She makes a small sound like a rabbit, a cluck meant to be cute, and I can see the sympathy wash across his face. It reminds me of something, but I can't remember, and when they finally kiss, Hilary and I relax, sit back in our own bench seat, and spread our own fingers wide on the plastic surface.

I want everything on the dessert menu. Everyone else passes, so I pass too, but Mr. Hulling grabs my menu before the waiter can take it and says, "Wait." He orders a white chocolate mousse and when it arrives he insists I eat the whole thing. He says Hilary and Kelly wouldn't touch it anyway. I hate him a little then, but I eat it, and it's like a cloud in my mouth, and then I'm grateful.

"Does your mom know about Luke?" Mrs. Hulling asks just when I've stuffed my mouth with chocolate.

"Yes," I say.

"Good. Moms should know these kinds of things. I'm lucky for Hilary. No withholding."

Hilary sits beside me and registers no surprise. Hilary tells her mom even less than I tell my mom. Maybe she tells her more about other people—my life, for instance—but Mrs. Hulling doesn't know that Hilary skips chemistry, or that Hilary's thinking about quitting swimming for lacrosse, or that she once made herself throw up for a week to see what it felt like. Hilary flips her hair and smiles like she's got brown sugar in her teeth.

"I can't believe you're going to be fifteen!" Mrs. Hulling exclaims, too loudly.

Hilary beams. "I can't either." She really can't. Hilary has acted all week like she was born to be fifteen, as if her whole life had been leading up to the moment she turns fifteen, at which point her life will flower out before her.

"You'll be fifteen soon, dear," Mrs. Hulling says to me. "Girls are so pretty when they're fifteen."

There is something big Mrs. Hulling doesn't know. She doesn't know that her own daughter has had sex. She's provided her with condoms and the pill, just in case, but Hilary hasn't told her she's done it. I know it, though. Mrs. Hulling keeps telling us there is danger out there, and we just don't know it yet. She says that's why we have curfew and why we can't talk to strangers on the boardwalk. But I know some things, I want to say.

Hilary convinces her mom that we'll stay on the boardwalk, in the lit parts, and be back by ten. We wave goodbye to them in front of the restaurant, Mrs. Hulling leaning her floral-clad body into Mr. Hulling's linen. Looking at Mrs. Hulling being held makes me feel sad for her, because I know it's the kind of feeling she feeds off of. How he made her feel when she leaned into him like that, when she was unable to stand up on her own. How he didn't mind that her dress started to sag around her neck. She'll remember his suit against her skin and the hard promise of his body supporting hers, and she'll remember that she felt completely comfortable.

Hilary and I set off on the boardwalk, which looks completely different at night, all lit up in silver light, the storefronts calling out in colors and music. People walk in clumps, but now they are clad in heels and hairspray. Everyone is laughing, and not paying attention to where they're going, except that they're thrust down the long, wooden planks until it ends.

"There's a boy I met earlier," Hilary says. "At that surfing store by the tiki bar."

"Who? I didn't see anyone."

"You weren't there, Beth," she says, as if it were a betrayal. "His name is Christian. He's seventeen. He graduated already."

I'm imagining the night before me, nights like others we've had back home. Christian and his friends in shorts and hemp necklaces. They'll make me drink beers on the beach and toss the bottles from the pier. Hilary will make out with Christian by a bonfire and his lanky friends will hover around me, shaky from being drunk, until one of them falls asleep on my foot. Hilary and I will walk back to the hotel at eleven and her mother won't say anything, and Hilary and I will hold hands all the way, she won't talk until we get back to the room, but I'll know she feels bad by the clamminess in her palm and the way her breath smells like his, like cloves and beer. I don't want to do this.

We walk past the ice cream cart from earlier in the afternoon. The same man is there, with a rainbow of stains on his apron. I don't look at him but I can tell his eyes are following us. I don't say anything about it to Hilary, but my heart is racing the whole time we're in his view.

Hilary groans. "I just wish it were here already. Friday. Fifteen."

"I know," I say. I wish it were here too, so we could stop waiting for it. When I am an adult, I know this: I will not have to do so much waiting.

"I'm sorry if my mom is totally annoying," she says.

"She's not."

"She drank too much. And really, Luke is awesome."

"I didn't think he wasn't," I say.

"She drank too much," she says again.

We walk in silence toward the surf store. The waves are on our right and the open air shops are on our left and the boardwalk is loud and clacky beneath our flip-flops. The tall lampposts bend over the walkway and lend an unnatural brightness to the night. It feels like we're in a grocery store, even outside, even at night.

"What was it like? With Sam?" I ask.

Hilary thinks about this for a minute. She grabs for her hair. "Not that much fun, actually. But good in another way."

"What way?"

"The way like, even though it kind of hurt, you knew someone else was really enjoying it. So it made you feel, like…necessary."

I don't know what she means, not exactly. I imagine it's close to what it felt like when Luke called me—the basic feeling of being missed by someone else, maybe even by their body, missing yours.

"I'm not like my mom, you know," Hilary says.

"I don't think you are."

"You don't? Because you know me the best and if you think I'm an okay person, then I am."

I put my arm around her. We're the same size right now. Thin-shouldered, exactly five feet four. I have a feeling this will change soon. She'll shoot up and I'll stay at this height. Short, dark haired, mysterious first girlfriend to boys like Luke. Friends with butter colored, long limbed, loud girls like Hilary.

"Your mom's a good person too."

"Why do people always have to take her side?"

I wish Mrs. Hulling had been the mother from this afternoon, the protective sunscreen mom, the sarong cover-all mom, who wouldn't let her child wander around Panama City at night, alone. Then we'd be in bed now, tossing the hotel bible back and forth in the dark, telling each other who we'd kiss from homeroom if we absolutely had to, if it were life or death.

"I'm not taking her side. I just don't think your mom is a bad person, and neither are you."

"Sometimes you're so—," she starts, and fumbles. "So boring!"

I think she expects that to hurt me more than it does, which is only a little. I've been called worse things, and I'd rather be boring than too loud. And she doesn't mean boring, she means I'm a goody-goody and too young, too sweet. Anyway, I already know Hilary will apologize for it later tonight, no matter how this turns out.

She stomps her foot on the boardwalk. "I'm just going to go meet Christian by myself. Tell my mom you're sick or something."

"Hilary," I say.

"It's okay," she says. "You guys would hate each other anyway." Which is a way of letting me know I'm hateable.

She turns and strides off toward Christian and her evening, her future mistakes, and a whole mixing bowl of choices. I'm left there, in front of the store window full of cameras and computers. The Beach Boys are blaring out from one store, The Doors from another, and a man is playing a Jimi Hendrix cover with his guitar case open in front of me. As if music stopped in 1970. Well, Panama City, I want to say, things have happened since then! People have done some living, get on with it.

I start walking back in the other direction, toward the hotel. The bright lights make it seem like a catwalk, and suddenly I am ashamed. I'm doing something awful. I'm leaving my friend *and* she left me, if both things are possible at once. I'm choosing to stay the way I am, pathetic and unwise. I feel in these lights as if everyone who passes me can tell what I am. A girl in department store shorts and sandals, who doesn't know how to have a boyfriend, who isn't even fifteen, who is pitied by everyone, even her friend's drunk mother.

Back at the hotel, I knock on the Hullings' door to check in. I don't know if they will be mad that I left Hilary alone out there. There are some muffled sounds after I knock, and then Mrs. Hulling opens the door in a long white T-shirt, so thin I can see everything through it, which makes me look her straight in the eyes, which is worse in a way, because her eyes are bright and alive and the skin of her face is red, and she is too happy. So I know it, now. And of course, I am the only one embarrassed.

"Honey, what's wrong?" she says, her voice all smooth.

"Um, I feel sick, I think from the fish, so Hilary was going to take a walk and be back soon."

"Hilary's out there by herself?"

"She said she would be back by ten."

"Ten was together! If she's alone, there's no curfew," Mrs. Hulling says, her face scrunched up. "Hold on, Beth. I'm getting my stuff, and then we're finding her."

She's doing her best to block my view of the bedroom with the door and her body, but she leans back to find her purse and the aspirin, and the door opens too wide, and I see in. A dark room, Mr. Hulling on the bed, the white of the tangled sheets and his shirtless body. And like a new dress, it just drops all over me. He's having sex. He's looking at me, his chest rising up and down. I look back at him, like I want to see him, and he sees me see all of him. His yellow suit is draped over a chair, I can see that, too, in the dark. Mr. Hulling props himself up on with his arm, which suddenly seems just that—a thick, athletic arm, muscles and skin, a part separated from the body of someone I barely know—and I think he almost says my name. I imagine the outline of it on his lips in the dark room. I start then, for the first time, to feel my embarrassment trickle away, and something else replace it. Something that makes the space I occupy, in the doorway, all lit up. Distinct.

Mrs. Hulling is wearing a pink cable knit sweater and jean shorts, and I don't think she put on a bra. She hands me baby aspirin—"for your stomachache," she says—even though I am too old to be taking that kind of aspirin. We walk back out to the boardwalk, me trying to keep up with her clip.

"Why would you leave her, Beth?" she says, in a voice not so much angry as sad. "I knew I should have given her a cell phone."

"I don't know. She said she was going to meet a friend."

"Who?"

"A surf guy. Christian or something. We met him earlier."

"When?" Mrs. Hulling is nearly shrieking, and she catches her throat, lowers her voice. "You were with me most of the day."

"Well, I didn't meet him," I said. "She did. I don't know, it feels like I met him, though."

"Don't lie, Beth. It's not pretty."

Mrs. Hulling wraps her arms around herself, hugging and shivering even though the night is sticky and the gulf breeze is warm. She is leading me down a set of stairs leading to the beach. We pass couples clinking plastic cups together and a little kid, seemingly belonging to no one. She stops just short of the lifeguard stand, and makes a visor with her hand, as if blocking out moonlight.

"Where is she?" Mrs. Hulling asks, but she's certainly not asking me. "I'm so worried. I know I'm not supposed to tell you that, that I'm really worried, but I am."

The waves crash mildly on the shore. There is nothing wild about the gulf tonight. "What are you worried about?"

She scans the beach, then brings her hand down from her face and looks at me. "Beth, you wouldn't understand."

I'm not angered by this—Hilary says it to me all the time—and instead I feel empathy for Mrs. Hulling. She must be so lonely. It seems like she thinks no one understands.

"There are things—it's hard to say what's good and what's bad," Mrs. Hulling says, wringing her hands together. "You know?"

"Yeah," I say. I look for some stars past the waves. The clouds have come in.

"If I knew where she was, I would know if it was good or bad is all I'm saying. Never mind." Mrs. Hulling stops scanning the sand and looks down at her feet, coral toenails popping out from sandals. "You girls. You're in a time, and you don't even know it."

What was scrunched up worry on Mrs. Hulling's flushed face is now turning into something else. To ward it off, I say, "Hey, I have an idea. That Ferris wheel at the end of the boardwalk, you can see everything from the top. We could see if there was a bonfire on the beach."

Mrs. Hulling's face warms, her wrinkles show around her small smile. "Oh, Beth. Such a good idea. Smart girl."

We make our way back to the boardwalk and walk with purpose through the crowds. Mrs. Hulling starts to hum along with a rock song playing over a store speaker. From what I can tell, the song is about a guy and a girl in a car, driving nowhere, and also freedom. She hums it until we are out of reach, and then we get to the Ferris wheel. Mrs.

Hulling flips her hair, reaches into her back jeans pocket and pulls out a ten dollar bill. She tells the ride operator to keep the change and smiles brightly as he pulls the bar down tight over our lap. It's almost as if she's forgotten what we're going up for.

The ride jerks forward and we are slowly rising. "Maybe we'll be able to see something even from the middle height," I say to remind her of our goal.

She gets serious again. "Yes, maybe." She looks all around her. "I used to come here when I was a girl. My parents never let me take friends, though. Said it was too expensive. It's okay to bring you, though. You're so easy."

I don't say anything and the ride stops while we are halfway to the top. I can't see much beyond the other rides at this point, teenagers sucking on Cokes in lines to get on. The ride jerks again and then suddenly continues up, and Mrs. Hulling puts her hand on top of mine as the seat we're in rocks wildly back and forth. I look at her, and her eyes are almost glistening.

The rocking slows, and just our luck the ride pauses again and we're at the very top, at the top of Panama City. The boardwalk looks different from up here, like a shiny game piece, and the beach next to it appears so much farther and darker. I look for a fire.

"I've never seen it like this," Mrs. Hulling says, leaning forward, and when she does, the seat propels me a bit forward, too. It feels like we are teetering, and my heart starts to race. It's safe, I say to myself, again and again. It's safe, we're safe.

"Do you see anything?" I ask.

But Mrs. Hulling's cheeks are wet. She doesn't wipe it away. "I'm sorry. Sometimes I cry after—," but she stops.

"After what?" I ask.

She looks at me and smiles again. "After it's over."

"Oh, I know," I say, which is maybe the wrong thing to say, because she looks hard at me. I say, "Because I saw Mr. Hulling."

She sighs and squeezes my hand, and when I don't squeeze back, she says firmly, "Hold it. It'll make you feel better."

So I do. But I don't feel like I need to feel better. I feel revved up, or filled up, looking out across the city. A full person. The night is at once thicker, and I don't feel responsible for figuring it out.

It's a disappointment when we descend, backwards-facing, all of the night slipping out of view.

"We didn't find her," I say.

"We will," Mrs. Hulling says. We start the long walk back toward the hotel. Mrs. Hulling is quiet, no chatter for once. Her strides are longer than mine, and I fall behind her. She doesn't seem to need me anymore for what we're doing. She thinks I understand, and I do now. The ice cream man is coming up again. My heart starts to race, but this time I recognize what it feels like. It feels like Luke approaching me at my locker, a note in hand, his hair still wet from swim practice. It feels like Mr. Hulling, his chest showing the speed of his breathing and his hand recognizing my back. It feels like looking over the bar of a seat in a Ferris wheel, throwing your gravity ahead of you, knowing you won't fall, feeling like you will. The ice cream man looks at me as if I'm something to buy, a magazine on a rack in one of these shops. I tell myself to breathe and put one foot in front of the other.

After we pass him, it is not Mrs. Hulling's swaying backside in front of me but Mr. Hulling's face, hanging like a new moon in the sky ahead. He was looking at his wife back in the room, I know that, her shirt lifting up over her bottom, the curve of her thighs where her underwear should have been. But I was right in line with her and he saw me in his state. I was, even if by default, an object of his desire. And really, it didn't matter where his gaze landed. It was that I wanted it to land on me.

Hilary is waiting in the lobby when we get there, smelling like woodsmoke and saying she lost her card key. She hugs me like it's been days since we've seen each other, and Mrs. Hulling is not mad and gets her a new key. She stands outside the door of our room to make sure we go inside, and then we hear the heavy door to her room click shut next to ours. The day finally seems over. When we are under the covers with the blackout curtains drawn, Hilary says she only drank one beer and kissed Christian, but it was boring, and she was thinking of calling Sam in the morning, and what did I do. I tell her I did nothing.

When I hear Hilary's breath deepen and slow, I open my eyes wider, try to make out shapes in the heavy dark. I think, for just a moment, I can hear what's happening in the next room, the brush of cold sheets against warm skin, and warm skin against other warm skin. I think I can hear it so clearly that I think I can see it, and in the dark, the hotel wall comes down, and nothing is mysterious.

So Hilary turns fifteen. She does it in her dress, with her hair and her tan, and I help her blow out the candles, which are trick candles, so by the end of it, the red icing roses are covered in our spittle. The Hullings applaud, and they give her a new and sleek cell phone, which she waves around for weeks in class. Mrs. Hulling never says anything to me about the night at their hotel door and the Ferris wheel. But I remember. I stash it away, so when Mr. Hulling cups my arm and says, "Nice cake," or Mrs. Hulling glances at my own expensive dress, I lift it up inside of me, a shield. An emergency secret. The way Mr. Hulling looked wolfish in bed, and the way I was something, too, even in the dark.

Me and my brother, Hawks Nest Beach, Old Lyme, Connecticut.

Karen Brown was born in Connecticut. Her first collection of short stories, *Pins and Needles*, was the recipient of the Grace Paley Prize for Short Fiction, and her 2012 collection, *Little Sinners and Other Stories*, won the 2011 Prairie Schooner Book Prize. *The Longings of Wayward Girls* (Washington Square Press)—her first novel—is just out. Her website is karenbrownbooks.com.

GEORGETOWN

Karen Brown

Last night before he fell asleep Mooney told her about his little boy—how he'd taken him once when he was small to the old Lowry Park Zoo, where the lion hid away in the artificial cave, and the bear had an ankle chained to the concrete floor of his cage, the floor wet and smelling of bleach. The boy had played in the park there, among the painted statues of fairy tale characters. The paint had chipped away from the characters' clothing, their faces. Spanish moss clung to the old, low hanging branches of oak. They followed the path through the Fairyland, over the rainbow bridge to the old band shell. Mooney got up on the stage with his son and they looked out at the empty seating area, the squirrels darting between the chair legs. "I sang Iron Maiden's 'The Evil that Men Do,'" he told her. He chuckled, his voice slurred with sleep. "We played air guitar."

Every night was the same—the dark, the no-see-ums that flew out of the mangroves, Mooney slipping into the abandoned apartment and lying down on the floor beside her, his voice a deep, rolling tenor. It was spring. His clothes smelled of the fire he'd come from, his breath of whiskey. It wasn't about sex, this lying down beside her every night. Mooney had chosen her to tell his story to—each night a new install-ment. *Nineteen eighty-nine*, he'd say, *apartment four-one-six*, slipping into the past like the characters in time travel books she'd read as a child:

Girl trips over tree root walking in the woods. Girl takes elevator up to nonexistent floor. *Time at the Top, A Stitch in Time.* She spent a long time trying to remember the names of the books, but could not.

Near dawn the abandoned complex breathed out its smell of rot. The apartments, five hundred of them in two-story brick buildings, softened like something going bad. Mold spread along the ceilings first, then moss-colored down the walls. Two years ago the property had been sold to a developer, and then fallen into foreclosure. The mangroves sent their bony arms into the muck. The tide slid in with a hushing sound, filling the canals, slapping the beach—white and pretty, populated by sand fiddlers. She listened and remembered the tree frogs outside her window as a child, the hum of the power lines, the moan of the train that passed along the tracks by a house she lived in once.

"What did you dream, Lucie?" Mooney asked her, awake now beside her.

The tide sucked at the mangroves.

She told him about the train again, painted bright and cheery like a circus train. The windows lit the people inside with their cutlery, their wine glasses. Before he could ask her any more she rolled away and stood up. Mooney reached out and grabbed her ankle, his hand big enough to fit around. He held her there a moment like the bear in the cage. The sliders were open and the sky lightened so that the shapes of palms appeared. They waved and bent, waved and bent. A glitch in a film reel.

"What?" she asked him. She tugged. "I have to go." He said nothing, and she kept silent and still until he loosened his grip.

She went to her bag in the corner and took out a dark T-shirt, a pair of black leggings, and dressed. Outside the breeze touched her arms, her throat. She secured her hair back. Basha was already there with the jugs. She stood by the curb smoking, the jugs lined up on the broken asphalt.

"Beachway today, Beauty?" Basha asked.

Lucie glanced at her, alert with suspicion.

"Your Highness," Basha said. She did an awkward curtsy.

"Don't," Lucie said.

Basha handed her a crumpled cigarette, extended a lighter and cupped the flame.

"It's late," she said. "Let's go, your Majesty."

They took the jugs and started through the complex. The brick buildings lined up the same. Lucie had imagined the iron balconies once held potted tomatoes, zinnias, herbs, children's plastic toys, strung Christmas lights, pumpkins with carved toothless grins. Cars filled the parking slots. There might have been the smell of charcoal briquettes and grilled meat, the sound of children playing Wiffle Ball, or freeze tag, the hum of all the air conditioning condensers. Now she could hear the warblers and jays, the cardinals she'd seen flitting about the oaks near the apartment entrance. As they passed the last building she heard the wind chime left behind, tangled in the lower branches of a tree. She and Basha didn't leave through the main entrance. Instead they came up through the small woods. They would walk ten minutes on the sidewalk. It was dark enough to see the cars' headlights approaching. They were invisible, the jugs pale and bobbing.

They turned onto Beachway Drive. The homes here were mostly new, Spanish Mediterranean style, two-story, some with clay roofs and brick driveways. They came here often mid-morning, walking the stray Mooney kept. Albie got the dog a collar and a leash. Lucie and Basha wore visors, running shorts, a tennis skirt. They waved to the neighbors heading off to work, to other women walking children in strollers, to the mail carrier.

"Forty-nine ten," Basha said.

It was a new house they'd watched go up. On this spot was once a low-slung brick ranch.

An old woman lived here, and they used to see her mornings retrieving her newspaper, a bent shape scuttling in a housedress, her hair soft white curls. One day they'd gone by and there were two newspapers at the end of the old woman's driveway, the woman nowhere in sight, and Lucie wondered. The next day another one, the three newspapers turning to pulp in their plastic sleeves, and she knew. They stopped in front of the new house—Tuscan-inspired, with clay tile awnings and a fountain built into the wall. The only trace of the old woman's house was the open bay view in the back. Yesterday, walking past, they'd heard the woman who lived here ask her neighbor if she'd pick up her mail for her. Just leave it on front table, she said. What about the alarm? the neighbor asked. Don't worry about the alarm, the woman said. She waved her hand, and rolled her eyes. She stepped carefully across the grass in her patent-leather mules.

The streetlights and the automatic lights surrounding the houses shut off before dawn. The house was shrouded in darkness. They went in through the back French doors off the paved patio, jimmying the lock. The pool shimmered and the pump clicked on. Beyond the pool the bay looked skittish. Basha told her to fill the jugs in the kitchen sink. Usually they did this from someone's hose. Basha filled plastic grocery bags with food from a refrigerator large enough to step into. She found the pantry and sorted through the cans and packages. They could be trusted not to walk through the house, or take anything else. Food and water, Mooney said. The house was cool and smelled of cinnamon. Lucie understood why others had wanted to wander through rooms, to explore the clean spaces. Once someone came back with lacy bras—another with jewelry and high-heeled shoes. Some returned smelling of expensive soap and shampoo. She'd only want to touch the coverings on the beds, to sit on them a moment, to find the children's rooms and touch their books, their piano trophies, their little clothes. But he sent them together, knowing they would watch each other. The house was dim and by the sink was a pile of bills, a checkbook.

Basha had loaded the bags and stood in the arched doorway facing the dining room, looking up at the chandelier. Daylight touched the crystals that revolved and spun in the air conditioning.

"Fit for a queen," Basha said.

Over by the sink, under the cover of the running water, Lucie tore out a check and slipped it into the waistband of her leggings.

The morning she saw the old woman's third newspaper she had been alone. She'd gone around to the back of the house, where a concrete patio table with a mosaic tile top sat on a cement deck. A frangipani dropped its flowers, pink and heavy. There was a sliding glass door.

Mooney had shown her how to get in through one before, and she did that, and stepped into a large room with a brick floor, a built-in pool, and rattan furniture. She told Mooney the story after, and he didn't believe her.

"A pool in the house?"

"The water pale blue and still, and skylights on the ceiling," she told him.

Beyond the room with the pool was a carpeted living room, dark with the drapes drawn. All around were the woman's quiet things: a salt cellar collection—tiny bowls of painted porcelain and crystal, a photograph of a smiling man in a graduation cap, wearing outdated glasses. She looked in the kitchen next, at the plate and fork propped in the drainer, the magnet on the refrigerator holding up a list written in beautiful cursive: *28 oz. can plum tomatoes, garlic, laundry soap.* She moved down the hallway to one bedroom, then the other, before she saw the old woman lying on the back bedroom floor. She wore a yellow nightgown. There was a small spot of blood by her mouth, dried into the carpet. The bay wavered beyond the window blinds, filled the room with a silvery light.

"She was gone," Mooney said.

"Probably the two days," she told him.

They'd been lying on the floor of the apartment, and she flipped onto her stomach and showed him how the woman looked.

"Heading to the kitchen for a glass of water," Mooney said.

"Thinking that would help her," she said.

The crystals on the chandelier spun. Basha turned to her. "Ready?"

They slipped quickly out the door and around the house to the street. If someone saw them now they might report them to the police, but by the time the patrol car came they would be gone. *Suspicious Person* and the date would appear in the newspaper under the city zip code. That was all. They walked the sidewalk without speaking, over the narrow canal, smelling the last of the perfume tree's blooms. The daylight made them uncomfortable, though they might easily have said they'd just come from the grocery store. Across the street was the neighborhood they usually visited, filled with smaller cement-block homes, ranches from the fifties, older bungalows with metal awnings, and doors and garages that were often left open in a hurry to drive children to school, in a rush to leave for work, out of an old-fashioned habit formed of trust. Inside they found the clutter of families with small children—bowls in the sink with remnants of cereal, scattered action figures clutching miniature weapons. Or the tidy rooms of the old man who rode his bicycle up and down the grid of streets, his two dachshunds in a wicker basket attached to the front.

They waited until no cars were in sight before they ducked into the woods. She listened to their footsteps, the plastic rustle of the bags. Once inside the complex they slowed their pace.

"Cigarette?" Basha said.

She had one left. They sat on a curb on Fayette Street and smoked it. Black iron posts held street signs with worn white lettering: Congress, Montgomery, Washington. The streetlights' lantern heads tipped or hung from useless wiring. The birds swarmed the overgrown oaks and magnolias. It was warm with the sun up. Basha brushed her blond hair out of her eyes. Her arms were thin, the bones delicate.

"There've been others before you," she said. "Yolanda, Mary Rae, Donna."

Lucie looked at her. "So?"

Basha shrugged. "Just don't think you're so special," she said.

She put the half-smoked cigarette out on the curb and pocketed the butt. They had perishable food that needed to be eaten.

The sun was up, the sky a bisque-colored haze. A group had gathered around the abandoned picnic table. Today there were ten of them. Some came and went, and each day was a different number. Mooney had caught a redfish. He kept it in the bucket, waiting to assess what they had gotten at the house, what could be eaten for each meal that day, before he cleaned it. They had brought frozen plantains, and Marilee remembered eating Sunday dinners with her grandmother—the *plátanos* and pork roast with *mojo*, the black beans and rice. They'd sat at the dining room table on velveteen cushions, surrounded by the figures

158

of frogs and cats her grandmother made in ceramics class. There was a celery-green cat that she loved.

"I want that cat," she said.

"You can't eat that," Basha said.

Marilee turned on her. "Fuck you." She was sensitive about her weight. She mourned food the way others mourned a lost parent, or child, or husband. Lucie didn't find it hard to imagine the feeling of being hungry as loss, as sadness, as a step before death, a lightening of the mortal body. Everyone had their own interpretation.

"Whoa, whoa," Mooney told her. He held up his hand with its long fingers like bones in the sunlight. Marilee scoffed and turned away. She took her plate of food to one of the molded plastic lawn chairs and sat to eat with a small group of newcomers Lucie hadn't met yet. One woman looked like a secretary wearing a cardigan sweater. Another had on a windbreaker, skirt, white socks, and loafers, like a fifties teenager. Clothes were fashionable and then they were functional, and then, layered out of necessity, they became their own sort of fashion again. Almost everyone carried a backpack. Inside, if they were new, they kept small rolls of cash, old credit cards, and family photos. A signed Norman Mailer first edition, a baseball with tiny scrawled signatures. Some people had cars where, like houses, they kept more things than they would ever need.

After the meal Lucie cleaned up. Trash was saved to be burned later. Plasticware was taken to the dock and dipped into the water to be rinsed off. She brought bread and watched the fish surface, darting and quick from the murky bottom. There were a handful of unusual breeds, dumped here, Mooney claimed, from someone's saltwater tank. A bright blue one with white stripes was an Emperor Angelfish, he'd told her. She watched now for this one, over a foot long, its colors brilliant in the sun. Mooney appeared behind her, a shadow thrown over the water. She ignored him and he waited. She'd learned if you ignore most people long enough they will give up and go away. But he didn't. He shifted his weight and the old dock groaned.

"I thought we'd take a trip," he said.

She rolled the bread into tiny balls and tossed them into his shadow that lay dark on the water in front of her. She remembered the fairy tale about the fisherman and his wife, and the magic fish who granted wishes. She remembered her kindergarten teacher who refused to let her remain silent in class. We're waiting for you, Mrs. Pearl said. She felt the same anger and resentment now, a childish fury.

"We'll leave in an hour," he said. "Wear something pretty." His shadow moved away down the dock.

When she'd been a teenager she competed to be Strawberry Queen. The festival was a yearly event. The Queen was presented at the Straw-berry Festival with her ladies in waiting, all of them in gowns like wedding dresses, tiaras, and rhinestone earrings. She dreamed of her picture among the others—girls from all the way back to the forties, in flipped-up hairdos waving gloved hands from the parade float. The strawberries lay waiting in rows under green leaves, in flats in stalls, smelling sweet and moldering. The Mexicans came in open trucks to pick them—boys who were sly and quiet and mysterious, dark-skinned, with agile fingers. She and her friends drove by in their Mustang and called out the window of the car: *Te amo! Bésame!* The only things they cared to remember from Spanish class. She was in love with one of the boys, Domingo Lopez Portillo. She called him Dommie. He was in her history class, and she flirted with him and treated him like a pet, and he resented her and ignored her, though she didn't know it. One night she and her friends went to a club and parked out in the lot and Dommie was there. He led her into the smoky bar to show her where the bathroom was. At first she thought he just wanted to kiss her. It started like that, just the kissing. In the middle of it happening she couldn't quite believe it. She didn't fight him off. She became limp, so that he had to hold her up. *Muñeca de trapo*, he said. He was angry, and he spit the words at her. She could see his beautiful teeth. *Te amo*, she thought sadly. She would have bruises on her upper arms, on her buttocks. She had to hide these from the other girls in the competi-tion. When she got pregnant she knew she could not be Queen. No pregnancies. Those were the rules.

It wasn't the saddest story he'd ever heard, Mooney said when she told him.

She'd laughed. "No, not the saddest."

Still, she'd asked him not to repeat it to anyone, and he'd given her a long look, his pale eyes flicking over her face. "What do you take me for?" he'd said. She understood now it was not a promise. It was only what she'd wanted it to seem.

When they left the complex that afternoon Basha watched from an upper-story window. Mooney took her straight down Montgomery to the apartment entrance. The weeds came up through the asphalt. The entrance was barred with a high chain-link gate. The old brick guard booth sat empty. They slipped through the gate, and walked past the ornate iron lettering on the sign: *Georgetown*. The lunch hour traffic rushed past, a blur of cars and exhaust.

"When will we be back?" she asked.

Mooney shook his head. She noticed he had recently shaved, but she refused to meet his gaze. He didn't look back at the sign, at the gate, or the empty guard booth. She had her nice bag, and wore a long skirt and flat sandals, earrings that kept tangling in her hair. They took the bus downtown and transferred to a Greyhound. The seats were soft, with high backs that afforded them privacy. Mooney had brought a bagel they split. He had paid for the bus tickets, but she wasn't sure if they were round trip. She didn't watch him buy them. She was cautious of him now, but uncaring where she ended up. He could lead her anywhere. She was a *muñeca de trapo*. Portable.

She slept and dreamed, but when she awoke and Mooney asked her what she dreamed she told him, "Nothing." It was late afternoon. She watched the flat land and the few trees and saw palm, the cows huddling by sad water holes. The dream had been of a house with terrazzo floors, and a sliding glass door, and a man with sunglasses and a white T-shirt. He sang "Santa Lucia" to her. She had a pallet on the floor in a spare room. The house was not theirs, but an abandoned house. At night teenagers would come and do their drugs and have sex, but she would not. "Saint Lucy," the man said. "Take out your eyes." She wondered if Basha would get the water in the morning, if the food they took would last until they got back. She worried about Marilee, about

Albie, and the others. She worried about them the way she worried about the old woman whose newspaper sat at the end of her driveway.

The bus engine's drone almost lured her to sleep again.

Mooney said, "Anytime now."

He worked in a revival tent as a teenager. The sound of his voice saying the words of scripture was thrilling, and when he recited in public places people stopped and looked at him. He held his hands out in a beseeching gesture. One arm was a tattoo sleeve—a wave's curl, a bird on a twig, flowers he'd identified for her, the species of which she pretended she could never remember. Hyacinth, she'd say. Hydrangea, hibiscus. He'd laugh. She found he liked her best when she was stupid. He claimed he knew the Bible so well that he had learned to look beneath the words, to the hidden subtext. There, he claimed, was the real story. He believed her dreams were portents, that they revealed landmarks and secret directions. When she told them to him she made sure to describe everything. In the room, she'd say, there are small items spread all over the tabletops: thimbles, whistles, tiny dolls, buttons made like amber colored flowers, dark green plastic knots, metal ones with anchors, small silver ones with mother-of-pearl, buttons you'd see on a little girl's white cardigan. Outside the room is the sound of water, rushing up close to the front door. She knew she couldn't lead him to the place he was seeking, and yet she had continued to tell him the dreams, biding her time with him.

The bus pulled into the transfer station in Fort Myers and they got off. It was five o'clock. She had lived here once, but she said nothing to him.

"It's about four miles," he told her. "We'll make it."

She'd asked him twice where they were going, but he shook his head. "It's a surprise," he said. The heat of the day sat in the pavement. The road was a three-lane highway with stoplights and strip malls. There were palm trees in the median, and traffic with a definite destination. As they walked past the cars waiting for the signal to change, the occupants stared at them: a vanload of kids in baseball caps, all of them turning like a clutch of birds, a man in a suit, a woman wearing pearls, her eyes flashing toward them, away, and then back again, a young man whose face seemed stony with grief.

"His father has died," she said. "He's driving to the funeral home, thinking about the only time they went fishing and he caught a speckled trout."

Mooney nodded, and smiled. "Ah yes," he said. "Ah yes." She told him that in Rodgers and Hammerstein's *Cinderella* the prince said this during the ball scene when women try to interest him in their daughters. Mooney laughed and looked princelike. "Ah yes," he said again, holding up his hands. She had nearly forgiven him for telling Basha her story, but then she remembered and was silent until they arrived at Colonial Station.

"What is this?" she asked.

Mooney told her it was where the Mystery Train departed and returned. The train sat steaming in the station, bright blue with orange stripes. People parked their cars and filed into the station house. She waited on the grassy embankment while Mooney went inside. She watched people step up metal stairs and enter the cars, a wash of colorful clothes, and then when it seemed the train was about to depart, Mooney emerged from the station house with two tickets. She didn't ask how he had gotten them. In the *Sanibel* car they found their table, and sat across from each other by the window. The interior was a reconditioned 1930s dining car with rows of tables filled with couples and families, assorted groups of friends, retirees, and people on vacation. The tables were set with china and silver and wine glasses. The waitress came in when everyone was seated and told them what would happen once they were underway. The performers would come into the car, and the diners would listen and mark down clues. The play was a murder mystery. At the end of the night the person who guessed the murderer correctly with the most clues would win a prize. The train lurched and started off down the track. The setting sun flickered through the dirty windows. Mooney ordered a bottle of wine. The waiters and waitresses brought in large baskets of bread, holding them on their hips like peasants.

It grew dark. The train moved through intersections where the lights flashed a signal and the traffic stopped. She looked down through the windshields of the cars, into the faces of people who didn't notice, who thought about other things. They passed behind warehouses, and through the center of small towns, and then through the hammock of pond apple and cabbage palm, button brush and strangler fig. They drank the wine. Mooney smiled at her, a man mothers might call dashing, or charming.

"This is it, isn't it?" he said. "Your dream?"

She smiled, leery.

"You can't say I didn't make your dream come true," he said.

The actors came into the aisle and said their lines—a short, plump woman with a wide-brimmed hat, a femme fatale in a gold sequined gown and a black shoulder-length wig, a man in a white tuxedo, a man wearing glasses, a plaid sweater vest, a short-sleeved shirt with a hole in the armpit. She imagined the actors purchasing their costumes in the Goodwill store, wearing them for the month or two of the play's run. They were well trained, and enunciated their lines so that anyone listening might hear over the murmur of low voices, the clank of the train on the tracks: *Getyourpick, Getyourshovel, Getyourpick, Getyourshovel.* The water in their glasses lolled back and forth.

Occasionally the actors broke into song. The play was about former USO performers trying to find jobs after the war. A famous producer is on the train, and they all want to be signed to play in his Miami club. Then his body is discovered. Each has the ability to shoot a gun, a sad history that might prompt vengeance. She didn't write anything down on her clue sheet. Mooney leaned forward, his eyes level with hers.

"Whodunit?" he said, laughing, his teeth flashing.

The wine made her dizzy, so that when she stood to make her way to the ladies' room she fell into a man's shoulder, and he reached up to steady her. She promptly shifted and fell into someone on the other side of the aisle. Inside the ladies' lounge was a three-sided mirror, and one of the old train seats, long and upholstered in red. The door banged open and shut, open and shut. Everything smelled of oil paint. She sat on the couch and listened to the door bang, stared out the window as they crossed the Caloosahatchee River on a narrow trestle, until Mooney came and knocked and asked if she was all right. She slipped the steak knife from the man's table into a pocket of her purse.

In 1989 Mooney had lived in the Georgetown apartments. He rented a one-bedroom there while he was separated from his wife. It was a trial separation, he'd told her. He never believed they would stay apart. He kept his apartment nearly empty of furniture, in the prospect of soon returning to his house. There was a couch, a bed, a television. He ate his meals out. After work each day he would drive to his house out of habit, and realize his mistake. One day he drove past and saw his son in the front yard with a babysitter, and he stopped and asked the boy for his mother.

"She went out," he said. He was four, and still at the age where he might be held on your lap, or in your arms. Still honest, Mooney had said.

"She's on a date," the boy said.

The babysitter, a chubby neighbor girl with a knowing expression named Patrice, took the boy's hand and yanked him in close. "Don't be silly," she said. "She went out with some girlfriends to the movies."

They were lying on the floor of the apartment when he told her this story.

"I never knew I could feel that sort of rage," he'd said. The dark surrounded them, oppressive and charged. She didn't ask him what he did. It was clear that what he did had led him somewhere that would point, finally, back to this place. Mooney believed you had to revisit the scenes of your mistakes. "Take a fresh account," he said.

Basha had told her the rest of the story just that afternoon, taking her arm after she'd washed the plasticware and sorted the trash, leading her down onto the beach where they could be alone. She said that after he'd found out about his wife and the other man, he'd gone to his house in the middle of the night. He'd wanted to see his son sleeping. He'd wanted to pick up some clothes. The wife had changed the locks, so he broke in and took her in her T-shirt and panties while the boy slept. He'd brought her to the Georgetown apartment and kept her there, a prisoner, watching the police swarm his house on the news, listening to the statements of neighbors, the little babysitter, Patrice, with her round cheeks, and then the man his wife had been seeing, swarthy looking, in tinted aviator sunglasses. Basha didn't know what he did to the wife while he had her. When she'd asked him he only said, "Nothing I wouldn't do to her again."

As they left the ladies' lounge the train slowed and stopped for the dinner service, and they took their seats and ate prime rib and parsley potatoes. Mooney smiled at her over his fork.

Their reflections were in the windows, and the world beyond the train was in darkness, and hidden from them. She ate quietly, only a portion of her food. She would take the rest back with her, she told him. He looked at her for a long time, and shook his head slowly. She felt the food in her throat.

"Why?" she asked. She tried to keep all emotion from her voice.

"We'll find a better place," he said.

She'd been a cocktail waitress at ABC Liquors, a bartender at a strip club in Tampa. She met people who wanted her to do other things, but she declined their offers, and when they insisted she refused. Basha had told her she was lucky she'd never met any men who would force her. When she was pregnant she'd left home and come here, to Fort Myers. She had money saved from birthdays. She sold her Strawberry Queen gown and her shoes. In Fort Myers was Thomas Edison's summer home, a place she had visited on a field trip once. She worked in a shoe repair store, and a Denny's restaurant, and when she was too big she worked in a small telemarketing office with older women who were sad about their children moving out, who spent their days at the hairdresser, or in front of the television, wondering what to do with themselves. They gave her a baby shower, brought gifts wrapped in pastel paper—tiny undershirts, pacifiers, and receiving blankets. They had a cake with buttercream icing, decorated with miniature baby bottles that they cleaned off in the break room sink and handed to her to save. She had rented a small, pink stucco house she found advertised in the newspaper. Behind it ran the train tracks, and at exactly the same time every night she'd be at her sink, washing up her plate, her Pyrex dish, when the Mystery Train passed by. She'd press her belly up against the counter and look out. She would see the faces of the diners, the shimmer of an actor's costume, sometimes even hear the performers' voices in song, or the roll of applause. The sound of the train, the low whistle signaling its approach, the rush of air as the cars passed—*Sanibel, Marco, Gasparilla, Captiva*, the faces of the diners, their mouths open in laughter, their glasses raised in the warmth of the lights, all of it filled her with uncalculated joy.

She looked at Mooney and smiled.

"I can't believe I'm here," she said. The plates were taken away and dessert and coffee were served, and the train started up again, reversing, heading back to the station. She stared out the window into the darkness. She asked Mooney the time. Now they were passing the little pink stucco house. They were passing children playing manhunt in backyards with flashlights, women turning off lamps in living rooms, men slumbering in front of ball games. She had wanted to have that sort of life. When the baby was born she took him home in a cab and settled him among the beautiful things the old ladies had bought for him. He was soft, brown-skinned, his eyes deep and dark like Dommie's. He fit in her arms, a bundle of blankets and small bones.

Mooney reached out and took her hand in his. He smiled and showed his even teeth. She had been alone for a long time, and it was nice to be with someone who asked her what she dreamed. But she wondered why he'd told Basha about the Strawberry Queen pageant.

"I never told her anything," he said.

"How does she know then?" she asked.

He dropped her hand as if it was something he had decided to set aside for a while.

The waitress left the bills on each of the diners' tables, narrow black folders with the check inside. They both looked at it. Of course there was no more money to pay. She could tell that from the expression on his face. She was resigned to what would come next—first a story, and an excuse, then a distraction they would use to get away. The waitress collected the clue sheets and the winner was announced, a woman who had not only guessed the murderer and the most clues but had drawn little caricatures of the players. Everyone clapped. There was laughter and a shuffling of chairs, a gathering of purses and sweaters. The waitress returned, huffy and impatient. My wallet, Mooney said, was left in the car in the parking lot. The waitress stared at both of them in turn. This wasn't something that normally occurred. She sighed, exasperated, as if they were children.

"Go then," she said. "Go and get it." She threw her hands up.

They stepped off the train with the rest of the passengers. The actors had lined up in their shoddy costumes to say farewell, their makeup garish in the bright lights of the station. She and Mooney walked down the line of cars, purposefully, and then they disappeared from the parking lot altogether. They took a side street where they would not be detected. It was an alley lined with trash cans and overhanging trees draped with kudzu. Mooney was laughing, exuberant. She stood a little ways off, watching him, wanting everything that Basha had said to be a lie.

"I'm going back," she said.

"Back?" he said. "Back where? To the train?"

"To Georgetown," she said. She turned to leave him in the street. A dog began to bark. Cicadas wound up.

He stepped beside her, still laughing. "What will you do there?" he said. "The property's been sold again. It'll be torn down soon. No one there cares about you."

She stared at him, waiting for him to say he was the only one who cared about her.

"You're an odd one," he said. "I always knew it. You're off."

She turned from him again and he took her arm and she pulled her arm away. He'd stopped laughing. He grabbed her arm again. He pulled her up against him and twisted her arm back and put his mouth in her hair, by her ear. "You aren't going anywhere," he said.

The baby with Dommie's eyes had died on his fourteenth day home. She'd woken up one morning, her breasts engorged and painful. He was there in the bassinet beside her, the little blanket still, his lips blue, his eyes closed to her. One of the old ladies paid for his funeral, and a small flat stone she has never visited. She hadn't thought about the baby or the pink stucco house in a long time. But now she remembered those weeks of bliss, the baby at her breast, the smell of her own milk on the sheets, the books on how to bathe, and feed, and tend spread out on the bed, the Mystery Train's passing at night, its plaintive whistle, its flash of brightness and hope.

Mooney will wrestle her down onto the asphalt, and tell her things that make him feel better about what he's doing. There will be that press of broken rock and sharp gravel, the mortification of her clothing tugged away, the soreness after, the ache on her face where he'll strike her. None of this will matter. She will wait until he believes he has subdued her to use the knife. Afterward she will walk away. She will be a woman on the side of the road in a flowing skirt with a stolen check slipped into its hem. She is there at Kash n' Karry supermarket pushing an empty cart, watching the people pass, or in the drugstore looking at the hair dye, the nail polish, perusing the magazines. She is in the mall, or the library, or walking with a tour at a museum. She could be anyone. She has nowhere to go in particular. She knows the old houses will be demolished. Under each newly built house will be the ghost of a woman who was forgotten, her corpse left to rot. Georgetown will be cleared up to the mangroves and the bay, and they will build over the remains—bobby pins, eyeglasses, pennies, wedding rings, keys. In the fairy tale the fisherman's wife with her greed and shrill demands has her final wish to be God, and ends up with nothing. The beautiful fish ventures out to sea.

*My father took this photo of my mother giving me a ride on her bike.
I could have known right then that I would settle down in the Netherlands.*

Stefani Nellen studied psychology in Heidelberg (Germany) and Pittsburgh (Pennsylvania), and now lives in the Netherlands as a writer and (sometimes) translator. She graduated from the Clarion Science Fiction & Fantasy Writers' Workshop at UC San Diego. Currently, she is working on a collection of short stories and two novels, which are inspired by science, "the mind," and the many aspects of running. She is a decent recreational runner, and hopes to qualify for the Boston Marathon in the future. Other stories can be found in *Inkwell*, *Web Conjunctions*, *Apex Digest*, *Cosmos Magazine*, *Best of the Web*, and online.

MEN IN PINK TUTUS

Stefani Nellen [signature]

Stefani Nellen

The Last Meeting

My father stood in my doorway at five in the morning. He wore a pink tutu and his running shoes. The tutu's sequin-studded top shimmered when he inhaled, expanded by his still broad chest and his new beer belly. Layers of transparent, stiff skirts rode around his hips like a wedding cake decoration. He held a magic wand, a silver-sprayed plastic star glued to an ice cream stick. He had sprinkled glitter on his hair. I could smell the mint on breath and—more surprising than the tutu—cigarette smoke.

"Hurry up, Sarah. We're going for a run."

"Dad, it's the middle of the night. Come inside."

"No. This is important."

He had left my mother and me two years ago. Since then, he had sent me a couple of unicorn postcards. There was never much text, apart from the obvious. *Sarah: I'm alive, I'll be back, hang in there.* The real message seemed to come from the eye rolling, teeth baring unicorns who stared at me as if I was one of them.

I made a show of cursing under my breath while I put on sneakers, but the truth was, I had been awake anyway. Tutu or no, I had expected him at my door in the middle of the night, and now that he had showed up, it was as if no time had passed at all.

Glimmer Train Stories, Issue 88, Fall 2013
©*2013 Stefani Nellen*

Like many athletic people, my father had a sadistic streak.

"Small strides," he said. "Ease into the hill." He meant well. They all do.

We soon passed the convenience store where I worked with my college buddy Abe and his mother. Our stuffed crow, Fitzgerald, sat on top of a soup pyramid. A smile of tin teeth dangled from a hook above the dental practice next door. It was the night before bulk trash day, so we ran past ghost furniture, gutted sofas, skeletal lamps, deconstructed shelves. The cars on the curb guarded the furniture trash, metal turtles layered in a crystal pattern of frost. It was almost summer, but this was a cold night.

"Stop," I wheezed.

My father turned around. He waved the magic wand at me with the gesture of a child in a booster seat spilling puréed carrots all over the table with glee, and I found my breath again. What a strange night, I thought, in a slow cadence that reminded me of Abe. What a sta–range night. Sinews rose from my father's neck, and he bared his teeth. He screamed without making a sound.

"Dad?"

He didn't try to catch his fall. He hit the asphalt like a corpse cut from a rope. The wand flew out of his hand.

I waited.

His white satin butt stuck up, right in the center of the lantern light.

What a strange night. And here came a click of a screen door, the curious neighbors, and the porch light without comment, an ochre light that made my father look ugly and human. I walked toward him and blocked it out. My belly wobbled like the chest of a sage grouse. I hadn't felt it at all while running.

His left leg jutted out from under the pink tutu skirts, and his hair was stiff with glitter. A little warmth was left under his hair and close to the skull, but it was soon gone, and when the blue light of the ambulance washed over us, there was no doubt anymore that he was a dead body. But no, he gave a last gasp! Sequins scratched across the asphalt. That was the last sound he made.

My Father's Family

(a) I, Sarah; Don't Look

I wished I could have hated my father. He stood at the side of the track in his navy running tights and stared at the stopwatch in his palm. My mother circled the track, as metronomic as a plastic horse in an amusement park ride. She wore apple green compression socks and a matching baseball cap. The grass on the infield was hot and raspy, and the crickets chirped under the stands.

I walked down the track, pushed small stones off the tartan surface, and counted the times my mother lapped me. I made my own jackets out of felt or corduroy and lived inside them, all sweaty, in my underwear. If my father had forced me to put on compression socks and run, I would have hated him.

Instead, he played me videos of miracles. Running miracles. Rod Dixon won the New York City marathon in the driving rain, his shirt sticking to him like transparent skin, his moustache a soggy brush. Abebe Bikila floated over the cobblestones of Rome, his calm face illuminated by flickering torchlight. Joan Benoit waved her cap at hundreds of thousands of candy-colored faces at the L.A. Coliseum. Other families have movies of children splashing in pools, or close-ups of Polish sausages burning on a grill while Uncle Herb is strumming "I Shot the Sheriff." Our family memorabilia were of runners.

Once, he let me hold his medal from the Boston Marathon. It was cold and heavy and about the size of my palm.

"Great," I said, when I saw what it depicted. "A unicorn head on a platter."

He squinted, raised his hand, and stroked my eyebrows with one knuckle.

(b) The Kids

That's how my father called them. He was the distance coach of our college track team. The head coach, Salvo, wore a whistle around his neck. It hung there like a threat of something that could sound really unpleasant if he wanted it to.

We had issues of *Track & Field News* in the bamboo husk basket in the bathroom. We had stacks of coaching drills manuals and nutrition journals on the couch, in the kitchen drawers, and next to our shoe rack. Sometimes, a cover showed a pack of young runners cresting a hill: *The College Issue!* The teams in the College Issue had names: Wildcats, Razorbacks, Huskies. Never Poodles, Ringworms, or Armadillos. Our team didn't have an animal name. I called them The Speedsters, because it is one of the words outsiders use when talking about runners. Meteor Miler. The Eldoret Express. The Jamaican Jet. The Sunnyvale Speedsters.

To me, they were the best runners in the world. At one moment, they shuffled around the track and bumped into each other in a show that I mustered effortlessly every morning, and the next moment, at a signal from my father, they were flying. At the end of a workout, my father had the boys chase the girls. I always hoped that one of them would get away, but it never happened. My father wanted the girls to last longer each time. That was enough for him. The chase always came down to the same couple: a strong, red-haired girl and an African boy with glasses. She ran like a boxer, her face and belly flushed red, and he stayed right on her shoulder, light as a spider. She refused to fall back and end it, and he refused to overtake her, until, finally, out of mercy, he did. The moment he was clear of her, she staggered to the infield and sprawled on her back, her arms and legs a big X.

(c) My Mother

My mother, Lauren, was part of my father's memorabilia collection. She lived in movies, in pixels, in the land of red tracks and plastic bottles and bouncing triple jumpers. She had made the Olympic team in the 5000m just out of college. In the Trials video they referred to her race as her "coming out party," although the idea of this girl partying was ridiculous. She tried, though. She wore glittering red–white-and-blue hairpins, waved at the crowd, and put her hands on her nonexistent hips when they introduced her at the starting line (but later, she said: the favorites were all injured that day, so it didn't count).

She and my father met later, at the expo of a race she was meant to run but couldn't, because of yet another injury. Her bones were as stable as baked sawdust, and her muscles were sheets of inflammation. At the time, the Olympic semifinal was already history. This was one tape we never watched together, but my father had it, I knew he did, and one day I found it at the bottom of the drawer. *Lauren, Beijing.* The runners lined up without much fanfare; it was only the semi, after all. My mother was one of many, not much taller than the Africans, her hair pulled back in a ballerina bun, her shoulders bony and wet from sweat. A shot sounded, the women started. She flew along with the leaders. A couple of laps in, she started limping. The right side of her body stiffened up. Her hairpins kept on glittering, and she kept on running, dragging one leg behind her. The commentator (the same one who had called her win a coming out party) said that that she was putting up a gutsy performance, but he sounded disgusted. The leaders lapped her and elbowed her out of the way, and an official pulled her off the track. She finally tore the dumb pins out of her hair, wrapped a towel around her shoulders, and strode away. "And thus," the commentator concluded, "Lauren Kelly's Olympic dream comes to a sad end."

She trained with my father. She was on an eternal comeback trail. She raced on the road, in small local races she often won, and trained on the track. On the track, she moved fast, much more smoothly than the red-haired speedster. At home, she was covered in tape and ice packs. The rattle of pill bottles followed her around the house. She had ultrasound machines for her bones, slept on a massage table, face down, and my father rolled out her muscles with a stick.

She and my father didn't talk. They were too busy taking care of their two children: her wretched body and her huge talent. I was probably conceived as therapeutic intervention, a hint for her body to do its job. I hadn't been very effective.

After my father had died, I brought the tutu to my mother's place. It sat on the couch like a guest.

"Have you ever seen him wear this?" I asked.

She leaned towards the thing, slowly, careful. "No. But I like it." She picked up a layer of lace and rubbed it between her fingers.

"Why?"

"It reminds me of my last race."

She had stopped running shortly after he left us. I never asked why. I wouldn't have asked her why she had stopped hammering her thumb, either. Some things just need to stop. But now she smiled. She let the lace travel between her fingertips.

The tutu was enormous. It looked custom made.

"During that 5K, I was hurting," she said. "I was working hard to beat high school girls, for god's sake. My knee was taped up again, I sweated, the tape came loose...I decided to jog it in. And suddenly, this guy was running next to me. He had a hairy chest and a beard, and he wore a pink tutu. You know what they say, if you're a runner, you don't want to be beat by the guy in the pink tutu. But he looked at me..."

I held my breath. *He lifted his magic wand,* I wanted to say. *Didn't he?*

"I *understood*," she said. "I understood that I could stop if I wanted to. I didn't have to do this. So I stopped. I dropped out right there, walked to the curb. And...the moment I did it, a weight dropped off my shoulders. It was over for good. I haven't run a step since then."

She let go of the lace. "And it feels fabulous."

"But why do you think Dad wore the tutu?" I asked.

She moved her jaw. Her face hardened. "Who knows why he did anything? Who knows why he had to come back that night, and make sure you saw him die." She got up. Her hand shot to her back. She froze in a lopsided curtsy position. "Damn," she hissed. I waited. When she didn't move, I offered her my arm, and slowly helped her upright.

"Anyway," she said, after a few deep breaths, "now you know about runners and the pink tutu men." She looked at me with that familiar look, which told me she didn't expect me to understand a single word of what she was saying.

But he has come to me, I thought. *And I'm not a runner.*

It has to mean something.

The Time He Left

He left us the summer I turned seventeen. Before he left, he stopped sleeping. He sat up all night, together with me.

School would be over soon, and I didn't feel fit for life at all. I didn't think I had earned it. To be on the safe side, I wanted a medieval job: bricklayer, midwife, gravedigger. These jobs weren't available, or if they were, I couldn't ask about them the right way. Excuse me, Ms. Career Advice, I was thinking about rat catcher. Exterminator. Pest Control. No, I'm not kidding. These are useful jobs, for god's sake.

I sat still for hours in the dark kitchen while the fan turned overhead. One word came up in my mind, then nothing, nothing, nothing, and another. At parties, I drank so I didn't have to talk. At night, when the Speedsters trained, I went to the track. I could lose myself in the pattern of their strides, warm-up jogs and laughs, the school colors tied into the girls' braids, the snot, spit, and shins torn open by spikes, the blood black in the floodlights.

Once, the African boy who always chased down the red-haired girl stopped at the edge of the track, right where I was sitting in the dark. He grabbed the steel fence with both hands, rounded his shoulders, and vomited with three coughs. The wet sound slapped me awake. He looked up, right at me, and wiped his mouth with the back of his hand. His lips were still wet when he was done. My heart was in my throat. *I need to get out*, I thought. *I need to get moving. I need to get out.*

"Is someone going to move their ass to the start?" Salvo shouted. The boy turned around and trotted back to the group. I scanned the bleachers, the infield, the top of the stairs, and the fence in front of the parking lot, but my father was gone. He had never been there. My head buzzed, like the intrusion of reality when I was about to wake from a nightmare, but I didn't wake up. I had never had a father. I had imagined him.

"He's sick," my mother said the next morning. "He is seeing a doctor. I told you?" He stayed home after that. "Stress." The Speedsters had a poor season. They gained weight, had mono, and tore tendons. Salvo killed them.

To Summarize

There were thunderstorms every night. My father and I sat in the kitchen and ate dry cereal. Lightning lit up our faces. He started to smell sour. I could go for days without sleep, he couldn't. My mother did contortions on a rubber ball. Salvo visited and banged his gym bag into a photo of Zatopek in the hallway. I sat in the kitchen and gave him the evil eye.

"Your father's not doing that great," he said.

I said I could tell.

"Let's hope he comes around," he said. The stubble on his cheeks moved while he chewed his gum. "See ya."

My father whispered to himself. His lips moved. Crumbs stuck to his lips.

"Dad," I said.

"I need to get out of here," he said. The kitchen was muggy, even at night, and my father was stealing my thoughts. We were entering each other's dreams.

This was in the time before he left. This is all I remember.

The morning he left, he was calm. He had shaved, he smelled better, and his face had settled down. He gave me a big hug I could feel all the way to my bones.

It could have been an awful morning: our family broke. My father left. Depressing books material, your entry ticket to Pitiful Central. Cue wistful memories: My dear old dad with his delightful stopwatch, which I would keep in a glass next to my bed, where other people keep their dentures.

No, I thought it was exciting. He left, but it didn't feel like an ending. It was the beginning. The first bird had left the nest. Why should families always work like this, with parents building the nest and feeding the children, who pay them back by leaving? In our family, there were no parents. There was just the three of us, and we fed each other for a while, and then we all had to leave.

My father had been the first bird out of the nest. I knew I would be the last.

My mother was next. By watching her struggle, I could forget my own future for a while. She was the girl left behind at the playground. Her running injuries had been perverse and glamorous. Now she was doing paperwork all night and trying to cook food that wasn't oatmeal or turkey salad wrap or muscle milk pancakes.

"I want to sell this place," she said. "I want to work."

She tried to train with Salvo, but they ended up fighting, and she stormed off the track wrapped in a white towel, like she had at the Olympics. "You can't beat yourself, Lauren," he shouted after her. I heard the chewing gum in his voice. "So stop trying!"

"I don't know," she said to me that night. She drank water out of a plastic bottle with a daisy print on it. "I don't know how this works. Would you like to do more things together? Would you like me to be more of a mom?"

"You're okay," I said. She kept playing with the green lid of the bottle.

"Yeah?" she said. Her fingers trembled. "You think so?"

About a year later, she was administrative staff at the School of Engineering. Salvo had gotten her the job. She had sold the house and most of the furniture, and the massage table had been the first to go. I had moved into my own place, a so-called studio in the apartment building of a distant cousin who needed tenants.

"I think he'll be back," I said, knowing she would understand immediately whom I meant.

"He had to leave," she said. "It sounds bad. It sounds as if it's no reason at all. It *is* bad. But one day, you might decide to do exactly the same thing. It happens."

My mother was right. The day after her pink tutu men anecdote, I decided to leave. It happens.

My Departure

Abe and his mother saw me off. I kept calling Abe my college buddy, even though we had both dropped out. He had been an experiment. His brain was brilliant. He had been on a six month internship in Switzerland along with fourteen other kids who had shown outrageous aptitude for language and simultaneous translation, and who were trained to translate and comment during minor business meetings of banks in Zürich in order to get a taste of a career in international trade. He had come back with a special headset, big plans, and a suitcase full of chocolate. The problem was his genes. He lacked an enzyme, one you couldn't afford to miss, and the medication he took to compensate sent his brain from overdrive to hibernation every couple of months. It wore him out. When we had met, he had been at equilibrium.

"I want to have a medieval job," I told him. "I want to do something I understand, I want to understand why I exist, what the fuck my point is."

He had eyelids like seashells, and wet-looking curls that always stuck to his brow. "You're dumb, Sarah," he said. We were driving around Morningside. The reindeer-in-bubble Christmas decorations were out, and he took photos with his cell, and I was at the wheel. "You can't say, Oh, a gardener has a useful job, because he's pushing a heap of weeds around in his wheelbarrow, and at the same time look down on the guy who is writing scripts that allow you to track packages online. The whole world is about pushing weeds around. Life is medieval."

"You're saying it's all good, and I can't make mistakes, because it's all the same."

"Yep."

I didn't mind being with him when he was in hibernation or in overdrive. I could do little more than sit and be in the same room with him, but this was more than most people put up with. It was easy for me, as easy as sitting in the dark bleachers when my father had still coached the Speedsters, but his mother was grateful—so grateful she granted both of us asylum in her convenience store. "You'll figure it out," she said to me on my first day. "For now, you're here." She was tall, tough, and bleached out, like wood that had dried in the sun. She had put her all into Abe's health and education, but his prognosis was bad.

"Well," she'd say, "here we are. Still afloat."

I left early in the morning. It was already hot, and Abe and his mother had put out the parasols and the ice cream trunk. Fitzgerald wore a mini straw hat.

Abe gave me a big hug that almost broke my ribs, like my father had that day. "Have fun," he said. "And take care of Pete." Pete was the name of his car. With his medication, he couldn't drive anymore. Pete was old, broad, flat, and maroon.

180

"Safe travels now," Abe's mother said. She shook my hand. "We really hope you'll be back."

"Fitzgerald is not going to let anybody touch a single can of soup before you're back," Abe said.

My mother wasn't there. She didn't want me to leave.

"You can't do this," she said. "You've never even driven out of town."

"It's summer," I said. "I want to do some coming of age stuff. I'm already behind the curve. It's my money, after all." Dad had left me some.

She scuffed, and rightly so. I didn't tell her that my coming of age didn't interest me, and that I had another mission: Find a pink tutu man. She had told me the anecdote of her last race, after all. *Runners and pink tutu men*, she had said, as if there was no hope in the world that I would ever understand her. But sometimes it takes an outsider to understand.

I wanted to surprise her. If she didn't understand why my father had come back wearing a tutu, I would.

She wanted an itinerary, a cell phone number, and GPS tracking. She did not want a lost or missing daughter.

"I hope you realize what you're doing to me," she said, her eyes and mouth scrunched up. "I'm already worried sick."

But she probably also knew that Abe wouldn't travel anymore, and that parents should be grateful for being worried sick about solo road trips in maroon cars instead of missing enzymes and eroded brains.

"Make sure you eat," she said. "And sleep."

The Way Out

I could feel it when I left the circumference of our town. My mother had been right: I had never driven out of town. Pete was an odd car to drive without Abe next to me. The seats were too broad, and so was the road. The steering wheel had grown. A couple of times, I thought the engine was roaring out of control, and took my foot off the accelerator. My hands were sweating ice cold, the way they had during my driver's test. I drove slowly, far on the right; I had memorized the route to my first stop. The car smelled of my new running shoes on the backseat.

I had found out that there was barely a set of coordinates in the country where people hadn't put up a start and a finish line and declared a footrace. All it took was some fences, volunteers in bright yellow jackets, and inflatable arches, and you had Uncle Bob's 10K, Fitt's Home and Garden 5K, the IKEA Half (with 1K fun run), and so forth. And after searching online race reports, I had found out another thing: Where there is a footrace, there are pink tutu men. My mother's encounter had not been unique. *Runners and pink tutu men.* You only need to put on a pair of running shoes to lure them out.

This was my plan.

There were two basic kinds of pink tutu men encounters.

One: He passes you. You quit.

"I followed Pfitz 18/70 and thought I'd run a personal record no matter what, but when this guy in the pink dress pulled past me and waved his magic wand, I knew it was over."

"Some might say it's weak to drop out of a race, but come on. How can you go on after that? He wore a wig, too."

"He grinned at me, and I thought, dude... At that point, I was done. I hit the wall so hard. The next six miles were a complete knuckle-drag. My first Boston where I didn't manage to re-qualify for Boston. I didn't bother to collect my medal."

Two: He passes you. You crush it.

"I wanted to give up. I had vomited twice. Please. But whenever I looked up, this guy in pink ran right next to me, and I refused to stop. I ended up running a PR by almost a minute!"

"If a guy in a pink tutu can finish NYC in less than three hours, so can I."

"I wanted to thank him after I finished, but I couldn't find him. I only saw him from afar, drinking beer with three girls."

An army of pink tutu men travelled the world, each of them on his way to meet a runner. What if my father had been part of it?

Pulling up at the parking lot next to the start of the Firecracker 5K, I thought that I would really like that.

Things I've Seen

I had a schedule of road races. My mother could see where I was because of my cell phone locator, but she didn't know what I was doing.

I tried to run. My new shoes became dirty.

This kind of running was so different from track races. There was music, there were buckets of banana pieces and sugar gels, and the slowest finisher was escorted to the finish by a bike. But the biggest difference was in the shapes and sizes of the runners. My mother and her competitors had looked like siblings: Sleek panthers with delicate rib cages, lean thighs and androgynous hips. These road-runners could have been from different species. (i) Women in pink. (ii) The leathery, silver-haired metronomic types. (iii) The surfer types with zinc ointment on the nose. (iv) The local elites with the sponsored gear. (v) The lumberjacks. (vi) The spiritual walkers. (vii) The tan ponytail girls. (viii) The memory people, with photos and obituaries printed on their shirts.

I had been scared to line up for a race. I expected to be able to run as much as I expected to be able to fly. But the crowd of people carried me along. We didn't compete, after all. We were making a statement. We were performing a ritual. For all I knew, we were making moving crop circles. I didn't have to explain why I ran, and no one told me I was too slow. The most difficult thing about running in these races, I soon found out, was pinning on the race numbers.

My life had a new rhythm: Sleep, shower, breakfast, plot out the way to the next race, enter, run, scout for pink tutu men, pick up dinner, search for a place to sleep (or prepare Pete's backseat for another night). In the beginning, each of these steps had taken me a long time, but soon the days rushed by. I washed my clothes, cut my hair, and increased my radius. I became an expert on different energy foods and sport drinks. I recognized the beep of the timing mat when I passed the waypoints of the race, and I learned to look out for the term *pasta dinner* in the race descriptions. I could sit at a table with strangers, and they asked me how long I had been running. Some asked where my parents were.

My parents. Before they had me—before they met—they had probably lived like I was living now. They had been traveling from one day to the next, busy with maintaining their lives, and planning treats such as a movie or a bath. My father had been living like this in the end, I knew. He had managed to find unicorn postcards at filling stations. He had worn a tutu.

I saw many people in costumes, but no pink tutu men. My father's death must have marked the territory. I had to move out.

Dan

At the Ocean Mist Marathon, I met a pink tube dress man. He sat opposite me at the pre-race pasta dinner.

By then, I felt easy inside my skin. Being away from home agreed with me. I was a ball of wool that had just about unrolled. Life was small and simple.

"So, you're going to run the full?" I asked.

"Sure," he said, mixing the tomato sauce with his spaghetti. With his light brown skin and black curls, he could have shepherded a flock of sheep. He reminded me of Abe, or of how Abe could have been with all his enzymes. Had I written to him like I had promised? I must have.

"Pass me the parmesan?" he asked.

I obliged.

"That's an interesting outfit you have," I said.

"I know, right? Look." He got up, put one leg on the bench, and pushed the dress up his thigh. The fabric snapped back into place the moment he let go, as if it were magnetic, and his skin made of metal.

"See?" He said. "It's special fiber. No seams, no chafing. I got it from a friend who works at the innovations lab of a dancewear company." He leaned closer. "It's the new frontier. Top secret."

"I see," I said. "If you tell me more, your friend will be in trouble."

"Yes," he said. "I'm Dan, by the way."

After the pasta dinner, we walked along the beach. It was a small beach. It looked as if the road had first crumbled and then stopped, and that was that. Tree roots, hydrants, and houses were all nearby, but it was still a beach, with a *No Camping* sign, and we took off our shoes. I wasn't keen on returning to the twelve-bunk-beds-and-one-bar-of-soap paradise that was the local youth hostel.

"I want to go sub-3 tomorrow," Dan said. "That would be a new marathon PR."

I had planned on dropping out as soon as I had found a pink tutu man—or verified there wasn't one in the field. Twenty-six point two grueling miles. Exactly. Why not stop at five?

"So what brings you here?" Dan said.

He was so similar to Abe. I felt I could trust him. And I was far away from home, far enough to talk about my life. No one knew me here.

"I'm looking for men in pink tutus. They show up in races and wave magic wands."

Dan dug his toes into the sand. He was barefoot.

"For how long have you been doing this?"

For a moment, I wasn't sure. How long had I been doing this? How did my mattress feel in the morning? What was the sound of my mother's voice?

"I've been doing this for a while now," I said.

"Why?"

The sand shifted underneath me.

"My father's a pink tutu man." I had never said it out loud before.

Dan pulled up his brown shoulders, the futuristic fabric stretching around his chest.

"How did you find out?" he said.

"He came to me in the middle of the night wearing his tutu. We ran together, he waved his magic wand, and he died."

He started walking again. I followed. He kept looking up at me in a way that would have made me uncomfortable at home. Now I felt powerful. *You think this is crazy? There's more.*

"I never thought of them as having kids," he said. "But sure. Why wouldn't they?"

And like that, from one moment to the next, I wanted to bail from this conversation. He had not only acknowledged the existence of the pink tutu men, he was speculating about their mating habits. He would be able to give my quest direction, and things would become serious. All these races had been nothing but a warm-up.

We waited, in front of each other. The sand turned to glass, prickling my feet.

"Come to my place," he said. "I want to show you something."

Dan's room had a view of the sea. I stepped inside and almost fell out again through the window. Plastic starfish stuck to the walls. Everything was made of plastic or glass, and smelled of sea.

I dropped my backpack and slid off my shoes.

"Have a seat," he said. I sat down on the bed. He pulled a drawer from underneath his desk, sat down on a swivel chair, and leafed through pieces of paper and photos.

Two computers stood on his desk. The screensavers bubbled and deflated in slow motion. I wanted to turn on the light, but I couldn't see a switch.

"Here," he said. "Arbies."

"Arbies?" I asked. "What does that mean?"

He held up a letter-sized photograph.

The photo showed a group of people who posed liked circus acrobats, all knotted together. A man in a pear costume lifted a woman in a mermaid costume. Three pink tutu men stood in the front, hands around each other's hips, with an expression that asked whether the photo was done yet. Everyone in the group, except the mermaid, wore running shoes.

At the top of the photo, it said, *Running Beauties—Chasing You Down!* Running Beauties. R–B's. Arbies. At the bottom were an address and phone number.

The middle pink tutu man—was it my father? I squinted. Impossible to tell. The only light came from the sunset now.

Dan turned around on his swivel chair. I stood up, reached out, and tousled his hair. He inhaled and tilted his face, and the light picked out his beard stubbles before he dipped back into shadow.

"I got this from a crazy guy," he said. "He was looking for his daughter. I had never heard of her. He acted as if I were a criminal. Later, I found this in my mailbox." He reached for the photo and turned it around. Someone had written on the back.

"I think he meant it as a message for me, in case I change my mind," he said.

My daughter, Carol Kruger, I read. *Please ask her to come home.*

This Really Happened, I Have Proof (Notebooks)

A woman named Bridget answered the door at Arbies. I had called ahead, and she had invited me without much fuss. Bridget's skin looked like fine, oiled leather. She had white teeth and a dancer's body, and she wore her hair in two gray braids that fell to her thighs. A lapel pin in the shape of a starfish gathered the scarf around her neck.

"Welcome to the perfect world," she said. Everything looked metallic: the sky, the red soil, the cacti. The land sprang to life at the mere hint of irrigation, and dried out just as fast.

"It never rains here," Bridget said. "And we hardly drink."

The house of the Running Beauties was a Mikado structure of pastel-colored wooden beams and cathedral-style windows. It balanced on the edge of a cliff above the ocean.

"There's a switchback path down, if you know where to look," she said. "We also have trails that go up into the mountains. Run with us tonight. Running is the beginning of everything."

The hallway was lined with shoe racks containing running shoes of all sizes, made of technical fiber, cotton, lace, velvet, leather, and dried grass. Pagodas of running shoes were growing in every corner, on the mantelpieces, and the windowsills.

"The others should be back soon," Bridget said.

We sat down at an oval table in a pentagonal room with four windows. You could see the ocean and horizon through each, and I wondered how this was possible. Bridget shoved a bowl of nuts and raisins toward me. I picked up a raisin and contemplated its wrinkles.

"I'm so sorry to hear your father passed."

I played with the golden elbows of cashews, and the dried blood of cranberries.

"Did he live here?" I asked.

"I don't recall hearing his name. But that doesn't mean he wasn't here."

"What about Carol Kruger," I said. "Is she here?"

"I don't think so."

The sunlight burned through the windows.

"What kind of organization are you?" I asked. The handful of nuts inside my fist started moving, like bugs.

"We're a charity," Bridget said.

Honey, she said. Relax.

Eat.
Lie down.
It's fine.

Arbies runners raised money, Bridget told me. They ran so AIDS patients could afford live-in nurses, cancer patients could afford wigs, and blind people could afford dogs. They didn't run for any particular group; they ran to even the scales. "Think of us as a meta-charity, honey." Two women with blond hair, who wore gray cardigans and lunched on steamed Brussels sprouts, did accounting in the attic. They used computers with big screens and ergonomic keyboards.

Every morning, when it was my turn, I walked up to the mailbox to retrieve bags of envelopes from all over the world, and brought them upstairs. In the afternoon, I stamped letters and deposited them in the mailbox. All the envelopes were pink.

From my notebook:

Three steel refrigerators. Pink meat marbled with seams of fat. Glass bowls with fruit. Twenty twin beds in the basement. Memory foam pillows, down blankets, a row of lockers in the hallway. Breakfast in shifts. Dinner standing up in the doorways, holding plates with one hand and forking up food with the other. Cooking and dishwashing according to a strict schedule. Weekly grocery runs. Bathrooms further down the road in a building made out of salmon-colored tiles. Showers forceful enough to hose down a mud-encrusted car. The water tastes salty. An enormous supply of Windex, Lysol, toilet cleaner, toilet paper in the basement. A dry cleaning van picks up the dirty laundry once a week and brings back scented duffel bags filled with clean clothes.

There are three pink tutu men, strong, with large hands. They are called Pico, Dico, and Nico. They perform acrobatic tricks while running. If they have to, they carry the wands between their teeth.

There are other costume runners. A pink tube dress man and two caterpillars. They all run up and down the road, past the house, again and again, all day. They do hills on the switchbacks. A few are away at any given time, at races, at home (!), and their beds are empty until they return and toss their backpacks on the beds and lie down, glad to be back at Arbies.

It's a zero distraction athletics camp atmosphere. It must have been Dad's paradise.

The Arbie runners took me out running. I couldn't keep up for long, but this time I didn't stop and push gravel out of the way. I kept on moving. And it was fine. The weight melted off my bones. I became a little faster every day.

The pink tutu men didn't have any secrets. I could ask them anything I wanted. They sat on fold-out chairs at the kitchen table, cleaning their shoes with toothbrushes. I mixed them sports drinks out of powder and filtered water and asked:

Why do you do this?

Because it's fun.

What are the wands for?

They do the trick.

What trick?

The trick.

I don't get it.

Yes, you do.

Are you real?

Of course. We snore, don't we?

Did you know my father?

Like you do.

Why did he die?

Heart failure.

Once, I found a pink tutu man—Nico, the youngest, who had a stutter—sitting on my bed. He turned the pages of my notebook with one hand, and adjusted one of his shoulder straps with the other.

"What are you doing?" I asked.

He dropped the book on the pillow.

"N-nothing," he stuttered. "I was curious."

"About me?"

He got up and raced past me.

"Two quick miles," he called over his shoulder. By then, my response was automatic. I always wore running shoes, a pair Bridget had given me, and ran after him without thinking. By then, I was fast enough to keep up.

Occasionally, a runner would leave Arbies for good. They took off their running shoes and put on the street shoes they had kept inside their lockers, packed their suitcases, and left. At breakfast, we observed him or her walking down the road. We waved in silence or raised a spoon. We never commented on the lives they returned to.

Then, with all the mailbox rituals every day, I wanted to send Abe and his mother a letter, and found I couldn't remember his address. I couldn't remember my own address, either. I found my wallet in my backpack and pried out my driver's license. Yes, that was my address. How could I have forgotten? I rehearsed it in my head. I covered it with my hand, and forgot it immediately.

"I'm losing my memories!" I said. "Did this happen to my father?"

"No!" Bridget said. "I don't know what happened to him!" She sounded as upset as I was. "Honey. Maybe you should go home."

I didn't want to leave.

"Sleep on it," Bridget said. It sounded like a line she had picked up somewhere. She wasn't used to taking charge. At Arbies, things happened. No interference was necessary.

One of the accountants made an ID card with my name and address for me. She punched a hole in the corner of the ID card and attached it to a bracelet she strapped around my wrist.

Echo of my steps on asphalt. Taste of stamp glue. Creak of the mailbox hatch. Buzz of the printer in the attic. Red dust on the switchbacks.

Being a runner. Lining up in the morning at a trailhead. Eucalyptus leaves, bird song, shade settling on our shoulders, and the first deep breath. My elbows in the same angles at theirs, my legs in the same rhythm. We chase our shadows. I look for my clumsy shape to stand out, and the only thing that marks me is the black square plastic ID dangling from my arm.

At night, in the hallway. I'm on my knees. I press a plastic handle covered with slime against the right side of my face. The handle beeps. I'm holding a phone. I don't remember a voice, but I'm talking, talking.

I walk from the bath/shower building to Bridget's Mikado house, barefoot, a towel folded over my arm. The baby blue van of the dry cleaner comes from the other direction and stops next to me. The windows are open. A country tune tells me not to worry.

"How are you doing," the driver says.

I look ahead at the house. The bags of dirty laundry have been picked up.

"Not too bad," I say. The sun warms my shoulders. It is always warm here, and very cold at night.

"I'm a bit thirsty," I say.

"You're not from here, are you?"

I hug the towel to my chest.

"No," I say. "I think not."

"You look lost." He has a moustache, like Rod Dixon and Bikila. He stops the engine of his car and gets out. He is a tall man.

"You remind me of someone," he says. "What's your name?"

He looks so normal. Graying hair, young skin, big Adam's apple. At first I think he takes my hand. Then I realize he only lifts it so he can see the tag on my bracelet.

"I think we should get you out of here, Sarah MacGuire," he says.

"I'm not sure," I say.

He pulls at the tag, still holding my wrist with his other hand. It feels as if he is tugging at my insides. I remove my hand from his, and my life becomes light again, made of technical fabric, and smelling of clean sweat and soap.

"I want to stay here," I say.

"I'll be back," he says. "In case you change your mind."

It is cool inside the house. I go to the basement. It is cold and quiet down here, and musty, as if the place had been deserted for a long time. My notebook lies on my pillow. I pick it up at the spine, and it falls open and spills its contents: E-tickets, business cards, race flyers, race numbers, and a long, narrow sheet of paper that isn't mine. I want to pick it up and read it when I notice the back of a photo, blank except for a few words:

"My daughter, Carol Kruger. Please ask her to come home."

I rush to the accountants' room. The accountants sit opposite each other and type. Bridget sits on the floor with her legs crossed, a stack of pink envelopes to her left, and a heap of folded pink cards to her right. The sun illuminates her pearly kneecaps. She dabs a finger against her tongue and picks up a card.

"Who are you?" I ask her.

"What?"

"Are you Carol Kruger?"

"No!" she says. Her teeth are translucent at the edges, as if she's been undernourished as a child.

"What's your name, then?" I ask.

"Honey, it's Bridget…" Her lips tried to form words, but nothing comes. I know how she feels. I can't remember my name, either. It's right there on the card dangling from my wrist, but unless I reach for the card and turn it around, I will never remember. I want to stay here, but I can't. I can't live without my own name. No one can live without a name. If I stay here, I'll die.

I'm itching to read the damn ID tag, but I won't. I have to remember on my own.

The accountants look at each other. They know I have figured it out.

I pull myself up on one of the accountants' desks. It's hard. No one helps me; the three of them just stare. When I stand upright, my scalp comes off. An air pocket is growing between my skin and my skeleton, and the air pocket is spreading. Now my face lifts, the back of my head, the neck. The air pocket runs down my chest and along my spine, over my hips and down my legs. I don't look. When I'm all surrounded by air, I expect to collapse, but instead—after a moment of panic, when I want to touch my face to make sure I'm still there—I feel normal again. A woman in a home office. Nothing to see here.

She's standing behind me: the runner whose shadow I borrowed. She turns and leaves. She can't help me now.

The dry cleaning man will help me.

What about my car?

My thoughts are sticky.

My father. He had been one of the runners who left. He had made it home, not in his civilian garb but in his pink tutu, all the way across the country, all the way to my doorstep. What a guy.

My Mother

"Here is the thing, Sarah." She put her water bottle on the table and closed her eyes, the way she used to before a race or a hard workout. Even her eyelids were perfectly still. When she continued, her voice was deeper than before.

"I am telling you this because I love you. You have to understand that your father wasn't perfect. He was a runner. He tried to be a coach, but in his heart of hearts, he was a runner. He ran away. That's what he did. He ran away from his family, and he started wearing a costume. These are the facts. This is what we have to work with."

I had arrived the night before. The dry cleaning van had dropped me off in front of my mother's new house. The address matched, but I didn't recognize it: Yellow bricks, a pine tree that almost swallowed the porch, a rusted mailbox, and an almost invisible dirt path through a patch of bumpy lawn. I had seen it before, but I hadn't bothered to remember.

My mother opened the front door and ran toward me. I hadn't seen her run in ages. She was still fast. She punched me in the belly with a sharp fist, and hugged me as if she wanted to strangle me. "Where have you been?" She only wore pajamas, and I could feel her wiry arms, her ribs, and her small breasts as she shuddered against me like a squirrel.

"It's okay, Mom," I said. "It's okay. I found out about Dad."

She took a step back, slapped me in the face, and started crying.

She turned around and limped back to the door.

Inside, she let me have it. She had waited, waited for my call. "What were you doing out there?" She had tried to reach me. If I hadn't called her that night—

"Come on," she said. "Spit it out!" We sat in the kitchen, on a table just big enough for two, and she let me have it. I didn't get a word in. I had stories of Arbies, and the Mikado house, and the eucalyptus trees, and the pink tutu men, and my mother asked me about sex and drugs and speeding tickets.

In between, she stood up and opened the fridge. Bottles cluttered. She took out a bottle of milk and a bowl of strawberries and put both on the table.

"Sorry, no cake," she said. "Or bread. Oh, hell." She sat down again and rubbed her face like my father had during our kitchen nights. Her lips were narrow, her lower arms white and sinewy. I could see her flat nipples underneath her shirt. She had always been like this. My life had always been like this. I had never noticed until now.

"I'm okay," I said. "Really."

"Abe and his mother were worried about you."

I started picking up the strawberries, and she watched me.

"Fine. Let's talk tomorrow," she said.

The next morning she wore her hair in a tight bun, track-style. She had put on makeup.

I had made the mistake of looking in a mirror before crashing. Choppy hair, dead skin, bloodshot eyes, yellow teeth. Clothes caked to my body. It had been too long since the showers at Arbies. I closed my eyes and thought of the scent of the dry cleaning van, and the warm, fluffy bags of clean laundry. Then I stepped into the shower and started scrubbing.

The next morning, my mother started to talk to me. "Here is the thing, Sarah," she said, and continued to tell me that she loved me, and that my father wasn't perfect...

I tried to listen, but I had already prepared my own speech. I mustn't mess this up. She didn't see me as qualified to talk about pink tutu men. My father was not a topic she enjoyed. But she and my father had been close once, closer than I had ever been to anyone. I wanted to show her I understood now: How she had felt in Beijing, before she tore a muscle. How much it sucks to be stuck inside yourself. Why my father had stopped making the Speedsters chase each other, and instead became a different kind of coach. Runners and pink tutu men. It all made sense now. We could all be free.

As it turned out, she simply tore me apart.

"Do you remember what you told me about your last race?" I said.

Confused stare, but still benign, willing to go there with me.

"You weren't the only one who met a pink tutu man. They're everywhere."

Leaning back into her seat. Very still.

194

"I tried to find them." My voice dropped to a whisper. "I think Dad was one of them."

A vein zigzagged down her brow, and her jaw muscles shifted. The new thing about it: Her reaction had nothing to do with what I said. It was about me. She stared at me, Sarah MacGuire, as if I had the power to hurt her.

So I tried to be gentle. I painted a nice picture with an extremely silky brush for her, making sure not to mess up the details: Dan's futuristic tube dress. The beach and the ocean that smelled like pine needles. The black-and-white photo of Arbies. Bridget's long, gray braids. Nico's little stutter. How I became a runner and lost my name.

She let me talk. I found this encouraging.

"Some of them go back home and visit," I said. "Dad came back home. And I did."

She nodded. *Go on.* I should have known that the quieter she is, the more dangerous she will be.

"Dad has become a spirit," I said. "He had a magic wand. He and the others, they appear at decision time, like witnesses. It's like you said. The weight comes off your shoulders. *You voted.* It's official. But in order to be who they are, they have to leave their old lives behind and live somewhere else. That's what happened to Dad. That's why he ran away."

She leaned forward and looked me up and down. The vein had disappeared.

"All right," she said. "I think I should tell you now."

Of course. I had dished out this story, this big, big miracle, and she was the one with the real news. She had waited all this time.

"Tell me what?"

"Your father…" She stopped. "Your father was sick. At first he couldn't sleep anymore, then he stopped talking. Finally, he wandered off at night. In the end, he didn't recognize me. He was severely depressed."

Now it was my turn to nod. *Go on.*

"We agreed that he should go home for a while. Being out there has always been good for him. But this time, he didn't get better."

"What do you mean?"

"He'd been living with his parents at first, and then with an uncle who has a resort of some kind, and they moved. I'm not sure. He didn't want you to know. And *I* didn't want you to know either."

"But he wrote…"

"The unicorn cards." She smiled for a moment. "I talked to a counselor about them. I wasn't sure whether it was good for you that he sent them. But she said it was. You have your own relationship with him, she said, and I had to trust it. She also said you needed your own place, and that you needed to get out. But now I think…"

Her words were too far away for me to comprehend. For now, I was simply miserable. My mother had lied to me. She had lied to me for two years.

"I think you need to be careful," she said.

This didn't make sense at all.

"Why?" I asked.

"I always worried about you," she said. "You were so quiet. So desperate."

A-ha, I thought. I was desperate. *I* was desperate.

"I told myself to give it time. I told myself, you're not your father. And you aren't. Of course you aren't. But now, after what you just told me…"

"I don't know what you mean."

"I'm worried about you. As the child of someone with mental disorder, you are at an increased risk…"

I stood up. I had to move or I would have thrown up. She looked up at me, about as intimidating as a gymnast with her neat little bun and her marzipan face.

"You scared me," she said. "I'm sorry, but you scared me so much. When you called me that night, you didn't make sense," she said. "You sounded like Abe when he's all over the place—"

"I'm fine," I said. "I travelled across the country."

"Honey," she said. "You were a two-day drive from here. There are no eucalyptus trees where you travelled. There is no sea. There's only a river, a couple of cabins, and a youth hostel…"

It was pointless. My lips and gums were hurting, and my body was squirming and wanting to get out and get away from her voice. I walked away and picked up my backpack. Good thing I hadn't unpacked. My toothbrush, that was all. I put on my shoes.

"I'm only saying you should talk to someone," she said.

There will be no official record of what I did next. No camera was there to record how I tied my shoelaces and picked my jacket from the coat rack. I would have deserved an enormous, shiny Most Excellent Restraint trophy on a marble base for holding back the following: You call me crazy. Because running with broken bones is not crazy. Training so much you need five thousand calories a day is not crazy. Running in a bucket of water because your bones can't handle the pounding is not crazy. Buying a machine that makes your bones grow back faster so you can break them again is so sane.

My mother sniffed and started losing it. "He was beautiful," she said, her mouth raw, and her face smaller than ever. "He was beautiful, but he broke. I don't want you to break."

Whatever. I didn't say anything, except one thing, when I was almost out of the door.

"Thanks for being honest," I said to her. "I didn't know you saw me like that."

What I Keep to Myself

After a minute or two, the shock and adrenaline started leaking out, and the pain had room to spread. My mother had punched me good. My eye sockets burned, and my nose felt like a stuck-on ball of pain. My gums were bleeding. She had caught my by surprise, and I hadn't had time to put my fists up. Now it was time to hurt. So she thought I was crazy. And not only now, at this moment—she had worried about me *all the time*.

Strange how, not long ago, this would have destroyed me. I had spent years cowering in the dark, afraid of being exposed as a flawed specimen. I had hidden and hoped no one would notice the odd rhythm of my breath. Now I knew better. Going crazy—being sane: It was a matter of giving in or holding off. Here, at the corner, stood Pete, Abe's poor, flat, dusty maroon car. Two memories lived in my mind:

The ride back in the warm, scented laundry van, country music, a crocheted pillow in my neck, and the hour-long zombification drive with my hands glued to the wheel, stopping only to pee and throw away my smelly running shoes. For now, both were true. For now.

No, what hurt me was to know that, *all this time*, she had seen me as a liability. *At risk.* She had been waiting, waiting for me to show the first signs of mental rot. I had never had a chance. And to think that I had pitied her.

The convenience store was closed. I stared through the storefront window, at the shelves with soup cans and pasta and diapers, the empty meat and cheese counter, and the scales in the corner, next to the broken cappuccino maker.

This is it, I thought. If I never get out of here again, this is it. Behind that glass is my life. A reaction. A reaction please. Is this horrible? Exhilarating?

It was Fitzgerald, the crow, who finally made it all right. There he sat, on his pyramid of soup cans, his feathers dusted off and shiny, and his glass eyes giving a sparkle of mischief. It was a weird shop run by two strange people and an exhausted mother, but you had to admit: Fitzgerald was the finest piece of taxidermy in town.

I sat down on the bench in front of the shop and opened my backpack. I took out my notebook and searched for the long, narrow sheet of paper with Nico's poem.

This was true, too: I had had my encounter with a pink tutu man. My father had run with me that last night. There had been no stardust when he waved his magic wand at me, no electric shock or quake or thunderclap. Only his smile and his death.

We, the Pink Tutu Men

Pick your story.

O.k., I was doing the truffle shuffle. My quads were screaming,
    and my hamstrings had died.
But I thought I could wing it until that guy in the pink
    tutu overtook me
That was the last straw
If a guy in a tutu
With pink dyed running shoes (yes, I had to check)
Overtakes me
It's over.
I walked
I dropped out
I'm done
I'm dog food.

Or:

He waved an ice cream stick with a silver star
And I knew I could do it
I ran Boston, New York, and Comrades (a long time ago)
No one waves anything at me during the last miles of a
    marathon
So I picked it up
And finished strong
You want to see my medal?
It's right over here, let me get it, it's no trouble at all

Whether you collapse on the curb
Or find another gear
Whether you finish now or later
We, the pink tutu men, approve

With my mother, California, 1979.

Danielle Lazarin's fiction has been published by *Five Chapters*, *Boston Review*, and *Michigan Quarterly Review*. A graduate of Oberlin College's creative writing program, she received her MFA from the University of Michigan, where her stories and essays won Avery and Jule Hopwood Awards. She is a two-time recipient of an individual artist grant from the Northern Manhattan Arts Alliance. She lives in her native New York, where she is raising her daughters and working on a novel.

SPIDER LEGS

Danielle Lazarin

When I leave to visit my mother in Paris, my father insists on driving me to the airport himself, although I could easily take a cab. The car is buried so deep in the parking garage that we stand at the entrance for twenty minutes before the attendants bring it up. My father speaks to me while staring down the ramp out of which the car is supposed to appear.

"I was thinking, while you're there, you might as well check out the American university."

We've had this conversation before. "I want to go to school in the States," I remind him.

I shift my carry-on bag, heavy with ten days of schoolbooks, from one shoulder to the other. I am missing a week of school for the trip; it times up with my brother Jack's fall break from college. My father pushes his hands into his pockets and toes a penny glinting on the garage floor. "Well, perhaps it could be on your list. I hear its art history department is quite good."

"That's Jill, Dad. I like science."

"I know that, Caitlin, but maybe you'll surprise yourself," he snaps at me, but his face is pink with shame.

A car alarm goes off on one of the sub-basement floors. We let its bleating take the place of our talking. When it stops, my father says,

"I've always thought you might like to spend more time with your mother, that's all," and shakes his head apologetically.

"I'm happy here," I say. "I'm happy in New York."

He nods and touches the back of my head affectionately, but he doesn't believe me; I can tell by the furrow still between his eyebrows.

Since their divorce eight years ago, my parents have been shuttling me back and forth between their apartments, and for the past three years, between New York and Paris, where my mother has taken a research fellowship of indeterminate length at the Bibliothèque Nationale. When she left, I moved in with my father and his second-chance family—new wife, new baby; I've never shaken the feeling that he thinks my stay is just temporary.

In the car, my father maintains his strained, guilty silence until he turns on the signal for the airport exit. Then he reminds me, as he likes to periodically, that I don't have to be afraid of Jill and Jack, not on this trip. In this way we share the same deluded hope that this time will be different. He hopes I won't call him in tears, asking to come home early like I did last year, after waiting three hours in a cold spring rain for them to show for a lunch they'd both forgotten about. I can still hear him asking me *why* I had waited so long, a scolding disguised as empathy. But what I hope is that despite seventeen years of feeling like an only child, on this trip I'll finally find a way in, and win my siblings' fierce loyalty that seems the odd and inaccessible nucleus of our disintegrating family.

"I'm not afraid," I say, which is a lie, but I know it's what he wants to hear, though he's not really listening. At the mere thought of them his face has gone hard and defeated, reliving all the anger and suspicion and fear he once had for them, and the shame that goes along with having those feelings for your own children. He nearly misses my terminal.

At the curb, when I've gathered my bags, his look softens. He pats my shoulder one last time and says, "Be good," as he always does when I leave him, because he knows I will be, because I am not one of his older children, because being good is all I know how to do.

When I see my older brother and sister, John and Jillian—Jack and Jill, as they have always been called—waiting beyond the customs gate at Charles de Gaulle with my mother, my chest tightens. They are like beautiful puzzle pieces, with interlocking features of high cheekbones and broad, easy smiles, the same shade of ashy blond hair tucked behind their ears. My mother still introduces them as Irish twins, no matter how many times Jill reminds her that no one says that anymore. Born less than a year apart, Jack on Jill's heels, they are as close as if they did share a womb, always in each other's friends and lives, always standing behind one another, no matter who stands against them.

I expect them to wave and keep walking, as they used to when I was little, shouting to me across the crosswalk that they wouldn't be home for dinner, laughing as they receded, while I headed home. But they don't. Jack takes my bags; my mother pushes my hair out of my face to get a look at me. Jill slings her arm over my shoulder and draws me to her, as if she has been waiting to see me, and while this feels like a mistake—a show, perhaps, for our mother—I let myself sink into her unexpected affection.

In seconds, of course, Jack is under her other arm, laughing at some inside joke of theirs from their mere hours together on French soil. Jill releases me from her grip within a few steps and I drift back to my mother, who takes my hand and squeezes it. "Here you are," she says to me.

"Here I am," I say.

We go to a late dinner to celebrate my arrival; Jill has been in Paris for a few days already, on vacation from the small, menial jobs she takes and leaves like a series of wrong turns; Jack since last night. From behind the rim of my glass, I study them as they lean in over their menus. I don't know my brother and sister well, despite these quarterly trips to Paris. While I spent my childhood perfecting how not to be a problem, Jack and Jill were at boarding school, special summer camps for troubled youth, with tough-love therapists and patient aunts in California. Jill puts down her menu and catches me looking at her; we trade nervous smiles, and I fill with the hope that rises up in me at the start of all of these trips: hope that our family will re-assemble in this small way here, as we never could in New York, that we'll make it past the small grievances that usually scatter us to different parts of the city within a few days—Jill and Jack together, of course, and myself, my mother's sidekick while she pretends that all is fine.

My mother orders champagne; the first glass of it fills my head like a balloon. The waiter asks if we want another bottle. Jill says yes. "We might as well, right?" She winks right at me.

When we're done with the meal, Jack takes out a cigarette. He tips the pack toward Jill.

"Don't anymore."

"Really?"

"Five months," she says.

"That's great," Mom says, reaching over to pat Jill's hand approvingly. "Now's the time to quit, while you're young." Her eyes are glassy from the champagne.

"By week's end, you'll be back," Jack says before sliding the pack into his coat pocket, his eyebrows crumpled into childish displeasure.

Mom turns to me, asks, "How's your dad doing?" My father will ask about her when I return, these public displays of civility part of the play they put on for me since the split.

"Oh, yes, how is Father?" Jill's voice is heavy with sarcasm. Jill lives in New York too, but we don't see her much; she and my father like it that way.

"He's fine. You know. He drove me to the airport."

"Did he bring the worm with him?" Jill crosses her eyes and wiggles her finger up and down, making Jack snicker.

The worm is their nickname for our half-sister, Isabelle; she's four now; my father brings her along when he doesn't know what to say to us.

"No, just us."

"Lucky you," Jack says. Jill laughs, snorting a bit of her water as she takes a sip.

My mother is too busy counting out bills from her wallet for the check, her eyes squinting in concentration, to say anything.

The four of us walk home that night along the Seine, waving giddily at the Bateaux Mouches, the big tourists boats, as they pass.

• • •

The next day, my mother meets me in the Luxembourg Gardens for lunch. I bring us sandwiches from her favorite *boulangerie* near the apartment. We sit on green metal chairs, watching the birds in the fountains, watching people.

"You know, I was thinking maybe you'd want to come here for the summer," she says as she unwraps the paper from her sandwich. She tried to get me to stay with her last summer.

"Maybe." I don't want to make another trip. I want her to come home. The longer my mother works here, the older she looks, the stranger she dresses, and, I think, the happier she becomes.

"How is the book?" I ask her. She seems busier than our last visit—more time at the library, longer hours.

"Good, really good," she says as she hands me a napkin, catching a tomato sliding out from my baguette. "The research part of it's almost done. Now comes the writing."

"You can do that at home, can't you? In New York?"

My mother puts her sandwich in her lap and takes my hand between hers. "Caitlin, look, I'm selling the New York apartment."

I spent my childhood in that apartment; we'd stayed in it after the divorce. A young couple is renting it now with all the furniture, and when I walk by there on my way to flute lessons I think of them and their two young children, living a life we never had in its walls—quiet, harmonious, intact. I probably won't see the apartment again, won't absentmindedly smooth the paper that's peeling back toward the walls, won't get a salute from Boris, the weekend doorman, or wait for the telltale flicker of the elevator lights before our floor.

"Why?" I ask.

"Paris is my home now."

"But it's not mine."

"It could be, if you just let it."

I look at my mother in this park in Paris where walking across the grass is a crime, at her soft, proud face, and I think, what could she know about home, about families, this woman who moved thousands of miles away from everyone else? I shake my head. "Don't you care about where I want to be?"

"Of course I care."

"It doesn't feel that way."

I pull my hand from hers, return to my sandwich. It's a beautiful late fall day, and the park is full of people having lunch, reading *Le Monde*, of tourists snapping photos under the foliage at the Medici Fountain. The voices of foreigners are all around me, speaking French and German and Japanese and Czech. My mother's voice, as she tries to explain why the move is good for all of us, is the only one I can understand. I let it bleed into the others, let it become foreign.

I don't expect to see Jack and Jill at the apartment, but they're there, finishing their own sandwiches at the small counter that divides the kitchen from the rest of the living space.

"What happened to you?" Jack asks.

"She's selling the apartment, in New York," I say, putting my bag down on the counter.

Neither of them look shocked. "That's too bad," Jack says, crumpling up the paper from his sandwich and aiming it at the trash can.

"Thank God," Jill says.

"Jill." Jack thwacks her on her shoulder with his knuckles. "She's upset."

"It's okay," I say, too quickly, because I don't want them to feel sorry for me. "It's just an apartment."

"Not all of us have fond memories of it, Jack. Caitlin can handle that."

"Of course," I say, and pull my calculus textbook from my backpack in the living room. I take a seat on the opposite side of the counter with my homework.

Jack peers over my shoulder. "You're sad and you're doing math?" He shakes his head.

Jill reaches over him and closes my textbook. "No homework today, good egg. Let's get out of here. You need to do something fun. You need an adventure."

Though I'd been trained by my parents to think of myself as an only child, to think that my difference in disposition from Jill and Jack was best for me—that I was too young, too good, to get mixed up in the trouble they always seemed to get into, I'd always wanted to go where Jack and Jill went without me.

That afternoon, Jack and I follow Jill from shop to shop, letting her dress us like dolls. She wraps Jack in scarves until she finds one she deems acceptable, a stretch of steel gray cashmere she carefully coils around his neck. "So handsome," she gushes, and she means it. Jack nods in appreciation. I feel a flash of jealousy stir in my stomach when I see them like this, for how they speak without words, for what, underneath their barbs and teasing, seems like a genuine desire to keep each other happy and safe.

For me, Jill chooses shoes from a small shop in the Marais. They are a warm pink suede, slim and sophisticated, with a tiny heel. When I look at myself in the store mirror, my jeans pulled up to reveal ankles marked by sock elastic, it seems the top and bottom parts of myself are two different people: the ponytailed, lightly freckled face of a child, and the calves of a woman. Jill smiles at me in the mirror with approval.

"You like them?" she asks.

"They're beautiful."

"I think so too."

"They're more you, Jill. You should try them on."

"No, they're yours. We'll get them."

I stand in bare feet as she puts them back in the box, tucking the tissue paper over them. She pays for them with Mom's credit card.

At my mother's request, I stop at the library before dinner the next night. The library is empty of its tourists and most of the other scholars, of the people who have people to go home to at night. Before we go into her private reading room, we wash our hands in the small bathroom. There's only one sink, and we let our hands run under the tap at the same time, the way we used to when I was a child.

In the study room, the walls are stenciled with the rules for handling the materials in French, the *ne*s stacking up neatly, a tower of don'ts. There's a laptop, its screen dark, on a pile of books on one desk. "Come here, I want to show you something," my mother says, her voice soft and secretive as though I'm still a girl. On a large table at the other end of the room, an open manuscript waits, fragile and faded and beautiful. We slide on pairs of cotton gloves, and she nods me toward it.

St. Agnes, she explains, one of the patron saints of girls, the subject of her book. Agnes was only twelve when the Romans tried to sacrifice her to the pagans as a virgin rape. But at the altar she crossed herself instead, refusing to turn against God, to marry any of the men who took pity on her and tried to save her afterward. "For that, she was tortured, raped, killed, of course." My mother clicks her tongue. "No sense of self-preservation, those saints," she says, and smiles.

There's a sword at Agnes's throat, but Agnes, pious, haloed, looks calm, accepting. It's rare, my mother says, to see such an image of her. "Mostly, they like to show her with lambs."

"It's nice," I say after a pause, unsure what she wants me to say.

"It's special, and I wanted you to see it. Just you."

She gives me this look I recognize from the divorce, the one that asks for my silent understanding, to be on her side. I was only seven then, when the family really started to fall apart. I can still see her so clearly by the phone in the hall, a hand covering her forehead, asking, "*Where?*" already reaching blindly for her coat and keys on their hooks. And then she'd give me that weak smile that asked me not to have seen anything at all, because by then she'd stopped telling my father about those phone calls, about the places she'd go to pick up Jill and Jack: police stations, store security offices, and once, when he was away on a business trip, the outermost tip of Long Island. She'd had to rent a car to bring them back that time. "He isn't built for children," she said to me one night, sitting on the edge of my bed. I'd woken up because my father had found out about one such omission and pounded a fist against the dining room wall, which was also the wall to my bedroom. "Your brother and sister, they're just *too much* for him." The rings under her eyes suggested they were too much for her, but she never said so. She tucked the covers in firmly, as if to hold me in place.

She shuts off the light above the manuscript. "I think I'm going to skip dinner tonight. I'm not too hungry anyway. But you guys go, and have a good time." My mother loves the library at night, its promised emptiness. "You know how it is, Caitlin. I just get so caught up in it."

She gestures to the room around her. She forgets I am only seventeen, that I do not know how anything is.

She reaches for her purse and pulls out some cash. "Take a cab to dinner, won't you?"

I take the money from her, but I walk.

At dinner, Jill holds the lip of a new bottle of wine over my glass, which is still half full. "You want more?" she asks, but this is not really a question. It's a test, a dare, an invitation. Jack and Jill's way of looking out for the hurt that must be on my face is to keep ordering wine. *Un plus, un plus*, they say, touching the tip of the empty carafe each time.

"Of course," I say.

"'Atta girl," Jack says, and they both beam their smiles onto me.

After a couple of bottles of wine, Jack begins to tell stories from their adolescence, of the years during the divorce, of the places they'd run off to—the park mostly, and friends' houses, and candy stores on the east side, where they'd have competitions to see who could pocket the most candy.

"It wasn't as much fun as he makes it sound," Jill says as she exhales out of the side of her mouth—her first cigarette in five months. "I mean, we also used to pretend we were orphans."

"It was fun, and you know it," Jack says, and tips the pack of cigarettes to me. Jill swats it away. "Dad would kill you," she says to both of us, and I leave the cigarettes alone.

We stay out drinking wine till the waiters start lifting chairs onto the tables to sweep underneath. We walk out into the crisp night of fall, drunk, full, pleased with ourselves. We decide to head to the Louvre to see the pyramid all lit up. Jack has the remainders of a bottle of wine tucked into his pea coat.

They whisper the plan to me, my brother in one ear, my sister in the other, in perfect synchronicity, as if they are speaking to one another through me. "So when the cab stops, you run," Jill says, smoothing my hair back behind my ear. "We'll come find you," Jack assures me as he hails a cab over to us. They shut the door before I can protest. I'm too drunk to say otherwise, too wanting to be full of faith in them.

I can see the cabby's jowls shake as he looks for the corner Jill has told him to stop at, a false address she delivered in her best French, with a smile.

When the moment comes, Jack tries to pull me in his direction by my jacket, but I freeze. I run away from the cab, back in the direction we've come from, to look for a bridge the cab can't cross, or a dark place to hide and wait for my siblings to come find me.

The cab sits in the middle of the block, its back doors open. For a few moments, the only sounds in the empty street are our footsteps pounding off in three directions. And then below the thrum of my thundering heartbeat, I hear doors slamming, and tires squealing, and the car is behind me, closing in.

I can't get out of the streetlights; there is no bridge. I try to turn a corner, but the heel of my beautiful new shoe gives out from under me, and my ankle takes a sharp twist; I fall forward into the curb.

The knee of one pantleg has split. My chest heaves wildly with my sobs. I give up. The cab's headlights illuminate the street that I had planned to escape to, a quiet residential block. When the driver gets out, he curses me in French. Shaking, I offer him the francs I have in my pocket, the remainders of the money my mother gave me. "*C'est tout,*" I manage to explain, *All I have.* He bends down, the folds of his fat face gathered up in disgust, grabs my elbow on the arm that holds the francs, and shoves me backward. The coins spill into the street. He raises an arm; he is going to strike me. I cover my face, bracing myself.

Instead he spits on me, spreading an ounce of thick phlegm that smells like tobacco and hate over my fingertips and hair. "*Salope,*" he shouts at me before he gets in his cab and drives away. I don't know what this means, but I can tell from the way he says it that it is something awful.

When Jill and Jack arrive, their faces are flushed and healthy. "There you are," Jack says, as if I have pulled off a very good game of hide and seek. I don't want to cry in front of them, but I can't help it.

"What happened?" Jill asks, her face falling into confusion.

I shake my head. My lungs feel as scraped as the heels of my hands, and I cough before I am able to speak. "He chased me."

He looks around, sees the skid marks on the street. "With the car?" Jack asks.

I nod at their knees; they both stand back from me in the empty street.

"You're okay." Jill bends over to put a hand on my shoulder. "You're fine," she says to me. I push her hand off.

Jack's fingertips hesitantly encircle my elbow and try to lift me. "Why don't we walk a little?"

I don't answer. I make myself heavy on the sidewalk. Jack looks back at Jill from his crouched position in front of me; I hear her long exhale.

"We're just a few blocks from the pyramid. We'll sit, we'll have a drink," Jill says, rubbing her arms in the cold.

"I can't," I say.

"Why not?"

The shoes dig into my flesh as my feet continue to swell. I am trying not to feel it, but I know blood is pooling in between my toes. I'm filled with a sudden hatred for the shoes; I take them off and put them on the sidewalk beside me.

"Shit," Jill says as she notices my bloody pinky toe. Most of the nail has come off.

Jack sits down on the curb next to me. He puts both arms around me, and pulls me in close. I've never been here before, so buried in his chest, but I imagine that Jill has, after a breakup or a failed test or during the divorce. My brother squeezes me with a force meant to bring me back to strength, but the weight of my own foolishness overwhelms me; I hate that I have done exactly as I've been told. And while I want most to shove him away, I don't, and I can't.

Jill takes the bottle of wine from Jack, uncorks it, and takes a sip. She passes it to Jack, who offers it to me; I shake my head no. "We can't stay here," Jill says to Jack.

"Give her a minute," he says.

I know in a minute we will still be here in Paris, my ankle will still be swelling, the night air will still be drying the blood across my toes like a swath of spilled paint. I wish I were little again, so little that one of them could lift me up in a piggyback, take turns with me all the way home. This is ridiculous; we are all the same size now, Jack a little taller, myself a bit stronger than Jill, and those were never the kinds of games they played with me anyhow.

Growing up, our mother showed us everything that was magical to children: the mechanical bear that blew bubbles outside the Penny Whistle toy shop, the quiet beauty of night sledding in Central Park, how to lengthen our shadows in the streetlights across the sidewalks of Manhattan. Mom, Jill, Jack, and I would walk the dogs we'd picked out at the pound after the divorce on Central Park West, and I'd stretch my arms up so far I'd lose sight of my hands in the distance, and give myself long spider legs, thick and lengthy and strong as they weren't yet. But then Jack would run up behind me and eclipse my shadow with his, and Jill would climb onto his back from a park bench to make it even larger. They became a giant bug with six legs and massive wings; they pretended to devour me. My mother laughed; we all laughed then, but that's how it's always been with Jack and Jill, a force bigger than I can ever imagine myself to overtake.

Jill finally sits on the other side of us. She takes off her shoes, uses the hem of her shirt to wipe mine out, and puts them on her own feet. "Here," she says, sliding hers toward me. "Let's go," she says a final time.

Before I go to bed, I notice my new, bloodied shoes tucked neatly in the closet. I throw them into the trash, taking satisfaction in their thud against the metal bucket, and go to sleep. When my mother asks about the scrapes on my hands at dinner the next night, I tell her I tripped in my new shoes coming out of the metro, and neither Jack nor Jill says a word.

I am scheduled to leave Paris on a Sunday night. Jack is already gone back to Boston; he'd muttered an apology as he hugged me goodbye, and while it felt like he meant it, I can't worry about trying to ever know. I decide to take a walk in the morning. My mother is sleeping in; the library is shut all day, even to her. Jill is packing in her room when I put my coat on. She sticks her head out of the door, asks me where I'm going.

"Just a walk."

"You want company?"

"Not really," I say. Maybe what I see on her face is hurt, or under-standing; I can't be sure she'd ever let either show.

"I might not be here. My train leaves at noon. Will you be back?" Jill is heading to London to see friends. She hasn't said so, but I suspect there isn't much waiting for her in New York except me and Dad.

"Probably not."

"Well, I'll see you when I get back then?"

"Sure," I say into her ear as we hug, but I don't expect her to call.

It's not eight yet, but near Notre Dame there is a crowd, amorphous and swelling, gathering for mass. I push through the crowd the way I learned to as a child of New York, weaving in and out of the devout, trusting that there is a open space just beyond the bodies moving against the direction I want to go in. When I get there, to a small street on the Île de la Cité, I hear the bells calling people in to services.

I keep going till the streets get quieter and emptier. When I find a small cathedral at the end of a narrow street, its simple gray facade is a relief to me, and I pull open the door without asking myself why. I'm wearing my American sneakers; they're silent in a sea of Sunday shoes clicking on the stone floor. It's cold in the church, and I can see my breath in the light coming through the stained glass windows. The ser-vice hasn't begun yet, but the church is full of people settling into their pews, pulling their coats tight around them in the chill morning air.

I stand off to the side in the nave and look for the saints I know—the ones my mother has taught me—in the stained glass, but they are not there: not Lucy, not Agnes with her lambs, not even Genevieve, the patron saint of Paris. What my mother said always fascinated her about the saints is the basic question of their existence, how little proof the faithful needed. Some saints didn't really exist, except through art and images and stories, through the collective imaginings of those who wanted to believe in them.

The things I want I can't will into existence: a version of my family that never was, a place we can all agree on as home. And maybe I am like my father, not built for this, not built for siblings, or family, or Jack and Jill. Perhaps it's a gene, a predisposition. When I think of it this way, as a malfunction, it doesn't hurt so much, though it seems like a waste of time, all these years of me trying to fit into them when I cannot, not by my nature, not by theirs. I understand what my parents have known for years: I am the proof, the last to verify that this thing we tried to make a family doesn't work. I am the piece that belongs in a different box, that comes from a different puzzle altogether.

As the service begins, in a tongue I've refused to try to understand, a young woman slides over to make room for me in her pew. I hadn't planned to stay, but I nod my head in gratitude to her. And even though I don't believe, I take a seat.

The
Last
Pages

*Lina (l), Lisbet (r), children Helmut and Helga, with the
Engelharts, their first landlords in America.*

Very little of my story is fact, but I did grow up with an heirloom dictionary from my mother's family that had a picture of the Indo-European language tree on the inner cover. I used to look at it a lot as a kid. Albanian is on the bottom right, and has two leaves, representing its two dialects (though based on the placement of leaves on other branches of the tree, this may just be a coincidence). The only limitation of writing, I think, is that most of us only have the opportunity to write in one language. Imagine having access to all of them: you'd always have the perfect word.

—*Michael Deagler*

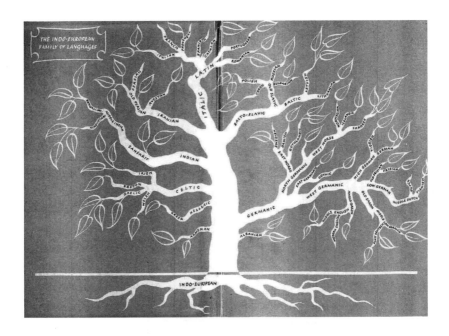

Two things happened:

I heard one gay man say disparagingly of another gay man, "He's got the inner life of a drag queen," spoken in a tone implying that all drag queens are vapid.

An editor at a small publishing house told me my work was "too gay" for a general readership.

So then I got angry, and wrote "The Manly Man's Guide to Virtue." Since I don't have the talent necessary to be a drag queen, I started with the initial discomposure the two above events elicited, mixed them together with disparate memories, observations, and inventions that clunk around in my head, and after a long struggle, I shaped them into a story.

—*Joseph O'Malley*

Below is a picture of my parents, probably around 1980. They were nothing like the Hullings couple in my story. But I had friends whose parents were like the Hullings, and I was and am endlessly fascinated by people like them. This story sat around for a long time. I wrote it years ago in Virginia, trying to get at the largely still mysterious (to me) exchange of power that can happen with young girls coming of age. I also wanted to look at the way we mythologize people, whether they are our friends' mothers or best friends or our love interests. But I couldn't get the story quite right for a long time, not until I moved down to Houston and spent a hot, sweaty summer here, staring out the dirty window, wishing for a beach or a boardwalk. Then it came to me—how Beth and Mrs. Hulling had to confront each other. I guess I owe a lot to the relentless heat down here, and also to my parents, for being nothing like the Hullings.

—*Aja Gabel*

In a recent issue of *One Story* magazine, Etgar Keret said of writer's block: "...you not only have a strong yearning to write, but you also have the bursting emotions, the skill, the vocabulary, everything. The only thing that is missing is the story itself." On hiatus from novel revising and longing to write a new short story, I found myself in a similar predicament. Then, one morning in February, I came across a news story about a fire at the Antarctic Comandante Ferraz Station, which caused the death of two Brazilian sailors. It was a terrible event, but also carried an air of mystery, and immediately I knew that I wanted to imagine myself into that world, into the stories and secrets the people in that station might have been carrying with them and who they might have left behind. Though the events in "Antarctica" only bear a passing resemblance to the fire at Comandante Ferraz, the central characters—Lee, her brother, and Eve—all grew out of that real life story.

—*Laura van den Berg*

Well, since "Stooges in Paradise" is a kind of sequel to my previous story published in this magazine, "Aliens," I suppose I'll talk once again about autobiographical fiction. As everyone knows, this sort of writing is discouraged by many "authorities" on the matter of fiction, while others want to regard it as memoir with fictional flourish. I dismiss the authorities altogether, and will meet the memoirists halfway, though I think there is a real distinction between memoir and autobiographical fiction. A memoir is, by definition, factual—a chronicle of real events that happen to real people. The trick is to write it in such a way that it could be deemed fiction, with, that is, literary tinsel. Autobiographical fiction goes further; it manipulates real events and even characters. The crux of the story "Stooges" is real stuff; it really happened. But as story, the reality is a bit askew, slightly or highly hyperbolic, double- or even triple-focused, intensified, or diminished—and all for effect, style, suspense, and story line. The process reminds me of cartoon art, and specifically, caricature. One zeroes in on certain prominent features of mind or body and from them broad-strokes new material. My process is a bit more complicated since I aim for humor as well, albeit a kind of dark humor. I believe, with the late author Walker Percy, that there are very few avenues of transcendence—sex, violence, and (though Percy didn't mention it per se, he practiced it in his writing) humor. If we add a sixth act to *Hamlet*, we would find ourselves in the realm of high comedy. Humor helps us transcend the often bleak human condition. Such transcendence may prove ephemeral, but for that splendid, ephemeral moment, we have triumphed as, again to cite Percy, neither angels nor beasts. (I think that goes for Pascal as well.) Finally, the four main characters of "Stooges" are actual people with personalities similar to their caricatures in the story; the set is impeccably accurate; the popular culture bits happened exactly as they are depicted. Nadya is half real; the "osprey guy," total invention. But the characters have stepped into new shoes and thus amble differently than their realistic counterparts. This is what I love about autobiographical fiction: it's a re-creation of the original creations. The writer feels a bit like, dare I say it? god (lowercase intentional). Ah, fiat flux!

—*Louis Gallo*

I took up running at the end of 2007, when we were still living in Pittsburgh. Soon, we would train with friends every Wednesday evening, either on the Schenley Oval or, as seen here, on the track at CMU. While I don't believe in writing about actual people, I'm fairly shameless about using locations, and I was thinking of this track when I wrote "Men in Pink Tutus." In another story, the Schenley Oval makes an appearance, and under its actual name, too. In some earlier drafts of "Men in Pink Tutus," I included a group of local runners modeled on the (very fast) Pittsburgh Pharaoh Hounds (you can Google Pittsburgh Pharaoh Hounds), but revision wiped them from this story. They are still active in the current draft of another story, though, so fingers crossed.

—*Stefani Nellen*

At eighty-four, the main character in this piece, Rabbi Stephen Smith, is one of the oldest characters whose point of view I've inhabited, and yet his perspective came to me quickly, nearly fully formed, and quite late in the process of writing my novel. Though we differ greatly in age and occupation, I think I related strongly to his sense of wonderment at the passage of time, his reflection on how, "The days passed, the months and seasons, not quickly at first, but with a certain driving cadence. And then... something shifted in that regard—a sudden acceleration..." When I began the novel from which "Year's Time" is taken, I was pregnant with my daughter, and my son was two years old. Now they're both in preschool, these amazing little humans learning to read and write and think for themselves. Our perception of the flow of time, of how it informs our identities and fears and longings, seems to me one of the great mysteries writers can explore. It's one of the themes at the heart of my novel and certainly at the heart of Rabbi Smith's struggle in "Year's Time"—his struggle to make sense of both the literal and figurative fires raging around him.

—*Kim Brooks*

I spent my freshman year of college in Paris. Both of these photos are from the spring of that year, 1997. The little boy is in the Luxembourg Gardens; he had defiantly stepped far onto the grass where, at the time at least, you were not allowed to be. The other is some months later, in Battery Park, when I returned home to New York for the summer.

Paris was a hard place for me to be. I had a boyfriend in the States and was, like all other college freshmen, making that transition from adolescent to grownup. As an independent city girl, I had underes-

timated what it would be like to live on my own so far from home. I learned a lot during that difficult year, including how much I truly loved New York, a city that welcomed all those people on the grass.

—*Danielle Lazarin*

Part of my writing process is finding old photographs to help me create characters and settings. I spend a good deal of time in libraries looking through art and photography books. The internet doesn't work in this way for me. The photo has to come from a book. Sometimes an odd or unusual expression can create a full character. In draft one of "The Lost Brother," Merrill was a very minor character, but one of my fellow writers/friends offered the opinion, "She's boring. Why would anyone drive all night to see her?" So I found a photograph of a woman drinking coffee in a kitchen and staring at the ceiling. Her expression seemed to say, I am not of this world, but I have learned much from my visit here. Merrill has an almost spiritual connection to Daniel, at least to my mind. They seem both hopeful and haunted. Oddly, Merrill keeps popping up in other stories of mine, when she's both old and young, with her brother and her mule and mice. When I find the right photograph for a character, or setting, or even just a mood, it's a very rewarding feeling.

—*Tom Kealey*

A few years ago a house went up for sale in my neighborhood. It was a 1960 ranch house on a canal that led to the open bay, a fixer-upper with an unusual indoor pool—emptied of water, but with a lingering odor of chlorine. The house had belonged to an older woman who'd died, and her daughter enlisted the longtime housekeeper to meet us there and show us around. The housekeeper, hunched and wild haired, led us through the still furnished rooms and told of parties held at the house in its heyday, of the death of the woman's husband, and then, with a dark look, of the woman's death—how she lay on the bedroom floor a few days before anyone knew it, and how it fell to her to clean the stain up off the carpet. "I couldn't get it all up," the housekeeper said. "You can still see it." The house was sold to someone who planned to tear it down and build something bigger. This sort of erasure, the impermanence of our bodies, our structures, prompted my story.

—*Karen Brown*

PAST CONTRIBUTING AUTHORS AND ARTISTS

Robert A. Abel • David Abrams • Linsey Abrams • Steve Adams • Hubert Ahn • Lynn Ahrens • Diane King Akers • William Akin • Daniel Alarcón • Susan Alenick • Xhenet Aliu • Ed Allen • Will Allison • Rosemary Altea • Julia Alvarez • Kyoko Amano • Brian Ames • Scott Alan Anderson • Selena Anderson • A. Manette Ansay • Graham Arnold • Joanna Arnow • Raymond Philip Asaph • Margaret Atwood • Dalia Azim • Kevin Bacon • Michael Bahler • Doreen Baingana • Aida Baker • Sybil Baker • Kerry Neville Bakken • Carmiel Banasky • Olufunke Grace Bankole • Russell Banks • Brad Barkley • Andrea Barrett •Victoria Barrett • Ken Barris • Marc Basch • Kyle Ann Bates • Richard Bausch • Robert Bausch • Charles Baxter • Ann Beattie • Sean Beaudoin • Brad Beauregard • Barbara Bechtold • Cathie Beck • Jeff Becker • Janet Belding • Janet Benton • Sallie Bingham • Kristen Birchett • Melanie Bishop • James Carlos Blake •Victoria Blake • Corinne Demas Bliss •Valerie Block • Carol Bly • Will Boast • Dennis Bock • Belle Boggs • Joan Bohorfoush • Matt Bondurant • David Borofka • Robin Bradford • Harold Brodkey • Barbara Brooks • Karen Brooks • Kim Brooks • Oliver Broudy • Carrie Brown • Danit Brown • Kurt McGinnis Brown • Nic Brown • Paul Brownfield • Gabriel Brownstein • Ayşe Papatya Bucak • Judy Budnitz • Susanna Bullock • Christopher Bundy • Jenny A. Burkholder • Evan Christopher Burton • Robert Olen Butler • Michael Byers • Christine Byl • Gerard Byrne • Jack Cady • Annie Callan • Joshua Canipe • Kevin Canty • Peter Carey • Ioanna Carlsen • Ron Carlson • Aaron Carmichael • H.G. Carroll • Paul Carroll • Nona Caspers • David Allan Cates • Marjorie Celona • Jeremiah Chamberlin • Brian Champeau •Vikram Chandra • Diane Chang • Mike Chasar • Xiaofei Chen • Yunny Chen • Terrence Cheng • Robert Chibka • Chieh Chieng • Jon Chopan • Carolyn Chute • Christi Clancy • George Makana Clark • Rikki Clark • Dennis Clemmens • Christopher Coake • Aaron Cohen • Andrea Cohen • Robert Cohen • Evan S. Connell • Joan Connor • K. L. Cook • Ellen Cooney • Rand Richards Cooper • Lydia E. Copeland • Michelle Coppedge • Rita D. Costello •Wendy Counsil • Frances Ya-Chu Cowhig • Doug Crandell • Lindsey Crittenden • M. Allen Cunningham • Colleen Curran • Ronald F. Currie Jr. • William J. Cyr • Quinn Dalton • Edwidge Danticat • Bilal Dardai • Peter Ho Davies • Tristan Davies • Bill Davis • C.V. Davis • Annie Dawid • Erica Johnson Debeljak • Laurence de Looze • Anne de Marcken • Toi Derricotte • Janet Desaulniers • Tiziana di Marina • Junot Díaz • Stephanie Dickinson • Stephen Dixon • Matthew Doherty • Leslie Dormen • Michael Dorris • Siobhan Dowd • Greg Downs • Eugenie Doyle • Tiffany Drever • Alan Arthur Drew • Andre Dubus • Andre Dubus III • E.A. Durden • Stuart Dybek • Wayne Dyer • Melodie S. Edwards • Ron Egatz • Barbara Eiswerth • Mary Relindes Ellis • Sherry Ellis • Susan Engberg • Lin Enger • James English • Tony Eprile • Louise Erdrich • Zoë Evamy • Eli S. Evans • Nomi Eve • George Fahey • Edward Falco • Anthony Farrington • Merrill Feitell • J. M. Ferguson Jr. • Lisa Fetchko • Lydia Fitzpatrick • Joseph Flanagan • Charlotte Forbes • Alyson Foster • Patricia Foster • Susan Fox • Michael Frank • Stefanie Freele • Jonathan Freiberger • Pete Fromm • Abby Frucht • Daniel Gabriel • Avital Gad-Cykman • Ernest Gaines • Mary Gaitskill • Riva Galchen • Tess Gallagher • Louis Gallo • Elizabeth Gallu • Kent Gardien • Abe Gaustad • William Gay • Abby Geni • Aaron Gilbreath • Ellen Gilchrist • David Goguen • Myla Goldberg • Allyson Goldin • D M Gordon • Mary Gordon • Peter Gordon • Trevor Gore • Amy S. Gottfried • Jean Colgan Gould • Elizabeth Graver • Lisa Graley • Jo-Ann Graziano • Andrew Sean Greer • Cynthia Gregory • Gail Greiner • Brian Gresko • John Griesemer • Zoë Griffith-Jones • Paul Griner • Lauren Groff • Cary Groner • Michael L. Guerra • Lucrecia Guerrero • Tracy Guzeman • Aaron Gwyn • L.B. Haas • Rawi Hage • Syed Ali Haider • Garth Risk Hallberg • Patricia Hampl • Christian Hansen • Ann Harleman • Elizabeth Logan Harris • Marina Harris • Erin Hart • Kent Haruf • Ethan Hauser • Jake Hawkes • Daniel Hayes • David Haynes • Daniel Hecht • Ursula Hegi • Amy Hempel • Joshua Henkin • Patricia Henley • Cristina Henríquez • Nellie Hermann • David Hicks • Patrick Hicks • Julie Hirsch • Andee Hochman • Rolaine Hochstein • Alice Hoffman • Cary Holladay • Jack Holland • Noy Holland • Travis Holland • Lucy Honig • Ann Hood • Linda Hornbuckle • Michael Horton • Kuangyan Huang • David Huddle • Sandra Hunter • Tim Hurd • Siri Hustvedt • Quang Huynh • Frances Hwang • Leo Hwang • Catherine Ryan Hyde • Stewart David Ikeda • Lawson Fusao Inada • Elizabeth Inness-Brown • Debra Innocenti • Bruce Jacobson • Andrea Jeyaveeran • Ha Jin • Joseph Johns • Charles Johnson • Cheri Johnson • E.B. Johnson • Leslie Johnson • Sarah Anne Johnson • Wayne Johnson • Bret Anthony Johnston • Allen Morris Jones • Nalini Jones • Thom Jones • Cyril Jones-Kellet • Elizabeth Judd • Tom Miller Juvik • Jiri Kajanë • Anita Shah Kapadia • Hester Kaplan • Wayne Karlin • Amy Karr • Ariana-Sophia Kartsonis • Andrew Kass • Kate Kasten • Ken Kaye • Tom Kealey • David Kear • John M. Keller • Andrea King Kelly • Jenny Kennedy • Thomas E. Kennedy • Tim Keppel • Jamaica Kincaid • Lily King • Dana Kinstler • Maina wa Kinyatti • Carolyn Kizer • Perri Klass • Rachel Klein • Carrie Knowles • Clark E. Knowles • Elizabeth Koch • N.S. Köenings • Jonathan Kooker • David Koon • Karen Kovacik • Justin Kramon • Jake Kreilkamp • Nita Krevans • Anasuya Krishnaswamy • Dana Kroos • Erika Krouse

• Marilyn Krysl • Frances Kuffel • Evan Kuhlman • Mandy Dawn Kuntz • Anatoly Kurchatkin • W. Tsung-yan Kwong•J.P.Lacrampe•Victoria Lancelotta• Christiana Langenberg•Rattawut Lapcharoensap • Matt Lapata • Jenni Lapidus • Danielle Lavaque-Manty • Doug Lawson • David Leavitt • Don Lee • Frances Lefkowitz • Peter Lefcourt • Linda Legters • Jon Leon • Doris Lessing • Jennifer Levasseur •Adva Levin • Debra Levy • Janice Levy • Yiyun Li • Jennie Lin • Christine Liotta • Rosina Lippi-Green • David Long • Nathan Long • Salvatore Diego Lopez • Melissa Lowver • Meredith Luby • William Luvaas • Clayton Luz • Barry Lyga • David H. Lynn • Richard Lyons • Bruce Machart • Jeff MacNelly • R. Kevin Maler • Kelly Malone • Paul Mandelbaum • George Manner • Jana Martin • Lee Martin •Valerie Martin • Juan Martinez • Daniel Mason • Brendan Mathews • Alice Mattison • Bruce McAllister • Natalie Teal McAllister • Jane McCafferty • Colum McCann • Sean Padraic McCarthy • Judith McClain • Cammie McGovern • Cate McGowan • Eileen McGuire • Jay McInerney • Susan McInnis • Gregory McNamee • Jenny Drake McPhee • Amalia Melis • Askold Melnyczuk • Matthew Mercier • Susan Messer • Frank Michel • Paul Michel • Nancy Middleton • Alyce Miller • Anne Walsh Miller • Greg Miller • Katherine Min • Lee Montgomery • Mary McGarry Morris • Ted Morrissey • Mary Morrissy • Jennifer Moses • Bernard Mulligan • Abdelrahman Munif • Manuel Muñoz • Karen Munro • Scott Nadelson • Paula Nangle • Jim Nashold • Micah Nathan •Antonya Nelson • Kent Nelson • Randy F. Nelson • Lucia Nevai •Thisbe Nissen • Katherin Nolte • Anna North • Miriam Novogrodsky • Sigrid Nunez • N. Nye • Ron Nyren • Joyce Carol Oates • Tim O'Brien • Vana O'Brien • Gina Ochsner • Mary O'Dell • Chris Offutt • Jennifer Oh • Laura Oliver • Felicia Olivera • Jimmy Olsen • Thomas O'Malley • Stewart O'Nan • Elizabeth Oness • Karen Outen • Mary Overton • Ruth Ozeki • Patricia Page • Ashley Paige • Ann Pancake • Michael Parker • Alexander Parsons • Peter Parsons • Roy Parvin • Karenmary Penn • Susan Perabo • Benjamin Percy • Marissa Perry • Susan Petrone • Dawn Karima Pettigrew • Jessi Phillips • Constance Pierce •William Pierce • D.B.C.Pierre •Angela Pneuman • Rebecca Podos • Steven Polansky • Michael Poore • John Prendergast • Jessica Printz • Melissa Pritchard • Annie Proulx • Eric Puchner • Lindsay Purves • Kevin Rabalais • Jonathan Raban • George Rabasa • Margo Rabb • Mark Rader • Paul Rawlins •Yosefa Raz • Karen Regen-Tuero • Frederick Reiken • Nancy Reisman •Yelizaveta P. Renfro •AdamTheron–Lee Rensch • Linda Reynolds • Kurt Rheinheimer • Anne Rice • Michelle Richmond • Alberto Ríos • Roxana Robinson • Anya Robyak • Susan Jackson Rodgers • Andrew Roe • Paulette Roeske • Stan Rogal • Carol Roh-Spaulding • Josh Rolnick • Frank Ronan • Emma Roper-Evans • Julie Rose • Sari Rose • Elizabeth Rosen • Janice Rosenberg • Jane Rosenzweig • David Rothman • Edwin Rozic • Sam Ruddick • Karen Russell • Elissa Minor Rust • Karen Sagstetter • Kiran Kaur Saini • Mark Salzman • Mark Sanders • Ron Savage • Carl Schaffer • R. K.Scher • Michael Schiavone • Robert Schirmer • Libby Schmais • Samantha Schoech • Natalie Schoen • Scott Schrader •Adam Schuitema • Jim Schumock • Lynn Sharon Schwartz • Barbara Scot • Andrew Scott • Andrew Thomas Scott • Peter Selgin • Amy Selwyn • James Sepsey • Catherine Seto • Bob Shacochis • Evelyn Sharenov • Hugh Sheehy • Cathal Sheerin • Karen Shepard • Maggie Shipstead • Sally Shivnan • Evan Shopper • J.Kevin Shushtari • James F.Sidel • Daryl Siegel • Ami Silber • Al Sim • Mark Sindecuse • George Singleton • Hasanthika Sirisena • Johanna Skibsrud • Floyd Skloot • Brian Slattery •Aria Beth Sloss • James Smart • Louise Farmer Smith • Janice D. Soderling • Roland Sodowsky • Stephanie Soileau • Scott Southwick • R. Clifton Spargo • Gregory Spatz • Diana Spechler • Brent Spencer • L.M.Spencer • Lindsay Sproul • Lara Stapleton • John Stazinski • Lori Ann Stephens • Barbara Stevens • John Stinson • George Stolz •William Styron •Virgil Suárez • Karen Swenson • Liz Szabla • Shimon Tanaka • Mika Tanner • Deborah Tarnoff • Philip Tate • Lois Taylor • Paul Theroux • Abigail Thomas • Randolph Thomas • Jackie Thomas-Kennedy • Joyce Thompson • Patrick Tierney •Aaron Tillman • Tamara B.Titus • Jennifer Tomscha •Andrew Toos • Daniel Torday • Justin Torres • Pauls Toutonghi • Johnny Townsend •Vu Tran • Patricia Traxler • Jessica Treadway • Eric Trethewey • Doug Trevor •William Trevor • Rob Trucks • Kathryn Trueblood • Eric Scot Tryon • Jennifer Tseng • Carol Turner • Christine Turner • Kathleen Tyau • Michael Upchurch • Lee Upton • Laura Valeri •Vauhini Vara • Gerard Varni • Joseph Vastano • Katherine Vaz •A. J.Verdelle • Daniel Villasenor • Robert Vivian • Matthew Vollmer • Sergio Gabriel Waisman • John S.Walker • Daniel Wallace • Ren Wanding • Eric Wasserman • Mary Yukari Waters • Claire Vaye Watkins • Jonathan Wei • Josh Weil • Eric Weinberger • Jamie Weisman • Lance Weller • Ed Weyhing • J.Patrice Whetsell • Sara Whyatt • Joan Wick-ersham • Vinnie Wilhelm • Margo Williams • Lex Williford • Gary Wilson • Robin Winick • Mark Wisniewski • Terry Wolverton • Joy Wood • Monica Wood • Christopher Woods • Leslie A.Wootten • wormser • Celia Wren • Callie Wright • Calvin Wright • Brennen Wysong • Geoff Wyss • Melissa Yancy • June Unjoo Yang • Kathryne Young • Rolf Yngve • Ella Mei Yon • Paul Yoon • Nick Yribar • Nancy Zafris •Yuvi Zalkow • Alexi Zentner • Jenny Zhang • Silas Dent Zobal • Jane Zwinger

Frank Mitchell, Henry's buddy back then.

COMING SOON

"You've been there a lot? When did you cross over?"

"I was born here," I tell her in English. Then I say it again to her in Spanish, then I let her stay silent for a moment so she can know who she's talking to.

from "The Happiest Girl in the Whole U.S.A." by Manuel Muñoz

"At first," she was quoted as saying in Ugandan sign language, "I was not accustomed to the hearing aids, which whispered in a raspy voice. I thought that they were broken, but the volunteers told me: what you are hearing is the noise of the wind. And I realized that the voice I heard was the voice of the world."

from "Everyone Is Waiting" by Soma Mei Sheng Frazier

It was one of those touching and tragic things you end up seeing over the course of a full life.

from "Levi's Recession" by Devin Murphy

And he laughed to think how all the Sundays of his life he'd sat in the pews of St. John the Baptist, trying to conceive of the afterlife, and here it was: you simply began again in youthful vigor and joy.

from "The Ghost Man" by Austin Smith

There are certain people in our lives, for instance, who can just say a few words—I love you, I hate you, I'm mad at you, you've disappointed me—that suddenly cause the chemistry in our bodies to change. It makes our heart race. Literally the words change us at the chemical level.

from an interview with Ben Marcus by David Naimon